Lunch At The Beach House Hotel

Judith Keim

BOOKS BY JUDITH KEIM

THE HARTWELL WOMEN SERIES:
The Talking Tree – 1
Sweet Talk – 2
Straight Talk – 3
Baby Talk – 4
The Hartwell Women – Boxed Set

THE BEACH HOUSE HOTEL SERIES:
Breakfast at The Beach House Hotel – 1
Lunch at The Beach House Hotel – 2
Dinner at The Beach House Hotel – 3
Christmas at The Beach House Hotel – 4
Margaritas at The Beach House Hotel – 5
Dessert at The Beach House Hotel – 6

THE FAT FRIDAYS GROUP:
Fat Fridays – 1
Sassy Saturdays – 2
Secret Sundays – 3

THE SALTY KEY INN SERIES:
Finding Me – 1
Finding My Way – 2
Finding Love – 3
Finding Family – 4
The Salty Key Inn Series . Boxed Set

THE CHANDLER HILL INN SERIES:
Going Home – 1
Coming Home – 2
Home at Last – 3
The Chandler Hill Inn Series – Boxed Set

PRAISE FOR JUDITH KEIM'S NOVELS

THE BEACH HOUSE HOTEL SERIES

"Love the characters in this series. This series was my first introduction to Judith Keim. She is now one of my favorites. Looking forward to reading more of her books."

BREAKFAST AT THE BEACH HOUSE HOTEL is an easy, delightful read that offers romance, family relationships, and strong women learning to be stronger. Real life situations filter through the pages. Enjoy!"

LUNCH AT THE BEACH HOUSE HOTEL – "This series is such a joy to read. You feel you are actually living with them. Can't wait to read the latest one."

DINNER AT THE BEACH HOUSE HOTEL – "A Terrific Read! As usual, Judith Keim did it again. Enjoyed immensely. Continue writing such pleasantly reading books for all of us readers."

CHRISTMAS AT THE BEACH HOUSE HOTEL – "Not Just Another Christmas Novel. This is book number four in the series and my introduction to Judith Keim's writing. I wasn't disappointed. The characters are dimensional and engaging. The plot is well crafted and advances at a pleasing pace. The Florida location is interesting and warming. It was a delight to read a romance novel with mature female protagonists. Ann and Rhoda have life experiences that enrich the story. It's a clever book about friends and extended family. Buy copies for your book group pals and enjoy this seasonal read."

MARGARITAS AT THE BEACH HOUSE HOTEL – "What a wonderful series. I absolutely loved this book and can't wait for the next book to come out. There was even suspense in it. Thanks Judith for the great stories."

"Overall, Margaritas at the Beach House Hotel is another wonderful addition to the series. Judith Keim takes the reader on a journey told through the voices of these amazing characters we have all come to love through the years! I truly cannot stress enough how good this book is, and I hope you enjoy it as much as I have!"

THE HARTWELL WOMEN SERIES:

"This was an EXCELLENT series. When I discovered Judith Keim, I read all of her books back to back. I thoroughly enjoyed the women Keim has written about. They are believable and you want to just jump into their lives and be their friends! I can't wait for any upcoming books!"

"I fell into Judith Keim's Hartwell Women series and have read & enjoyed all of her books in every series. Each centers around a strong & interesting woman character and their family interaction. Good reads that leave you wanting more."

THE FAT FRIDAYS GROUP :

"Excellent story line for each character, and an insightful representation of situations which deal with some of the contemporary issues women are faced with today."

"I love this author's books. Her characters and their lives are realistic. The power of women's friendships is a common and beautiful theme that is threaded throughout this story."

THE SALTY KEY INN SERIES

FINDING ME – "I thoroughly enjoyed the first book in this series and cannot wait for the others! The characters are endearing with the same struggles we all encounter. The setting makes me feel like I am a guest at The Salty Key Inn...relaxed, happy & light-hearted! The men are yummy and the women strong. You can't get better than that! Happy Reading!"

FINDING MY WAY- "Loved the family dynamics as well as uncertain emotions of dating and falling in love. Appreciated the morals and strength of parenting throughout. Just couldn't put this book down."

FINDING LOVE – "I waited for this book because the first two was such good reads. This one didn't disappoint.... Judith Keim always puts substance into her books. This book was no different, I learned about PTSD, accepting oneself, there is always going to be problems but stick it out and make it work. Just the way life is. In some ways a lot like my life. Judith is right, it needs another book and I will definitely be reading it. Hope you choose to read this series, you will get so much out of it."

FINDING FAMILY – "Completing this series is like eating the last chip. Love Judith's writing, and her female characters are always smart, strong, vulnerable to life and love experiences."

"This was a refreshing book. Bringing the heart and soul of the family to us."

THE CHANDLER HILL INN SERIES
GOING HOME – "I absolutely could not put this book down. Started at night and read late into the middle of the night. As a child of the '60s, the Vietnam war was front and center so this resonated with me. All the characters in the book were so well developed that the reader felt like they were friends of the family."

"I was completely immersed in this book, with the beautiful descriptive writing, and the authors' way of bringing her characters to life. I felt like I was right inside *her story."*

COMING HOME – "Coming Home is a winner. The characters are well-developed, nuanced and likable. Enjoyed the vineyard setting, learning about wine growing and seeing the challenges Cami faces in running and growing a business. I look forward to the next book in this series!"

"Coming Home was such a wonderful story. The author has a gift for getting the reader right to the heart of things."

HOME AT LAST – "In this wonderful conclusion, to a heartfelt and emotional trilogy set in Oregon's stunning wine country, Judith Keim has tied up the Chandler Hill series with the perfect bow."

"Overall, this is truly a wonderful addition to the Chandler Hill Inn series. Judith Keim definitely knows how to perfectly weave together a beautiful and heartfelt story."

"The storyline has some beautiful scenes along with family drama. Judith Keim has created characters with interactions that are believable and some of the subjects the story deals with are poignant."

SEASHELL COTTAGE BOOKS

A CHRISTMAS STAR – "Love, laughter, sadness, great food, and hope for the future, all in one book. It doesn't get any better than this stunning read."

"A Christmas Star is a heartwarming Christmas story featuring endearing characters. So many Christmas books are set in snowbound places...it was a nice change to read a Christmas story that takes place on a warm sandy beach!" Susan Peterson

CHANGE OF HEART – "CHANGE OF HEART is the summer read we've all been waiting for. Judith Keim is a

master at creating fascinating characters that are simply irresistible. Her stories leave you with a big smile on your face and a heart bursting with love."

Kellie Coates Gilbert, author of the popular Sun Valley Series

A SUMMER OF SURPRISES – *"The story is filled with a roller coaster of emotions and self-discovery. Finding love again and rebuilding family relationships."*

"Ms. Keim uses this book as an amazing platform to show that with hard emotional work, belief in yourself and love, the scars of abuse can be conquered. It in no way preaches, it's a lovely story with a happy ending."

"The character development was excellent. I felt I knew these people my whole life. The story development was very well thought out I was drawn [in] from the beginning."

THE DESERT SAGE INN SERIES:
THE DESERT FLOWERS – *ROSE* – *"The Desert Flowers - Rose, is the first book in the new series by Judith Keim. I always look forward to new books by Judith Keim, and this one is definitely a wonderful way to begin The Desert Sage Inn Series!"*

"In this first of a series, we see each woman come into her own and view new beginnings even as they must take this tearful journey as they slowly lose a dear friend. This is a very well written book with well-developed and likable main characters. It was interesting and enlightening as the first portion of this saga unfolded. I very much enjoyed this book and I do recommend it"

"Judith Keim is one of those authors that you can always depend on to give you a great story with fantastic characters. I'm excited to know that she is writing a new series and after reading book 1 in the series, I can't wait to

read the rest of the books."!

THE DESERT FLOWERS – LILY – "The second book in the Desert Flowers series is just as wonderful as the first. Judith Keim is a brilliant storyteller. Her characters are truly lovely and people that you want to be friends with as soon as you start reading. Judith Keim is not afraid to weave real life conflict and loss into her stories. I loved reading Lily's story and can't wait for Willow's!

"The Desert Flowers Lily is the second book in The Desert Sage Inn Series by author Judith Keim. When I read the first book in the series, The Desert Flowers-Rose, I knew this series would exceed all of my expectations and then some. Judith Keim is an amazing author, and this series is a testament to her writing skills and her ability to completely draw a reader into the world of her characters."

Lunch At The Beach House Hotel

The Beach House Hotel Series –
Book 2

Judith Keim

Wild Quail Publishing

Lunch At The Beach House Hotel is a work of fiction. Names, characters, places, public or private institutions, corporations, towns, and incidents are the product of the author's imagination or are used fictitiously. Any resemblance to actual events, locales, or persons, living or dead, is coincidental.

No part of *Lunch At The Beach House Hotel* may be reproduced or transmitted in any form or by any electronic or mechanical means, including information storage and retrieval systems, without permission in writing from the author, except by a reviewer who may quote brief passages in a review. This book may not be resold or uploaded for distribution to others. For permissions contact the author directly via electronic mail:

wildquail.pub@gmail.com

www.judithkeim.com

Published in the United States of America by:

Wild Quail Publishing
PO Box 171332
Boise, ID 83717-1332

ISBN# 978-0-9968637-6-6
Copyright ©2016 Judith Keim

Dedication

This book is dedicated to those who work hard in the hospitality industry and often go unnoticed and under-appreciated.

CHAPTER ONE

I'd just stepped out of the shower when my business partner, Rhonda—Rhonda DelMonte Grayson, as she proudly called herself—phoned in a tizzy.

"Annie, you've got to get over here right away. Something's come up."

She hung up before I could ask her about it, but I knew I'd better get moving. In the hotel business, there were a lot of "somethings"—some good, some bad.

My mind whirled with possibilities as I quickly dried off and dressed. After brushing my hair and dabbing on some lipstick, I took a moment to put on the chain and pendant Vaughn Sanders had given me. He wouldn't return from filming for another six weeks, and I missed him like crazy. The gold pendant spoke of so many things. His initial V formed one side of my A. Across the middle of it was a bar with five diamonds—a symbol of us, our collective three children, and the hope that we'd all share a life together.

I left my house on the hotel property and headed toward the hotel. Warm air wrapped around me, caressing my skin in silky strokes, and I joyfully inhaled the tang of the salty air. After living most of my life in Boston, I relished the tropical setting along the Gulf Coast of Southwest Florida.

As I approached the front of The Beach House Hotel, I paused to stare at the beachside estate Rhonda and I had turned into a small, upscale hotel. The pale-pink-stucco, two-story building spread before me at the water's edge like a palace, regal and splendid. Wide steps led to carved-wood, double doors that invited guests inside. Potted palms sat on either side of the doorway, adding a tropical elegance to the entry. Along the front of the hotel, brilliant pink hibiscus blossoms vied for attention with bougainvillea and other colorful plantings and softened the lines of the building.

Gratitude filled me.

In the troubling days following my ex's dumping me for his receptionist—Kandie with a K as she called herself—I would never have imagined being part owner of such a beautiful place. We'd started out better than expected, but the fear of failing kept me working day and night to make sure the hotel succeeded. So many didn't. And though I loved Rhonda, it was sometimes frustrating to be left with most of the detailed, follow-up work she disliked. Doing it as cheerfully as I could while she stayed busy doing the most-fun stuff was a way to pay her back for all she'd done to help me.

Rhonda appeared at the top of the stairway. Dressed in one of the light-weight, colorful caftans she loved to wear, she urged me forward, flapping the green sleeves of her dress like a tropical bird about to take flight. *Or more like the early bird who got the worm,* I thought wryly, as I got a closer look at the grin on her face.

She placed her hands on her ample hips and shook her head at me. "Annie Rutherford, how can you look so freakin' beautiful and put together at this early hour? I swear, if you weren't my best friend, I'd hate your guts."

I laughed. Rhonda was known for speaking her mind. It was amazing we even got along—we were as different as two people could be. My strict grandmother, who'd raised me after my parents died, would shiver in her blue-blooded Boston grave at the language Rhonda used. I'd gotten used to it, which was a good thing because Rhonda didn't even notice it. She'd come from a loud, Italian family in New Jersey.

"What's up?" I asked. "It better be good. I haven't even had my coffee yet."

"Oh, it's good all right. We have a decision to make—an important one that can't wait."

"And?" I prompted, giving Rhonda a dubious look.

"And I promised Valentina Marquis' agent we'd call her right back. She's at LAX, ready to put Valentina on a private jet to us."

"Oh, no!" My heart thudded with dismay. "Are you talking about the same Valentina Marquis who co-starred with Vaughn in that awful short film, the one he tried to get out of several times?"

Rhonda nodded. "The very same one. But, Annie, this could mean a lot of business for us."

As usual, talk of new business stopped me cold. Overseeing the finances of the hotel consumed me. At best, the hotel business was a series of ups and downs, fluctuating as bookings rose and fell. At worst, I had invested every cent of mine into my share of the business. Weather, dates of holidays, and fierce competition affected bookings for rooms reservations, which created a lot of uncertainty.

"Okay, you'd better tell me about it. Why does Valentina's agent want her to come here?"

An even bigger grin spread across Rhonda's face. Beneath her bleached-blond hair, her dark eyes sparkled with mischief. "You won't believe it! She's going to be shooting a movie in two months and has eight weeks to lose twenty-five pounds."

I frowned. "How's Valentina going to do that here? We're known for our delicious cuisine."

"The agent has requested us to provide a trainer to stay with Valentina, to keep an eye on her, and to guide her physical training. Because our guests know that The Beach

House Hotel assures them total privacy, she figures the director and producer won't find out what shape Valentina is in before she loses the weight. Cool, huh?"

"I'm not sure." Vaughn, sweet guy that he is, had ranted and raved about Valentina's *prima donna* attitude on the movie set. He'd declared her self-absorption and treatment of the people around her deplorable.

"It could be a bit tricky," admitted Rhonda, "but it's been a really slow fall season for us."

I couldn't deny it. In the past, we'd had a lot of VIP guests from the world of politics, but, with the latest mess in Washington, they'd been forced to stay put. Not that I minded all that much. The politicians were as egotistical as any movie star.

"Okay, let's call her back," I said reluctantly. Her visit could boost our cash flow, and who couldn't use a better bottom line?

On the way to our office, which sat behind the kitchen, I stopped and grabbed a cup of coffee along with one of Rhonda's famous breakfast rolls. Sweet and buttery, filled with cinnamon and nuts, their enticing aroma filled the air. These breakfast rolls had been instrumental in promoting the culinary reputation of the hotel since we opened it a little over a year ago.

After sipping my refreshing hot coffee, I carried it and the roll into the office and sat at my desk. A sigh of pleasure escaped me as I bit into the soft, warm breakfast sweet.

Seated opposite me, Rhonda dialed the number the agent had given her. I listened carefully as she informed Valentina's agent that we'd be delighted to have Valentina stay with us.

Rhonda stopped talking and then said, "Please hold. I'll check to see if we can make those arrangements." She turned to me. "Is it okay if I offer her the lower rooms at the far end of the hotel? If we give her rooms #101 and #102, Valentina will have the privacy her agent says she needs."

I quickly checked our online reservations system. "How long does Valentina's agent want her to use the rooms?"

"They want 'em for the full eight weeks, starting today. That takes us up to the Thanksgiving weekend."

I quickly looked at the reservations list. "We'll have to move a few people around, but we can do it." There were no full-house, wedding weekends planned during that time. Only smaller groups.

After she assured Valentina's agent she'd take care of everything, Rhonda hung up with a sigh. "It sounds as if this situation hasn't been easy for anybody. Valentina is getting on a plane within the next moment or two. We're to hire a personal trainer and meet her at the airport. She'll be traveling under the name Tina Marks, which I understand is her real name. And that's not all. I've agreed not only to provide special meals for her but to keep her out of the spotlight, so no one even guesses she's here."

"Okay, that's settled then," I said, suddenly overcome by the horrible feeling that this might be one of the biggest mistakes Rhonda and I had ever made together. And there'd been a few.

Tim McFarland, our young assistant manager, agreed to pick up Jerry Brighton, the personal trainer we'd hired through an agency, and to drive him in the limo to the airport to pick up Tina.

Rhonda and I stayed at the hotel to discuss the details of Tina's upcoming stay. Then I began my daily ritual of reviewing revenue reports, staffing schedules, and reservations to update my forecast. The sales weren't as strong as I'd hoped, emphasizing how important Tina's stay was to us. I resolved to make her visit go well. In addition to paying for the rooms, her agent was paying a hefty price for the hotel to cook special, low-calorie meals for Tina and her trainer.

I'd finished making some financial projections when Tim called from the limo to say he was approaching the hotel with our guest. As part of our normal routine, Rhonda and I went to the front stairway to greet them. From the hotel's beginning, it was something we'd done as often as we could. Our guests liked it.

Rhonda and I were standing by the front door in our usual stations when Tim pulled the limo into the front circle.

"Here goes," Rhonda said, giving me a high five.

As the car came to a stop, we watched closely.

Tim got out and raced around the limo to open the passenger door.

A foot encased in a high-heeled, gold sandal emerged. A young woman quickly followed, dressed in a denim skirt so short I knew she was wearing a thong. Her white tank-top indicated she wasn't wearing a bra.

My gaze lifted to her face. Large sunglasses hid most of it. Blue hair piled in a knot atop her head added a few inches to her height but couldn't hide the fact that she was short and ... well, wider than normal in places ... for a movie star.

We started down the stairs.

"Welcome ..." I started my spiel.

"What a dump," Tina said, cupping her hands around her sunglasses for a better view in the sunlight. "I asked for a big, fancy, glittery place if I have to do this stupid Hollywood thing."

Beneath her normal tan, Rhonda's face turned red.

I held my breath. Nobody bad-mouthed the hotel in front of Rhonda.

"That little brat," Rhonda murmured.

I grabbed hold of her arm. "Don't!"

She jerked her arm out of my hand and hurried down the rest of the stairway, her caftan flying behind her in a cloud of green.

Knowing what was coming, I raced past her. Tina might be a gigantic boor, but we would welcome her properly as my grandmother had taught me.

"Welcome to The Beach House Hotel," I said, elbowing my way in front of Rhonda.

A bald, muscular giant emerged from the car, looking like the smiling ad man on television who told viewers all about his cleaning products. Standing beside Tina, his bulk made her seem smaller than ever.

"I'm Jerry Brighton, the one you hired to keep tabs on Tina." Turning to Rhonda, he smiled. "This place is beautiful."

The lines of distress left Rhonda's face. She returned his smile. "Thank you. I'm Rhonda DelMonte Grayson, and this is my partner, Annie Rutherford. Among other things, The Beach House Hotel has a reputation for good service; we're here to help you in any way we can."

"Great," he said.

Tina's red-painted lips formed a pout as she glared at us. "I don't need anyone watching over me. I can do this myself. And nobody can know I'm here at this fat farm," said Tina. "That would ruin me."

Rhonda drew herself up.

This time, I knew I couldn't stop her.

Hands on hips, Rhonda stared down Tina. "This is not a fat farm. This hotel is a lovely place where guests can find some of the finest food in Southwest Florida." She paused for emphasis. "If they're allowed to eat it."

Tina gasped and stamped a sandaled foot. "That's it! I'm leaving!" She ruined the effect of her tantrum by teetering on heels too high for her. She regained her balance and turned to climb inside the limo.

In one swift movement, Jerry took hold of Tina's elbow. "Hold on. Let's at least give this a try."

Tina's shoulders slumped in defeat, allowing me to see a vulnerability that touched me. It couldn't be easy for someone so young to have so many demands made of her.

"Okay. I'll show you to your rooms," said Tim, who up to now had been standing aside wringing his hands. He urged them forward.

After Jerry and Tina had followed him into the hotel, Rhonda gave me a sheepish look.

"I'm sorry, Annie, but that little brat deserves more than a scolding. She deserves a spanking."

"No wonder Vaughn found it so difficult to work with Tina," I said. "I hope this isn't how she's going to act for the whole eight weeks."

A frown creased Rhonda's brow. "We can do this, can't we? Keep Tina here and get her thin?"

"We're going to try our best," I said with determination, "but, Rhonda, she won't be our only guest. We'll have to keep everyone else happy too."

"Eight weeks seems like a long time, huh?"

I nodded. "More like an eternity."

CHAPTER TWO

Tim came into the office shaking his head. "Tina is terrible. Now she's demanding to know what spa facilities we have. Apparently, she likes a lot of massages and other such treatments. Guess she likes being pampered."

Rhonda and I exchanged glances.

"It's a good thing we went ahead and put in the spa this year. Maybe now we'll finally get some good return on it," I said.

Rhonda gave me her impish grin. "After the phone call with Tina's agent this morning, I went ahead and ordered the monogrammed spa robes we've talked about getting."

I smiled. It was so typical of Rhonda. With her, things could and often did happen quickly. It wasn't all that long ago I'd been left without a marriage, a home, or a job. If Rhonda hadn't forced me to let go of my traditional ideas, I might never have decided to join her in this all-consuming project. Now, I was in it, and in it deep.

I thought about the spa, which we'd had built on the ground floor of the separate, multi-car garage, adjacent to a small laundry we used for towels and some special linens. We'd converted the top floor of the building into two very nice apartments. One was for Consuela, the number one person on staff in the hotel, and her husband Manny, who was what Rhonda called our "Manny around the house." He oversaw the landscaping and maintenance of the property. The smaller apartment was for Tim.

Concerned about the extra work of having Tina as our

guest, I turned to Tim. "With Tina here, it might be a little more difficult for any of us to get time off. You might feel as if you never have any peace."

"That won't be a problem." Tim's smile was devilish. "If it gets to be too much, I'll move in with my girlfriend."

Rhonda and I exchanged disappointed glances. Her daughter, Angela, had had a huge crush on Tim. We'd both thought it might evolve into a lasting relationship, but with Angela up north at Boston University, it now appeared that wasn't going to work.

We decided to speak to Consuela about what Rhonda privately named "The Tina Project." She and Manny had been with Rhonda since Rhonda and her ex-husband Sal bought the property. Without them, the hotel would never have gotten off the ground. Though our staff had grown, they were the two people we counted on most. We considered them family.

When we went into the kitchen, Consuela was there preparing lunch. With only ten guests here and no in-house events scheduled, the work-load was comparatively easy.

"Good morning," I said, giving her a quick hug before swiping a taste of her famous egg salad. The little bit of curry she added to the mixture, along with finely chopped mustard pickles added a zing that made it special. I licked my lips and gave her a thumbs-up.

Rhonda waved Consuela over to a seat at the kitchen table. "We need to talk with you."

We tackled the subject of a diet for Tina Marks, as she'd always be discreetly known to our staff and us .

"So we need to come up with plenty of low-calorie options for her," Rhonda ended.

A look of disapproval crossed Consuela's face. "*Si*, but we don't make food that has no taste."

"That's the challenge," admitted Rhonda. "She's a fussy eater who doesn't like so-called 'rabbit' food."

"She's fussy about everything," I said. "So if you have any problems with her, please let us know." We weren't about to let any guest abuse Consuela or anyone else on the staff.

I left Rhonda and Consuela discussing Tina's menu for lunch and went back to my house to check on things. I'd left in such a hurry I hadn't even made the bed. Besides, I wanted privacy when I called Vaughn. After he had resigned from the soap opera he'd starred in, he'd made one small appearance in a film, and now he was undertaking a bigger role in his first major movie. They were filming in Europe, and I hoped to catch up with him between scenes.

As I approached my house, I paused. It was sometimes hard for me to believe this perfect little house was mine. If Rhonda hadn't offered to sell me what used to be a caretaker's cottage on the property for a reasonable price, I might still be without a home.

I felt a smile spread across my face. Robert, my ex, had been shocked to see how well I'd landed on my feet. The house, with two bedrooms, an office, nice open living and eating area, and a fabulous little kitchen, was everything I'd dreamed it would be. The small swimming pool off the lanai was an extra I had decided to put in at the last moment.

Hurrying inside, I couldn't wait to talk to Vaughn. Our love was such a wonderful surprise to me. A well-known soap opera star, I'd met him when the show had done some filming at the hotel. He was the opposite of the egotistical character he played on television. That, and his devotion to the wife he'd loved and lost to an early death, made him more desirable to me than his dark, handsome features did.

Easing myself onto the desk chair in my home office, I settled down to talk to him. This was one time I didn't let financial worries interfere. My conversation with him was all I'd have for a while. I punched in his cell number, hoping I'd timed it right.

"Hello?"

The sound of his voice sent pleasure rolling through me. "Hi, Vaughn. It's me."

"Hi! I've been thinking about you. I've had to redo a couple of kissing scenes with Alicia, and the only way I could get through them was to pretend it was you."

I swallowed hard. I'd never get used to all the other women in his life.

"Ann?"

"I'm here. So, uh, she's not a great kisser?" I hated asking him, but the insecure part of me needed to know. I still couldn't believe that of all the women he could have, I was the one he'd chosen.

He chuckled. "Honey, she isn't you. That's for sure."

I drew a breath of relief. "Guess I'd better keep in practice. Maybe I'll have to find a substitute for you until you come back."

"Better not," growled Vaughn, and we laughed together.

"So how's it going?" I asked.

"Other than the constant rain in Ireland?" he said. "Can't wait for the outdoor shots to be over. The guy I'm playing is an interesting character, though. What's up with you?"

"We have a new guest, a VIP who's very demanding. Rhonda's already called her a brat. It's someone you've worked with. Guess who?"

After a moment of silence, Vaughn said, "You're not talking about my least favorite person, an actress by the name of Valentina Marquis, are you?"

"Afraid so. She's known to us as Tina Marks, but it's the very same young girl you complained about. She's hiding out here to lose weight for her next movie. Can you imagine? We're to provide low-calorie meals for her and her trainer."

"Ann, that sounds like a can of worms. How did she land at The Beach House?"

I filled him in on the story.

"Too bad. You really need the money?"

"Yes. I was even thinking of surprising you with a visit, but I can't consider it now. I wouldn't feel right about leaving, especially when we're starting a new ad campaign for the holidays."

"Well, I guess I'll have to make up for lost time when I get back to Florida." The note of regret in his voice made me feel a little better about not seeing him. I'd already learned what making up for lost time meant to him, and I couldn't wait to feel his arms around me, his lips on mine.

"I've gotta go," Vaughn said. "I'll call you as soon as I can. Maybe when you're in bed."

I laughed. "Oh?"

"Guess it's the best we can do," he said.

At the smile I heard in his voice, I grinned. I'd never had such fun with a man.

We hung up, and taking a chance that Elizabeth was free, I punched in her number. My daughter was so special to me, the child I'd always dreamed of. I'd wanted more children, but it hadn't happened. Liz, though, was a daughter any mother would treasure.

It was through Liz that I met Rhonda. As freshmen college roommates, Liz and Rhonda's daughter, Angela, became the best of friends. This year, though, what would have been her junior year in college, Liz was not at school with Angela but working in DC. After her father had admitted he'd used her college fund to build a house for his new wife, Liz decided to take a year off from school. I'd finally agreed to it, but every time I thought of what Robert had done to her, it made me bubble inside with anger.

Liz's phone rang and rang. When her voicemail came on, I left a message asking her to give me a call. It had been more than a week since I'd heard from her, and we usually talked every six or seven days.

I straightened up the mess I'd left behind earlier and headed back to the hotel.

A small, wiry man crossed the front lawn of the hotel toward me. Beneath a wide-brimmed straw hat, his dark eyes sparkled as he waved. "*Buenos Dias*, Annie! When is *Señor* Vaughn coming back?"

I smiled into his pleasant, brown-skinned face. "Hi, Manny! Vaughn won't be home for a few more weeks. Why?"

Manny shrugged. "I was hoping he'd help me with some new landscape designs around the pool. He and I talked about it before he left."

"Why don't I ask him to email you his ideas? Hopefully, I'll be talking to him again sometime soon."

"Okay," said Manny. "Paul is helping me with the new garden Rhonda wanted. We started this morning."

"Great. She'll love it." Rhonda and Jean-Luc Rodin, the French chef who worked for us in the evenings, had come up with the idea of a herb garden. In the Florida heat, it was a bit of a challenge, but having herbs freshly cut from the garden would be an added feature to the gourmet meals we offered our guests.

When I entered the kitchen, the look of fury on Rhonda's face stopped me. "What's wrong?"

"Look what Tina did!" Rhonda pointed to a noticeable spot on her caftan. "Annie, I swear I would've tackled her if Jerry hadn't been there."

I held back a laugh. With a rough and tumble older brother

and from a rather rough neighborhood, Rhonda had always been ready to defend herself.

"What happened?"

"Her agent told me Tina doesn't like 'rabbit food,' so Consuela and I made her a very nice gazpacho-type soup, without all the spice. She took one look at it and threw it at me. I ducked out of the way, but some of it splashed on me." Rhonda's dark eyes blazed with fury. "I'm tellin' ya, Annie, if she doesn't shape up, I'm gonna choke her."

"What about the other guests? Did they see her or hear anything?"

Rhonda shook her head. "I asked Jerry to take Tina inside. Maria's cleaning up the mess on the patio."

"I'm so sorry this happened. Tina hasn't been here even a day, and already she's causing trouble. Maybe." I said hopefully, "she just needs a little time to settle in."

"I don't know about that. Do we really need the money?" Rhonda gave me a worried look.

"I've checked our figures. We're going to have to get through these next eight weeks, Rhonda. Somehow."

She made a face. "Maybe a little arsenic would do it."

"Rhonda..."

She winked. "Okay, okay. It was just a thought."

Following the dinner hour at the hotel, Rhonda and her husband, Will, sat on my patio sharing a bottle of pinot noir. It was a good time to relax.

Though she'd recently turned forty-two, in Will's presence, Rhonda became like a young woman again. Love did wonderful things for people, I thought, watching the two of them flirt. Will lifted her hand and kissed it. Beneath her tan, Rhonda's cheeks flushed a pretty pink.

Will, tall, thin, and shy, was the perfect foil for Rhonda's exuberance. After living for many years with a sickly wife and caring for her to the end, he'd once told me he loved the way Rhonda charged through life with love and laughter.

Rhonda, I knew very well, had a big heart. Nobody would believe how much she did for others. But then she'd had a stroke of luck not many people receive. She'd won one hundred eighty-seven million dollars in the Florida Lottery. She'd kept control of the money. Though most of the winnings were tied up in various trusts, that's how Rhonda and Sal bought what she'd simply called The Beach House.

"So what are we gonna do about the brat?" Rhonda said. "Earlier, Jerry came to the kitchen to pick up Tina's food tray, but he returned it, saying she refused to eat stuff like that. She says she's going on a hunger strike until she gets what she likes."

"What does she want?" I'd been too busy overseeing a small private business dinner to pay much attention to the drama with Tina.

"She's asking for a ten-ounce filet and home fries." Rhonda snorted with disapproval. "I say give 'em to her. It would serve her right to lose out on the film. After knowing what she's like, I never want to see a movie of hers."

"How is Jerry handling things?"

"He doesn't look happy about the job. Their rooms connect, so they each have privacy, but he doesn't dare go into his room until he's sure she won't run."

"Hmmm. Maybe there's a way we can handle her."

Rhonda leaned forward. "Yeah? What do you have in mind?"

I grinned. "Bribery. It works on two-year-olds. It might work on her."

Rhonda, Will and I laughed together. It was worth a try.

CHAPTER THREE

The next morning, I dressed in shorts and a T-shirt, slipped on sandals, and headed over to Tina's room. I sensed that behind all the antics she was pulling there was a vulnerable girl who was acting out over something that had nothing to do with us.

Outside, thin spokes of sunlight radiated from the ball of light peeking above the horizon like a child playing hide and seek, barely illuminating the sky.

I knocked softly on her door.

As expected, Jerry answered. His frown turned to a smile when he recognized me. "Got food?" he asked hopefully.

I shook my head. "I have a plan to make Tina hungry enough to eat something healthy."

He grinned and held the door open. "Come on in."

Wearing a tank top and shorts, Tina was sprawled on the couch sound asleep. Even though we had a "no smoking" policy in the rooms, the place smelled like burnt tobacco. For that alone, I wanted to give her a good spanking.

"Should I wake her?" At my nod, he went over to her and shook her shoulders. "Okay, princess. Time to get up."

She groaned. "Go away!"

He shook her harder.

She rolled over and stared up at him. "What the fuck! It's still dark out, you jerk."

"Get up, Tina," I said, coming to Jerry's side. "I've got a deal for you."

She sat up, pushed the hair out of her face and snarled,

"Get out of here."

I forced a smile. "Aren't you tired of being a prisoner in here?"

She glared at me. "Yeah, so what?"

"I'm here to sneak you out of the room for a while. But it has to be now before any other guests see you. Come on. Let's go."

"I have to change, get some makeup on."

"No, we don't want anyone to recognize you. Follow me. We'll take a walk on the beach."

Frowning, she got to her feet. "This is your big deal? Doesn't sound so great to me."

I took her arm, handed her the baseball cap I saw lying on the floor, and walked her to the sliding door by the patio. "After you've been inside the room for another couple of days, it will seem like a dream to you to be able to run on the sand."

We stepped onto the patio.

It was quiet except for the movement of the waves meeting the shore and rolling back again and the cry of seagulls swooping in the sky above the water. I looked around. The pool was empty, and no one else appeared to be up and about.

"All clear."

Tina smirked at Jerry. "See ya later ... maybe."

"We'll be back before the sun is fully up," I assured him.

Holding onto Tina's arm, I hurried her across the bit of lawn leading to the white sand beach edging the Gulf of Mexico.

I slipped off my shoes and placed them on the lawn.

When I turned around, Tina had already hit the sand and was trotting away from me.

I caught up with her and pulled her to a stop. "We can make this work or not. Stay with me. Understand?"

She made a face and shrugged. "Anything to get away from

that guard you hired for me."

I took hold of her elbow. "C'mon! I want to show you something."

She jerked her arm out of my grasp. "I'm not a baby."

At her defiance, I fought to hold onto my temper. "I was only going to introduce you to something I love to do."

She remained silent but followed me to the water's edge. Standing on the hard-packed sand where the tide had ebbed, I took several deep, calming breaths.

"Go ahead, try it," I said to Tina. "Breathe deeply, close your eyes and listen. You'll hear all sorts of things most people ignore with their activity. It's a magical moment."

"What are you? Some kind of yoga instructor?" Tina sneered.

Frustration ate at me. I shook my head in disgust. "Are you always such a jerk?"

She clamped her hands on her hips and glared at me. "Are you always such a fucking freak? Don't you know who I am? I'm a star, and you're a nobody. So there." Eyes full of disdain, she spit at me, missing my face by inches.

My hand reacted before I thought.

"You bitch!" she screamed, fingering her red cheek.

"I'm sorry," I said, as shocked as she by the slap I'd given her. "But it's time you learned you aren't any better than anyone else. If my daughter ever treated people the way you do, she'd get the same reaction from me."

"Yeah? Has she told the authorities what kind of bad mother you are?"

"Elizabeth and I ..." I stopped. Tina would never understand that my daughter and I were the best of friends. In Liz's entire lifetime, I'd rarely had to act with force. "C'mon. Let's take a walk and cool off before it's time to go back to the hotel."

She gave me a challenging look. "What if I run away? God knows I could use some real food and I'd like nothing more than to get away from people bossing me around all the time."

"Do you honestly think that's going to help your situation?" I didn't mention that Jerry was ready to bail from the job of keeping tabs on her. He'd told Rhonda last night he didn't know how long he could last.

Tina gave out a sigh. "Okay. Let's go."

Together, we headed down the beach.

The sand felt cool on my bare feet. Knowing how hot it would get later in the day, I enjoyed the cooler sensation on my toes. Walking along in tandem, I studied Tina out of the corner of my eye. Without the amount of makeup she usually wore, her face was attractive. But the pout of her lips ruined the effect of her other pretty features. I couldn't help wondering about her family. Did her mother allow her to act this way?

"What are you staring at?" Tina snapped at me.

"Nothing," I said. "It's a beautiful morning, huh?"

She shrugged. "Like you said, it feels good to be outside, away from Jerry."

I heard the sound of footsteps behind me and whipped around.

"Hi, Ann." Brock Goodwin smiled at me.

My insides turned cold. His well-toned body in bathing trunks, his sleek gray hair, and his handsome features did not interest me. I detested the man.

To avoid being churlish, I said, "Hi, Brock." I took Tina's arm and started to lead her away from him.

She jerked out of my grasp and turned back to face Brock. "Who are you, handsome?"

His face lit with pleasure. It was exactly the kind of attention he sought.

"My name's Brock. How about you, sweetheart?"

I pulled Tina away. "She's a friend of Liz's and off-limits to you."

Brock called to me as we walked away. "You and Vaughn Sanders are never going to make it, and when he breaks it off with you, I'll be here waiting."

The look of surprise that crossed Tina's face was laughable. She stared at me as I kept the two of us marching back to the hotel.

"You're the hot babe Vaughn kept talking about?" Her shock was more than a little insulting.

"Hot babe?" Others might think of me that way, but heaven knew I didn't. Forty was on the horizon, and I had a twenty-year-old daughter. Liz had once told me I was gorgeous, whatever that meant, but my self-doubts remained. After all, I apparently couldn't measure up to bosomy, empty-headed Kandie, the bimbo Robert left me for. That, and growing up with a rigid grandmother who thought I never did anything properly had pretty much convinced me I was nothing special.

"I thought Vaughn would go for someone like me," Tina admitted, "but he apparently likes much older women."

I gritted my teeth and let the remark go, though Tina once more had proved she was the brat everyone thought she was.

After showering and dressing for the day, I headed to the hotel. Brenda Bolinder, the travel consultant who'd arranged for Vaughn's former soap opera, *The Sins of the Children*, to be filmed at the hotel, was due to arrive that morning. She wanted to speak to us about another idea. I couldn't wait to meet with her.

When I walked into the lobby, Tim was busy with a couple from Australia, who were checking out.

"I hope you enjoyed your visit," I said, shaking hands with them. "It's always a pleasure to have guests from afar visit The Beach House Hotel."

"It was lovely, simply lovely," the woman said. "Can't wait to tell my friends about it. Such a relief to be away from Orlando's Mickey Mouse."

I laughed. "Even Mickey would be welcome here if he behaved well enough."

She chuckled, and I left Tim to complete his work.

Consuela looked up at me and smiled when I entered the kitchen. "Tina ate her breakfast this morning. What did you do to her?"

"Took her for a walk on the beach. Once we learn to trust her, she can do more things incognito. You'd think she'd understand that."

Consuela nodded. "Rhonda's in the office, but she's not feeling so good."

I went to check on her.

"Are you all right?" I asked Rhonda, swinging into the room.

She nodded. "I'm feeling blah. That's all."

"Any word from Brenda?"

"Yeah. She called to say she's coming from Miami. She'll be here in a couple of hours." A smile spread across Rhonda's face. "I've got a feeling things are going to look up, Annie."

"It would be nice if Brenda's visit brought another windfall to us. I wonder what could be so important that she needs to see us right away," I said, taking a seat at my desk.

"Maybe it's another film," said Rhonda, rubbing her hands together with glee. "That would help us."

A while later, when we got a call from Brenda saying she was in town and approaching the hotel, Rhonda and I went outside to greet her.

Brenda's white limousine pulled up to the front of the hotel.

Excitement filled me as I watched a tall, regal-looking woman emerge from the limo and stand before us. Deep-red hair was pulled back away from her face and tied in a knot behind her head, exposing huge but tasteful diamonds in her ear lobes.

Dressed in a light-turquoise sheath that brought out the green in her eyes, Brenda moved toward us easily, a woman who was comfortable meeting with clients of all backgrounds.

"Welcome to The Beach House Hotel," said Rhonda, approaching her and giving her a boisterous hug.

"Yes, we're so glad to see you again," I added, embracing her.

Brenda beamed at us. "It's good to see you both too. I can't tell you how many people I've told about the two of you and your fabulous hotel."

Optimism curled inside me. Maybe Rhonda was right. Maybe this visit would bring us a lot more business.

"Come inside," I said eagerly. "We thought we'd have lunch in the Presidential Suite where we can talk privately."

Brenda's face brightened. "That sounds lovely."

We led her inside and up to what had been Rhonda's private living quarters. After marrying Will, she'd moved into his oversized home where they could have more privacy. It turned out to be a good move in more ways than one. Renting out her old space as the Presidential Suite brought in a lot of revenue, and occasionally offering it on a complimentary basis helped to attract small, executive groups to the hotel.

As we entered the main room of the large suite, pale-blue walls greeted us. Their blue color duplicated some of the hues in the assorted fabrics on the overstuffed furniture and in the drapes. The blue and magenta accent colors in the plush, cream Oriental rug echoed the various shades of the Gulf's blue water and the bougainvillea displayed colorfully outside the window. In the middle of the room, a crystal chandelier winked cheerfully in the bright sunlight shining through tall windows.

"This is beautiful," said Brenda. "As I recall, you didn't have this suite operational when I stayed here before."

"Nope, we converted it after I got married and moved out," Rhonda said proudly.

"Oh, how nice!" said Brenda. "I thought I saw a wedding band on your hand, Rhonda. I'm so happy for you!"

"Will is the nicest guy. Wait until you meet him," I said sincerely. Will was not only my friend but my financial advisor. I loved him like a brother.

"That's so nice to hear." Brenda smiled. "I look forward to meeting him."

Maria, Consuela's daughter, delivered a tray to the suite. Instead of our sitting at the large conference table inside the suite, she set up our lunches at the round, glass-topped table on the spacious balcony that overlooked the gardens in the side yard.

"Mmmm, so peaceful," murmured Brenda, taking a seat at the table.

Plates laden with chicken salad, sliced tomatoes, and frosty, green grapes, all atop a bed of fresh red-leaf lettuce and arugula, sat at each place, along with a tall glass of Consuela's special berry iced tea. A loaf of warm, sliced French bread with a ramekin of whipped honey butter complemented the meal.

Rhonda fidgeted in her seat, as anxious as I to know the purpose of our meeting.

After taking the last bite of her chicken salad, Brenda dabbed at her mouth with her damask napkin and smiled at us. "Delicious. Thank you."

"Okay, I can't wait any longer. Why are you here?" Rhonda leaned her elbows on the table and stared at Brenda. Patience was definitely not one of Rhonda's virtues.

Brenda laughed. "Oh, my! Sorry. I was caught up in the relaxing atmosphere and fabulous food here, but I should've known how curious you'd be."

She leaned back in her chair, studied Rhonda and turned to me. "How would the two of you like to host a very special wedding?"

Rhonda sat up in her chair. "A wedding? Whose?"

"For the moment, that has to remain a secret. Let's just say royalty is involved."

Rhonda's smile was as big as the one I felt spreading across my face.

CHAPTER FOUR

Having the wedding here at The Beach House Hotel is one of three choices I will be offering the bride's family," continued Brenda. "Let's take a tour of the property. You've obviously made some changes since the soap opera was filmed here." She turned to me. "I understand you and Vaughn are still going strong."

My hand crept to the pendant I wore around my neck. I nodded happily.

Smiling, Brenda squeezed my hand. "I'm so glad. He's such a nice guy. We were neighbors in New York. We even considered dating, but after he had met you, I knew he and I weren't going to get together."

I stared at her with surprise. "You did?"

She nodded. "When he told me who he was dating, I thought you were perfect. Besides, my kind of life wouldn't mesh with his. Not really. And as it happens, it's all turned out for the best. That's how I got the job of finding a place for this wedding."

"You know the family?" Rhonda asked.

Pink crept into Brenda's cheeks. She nodded. "Quite well."

Intrigued, I got to my feet. "Let's start the tour here. We've used the Presidential Suite for weddings, both for the bridal party and as a honeymoon suite."

I led Brenda into the huge master bedroom. In addition to most features in all of our rooms, it had a nice sitting area that looked out over the beach below and beyond to the Gulf of Mexico. A small, private balcony facing the water was a favorite place to sit and watch the famous sunsets along Florida's western shoreline.

"How about the master bath?" asked Brenda, taking notes.

The marble floor and walls of the bathroom offset a large spa tub. Its brass fixtures in the shape of a dolphin and those in the two individual sinks were highly polished. The oversized shower had six large shower heads and was plenty big enough for two.

"This is a great playground for newlyweds," said Rhonda. Her cheeks turned a bright red.

"Guess you and Will liked it, huh?" I said.

"Aw, Annie, you know I can't keep anything to myself," said Rhonda, giving me a playful push.

Brenda smiled. "I like the whole set-up here in the suite. What else do you have to show me?"

"Come on outside," I said.

"Yeah," said Rhonda. "We didn't get permission to put up the little, open, grass-roofed, bohio-style shelter we wanted to place on the beach. But we did get permission to build a wooden deck under the palm trees where we can serve lunch in the shade to our guests."

"Lunch and cocktails," I amended. "Though most cocktail parties take place around the pool, the wooden deck is the perfect place to watch sunsets."

"Sounds good," said Brenda. "Let's take a look at that and anything else you think I should see."

After showing her the deck and then the spa, we went inside to the conference room and the private dining room we used for our VIP guests.

"Thanks for the tour," Brenda said. "If you don't mind, I'm going up to my room to rest for a bit."

"Of course. When you come down, we can have a glass of wine and perhaps watch the sunset over the Gulf."

I checked my watch and smiled at Brenda. "I think we have time. Come with me."

We walked outside to the new deck. The sky was awash with pink.

"If guests don't want to get dressed for dinner, they sometimes come here to watch the sunsets." I turned to Brenda. "Have you ever seen the green flash?"

"Green flash?" She grinned. "What's that?"

"They say if the atmosphere is right, you can see a bright-green flash at the moment the sun dips beneath the horizon. I've never seen it, but I never get tired of looking for it."

"It's become sort of a contest among our guests to see who can spot it," said Rhonda. "I swear I've seen it. It comes and goes so quickly you can't be sure."

"Hmmm, interesting," said Brenda. "Maybe I can use that in promoting the place."

We watched and waited. The golden orb of the sun dipped lower and lower. As it slid below the horizon, I groaned. "We missed it."

She turned to me with a smile. "It was fun to watch for it anyway. Say, how would you feel if we offered your house to the bride's family for the wedding weekend?"

I hesitated. I had grown up in my grandmother's house in Boston, which she had filled with antiques and priceless objects. I'd gotten rid of most of them as they'd become a burden. But I'd carefully chosen a few of them for the house I'd never dreamed of owning.

"Maybe that's a bad idea," said Brenda, seeing my hesitation.

"No, it's a fine idea." It was silly to be made a prisoner of material things.

"I'm thinking of the privacy aspect," Brenda assured me. "If they go for it, they might want to book all of the rooms at the hotel for their wedding party. Is that possible?"

"For what dates?" Rhonda said.

"I'd have to confirm, but they're thinking of early January," came Brenda's reply. "It's a hush-hush wedding under private circumstances. I know that doesn't give you much time, with Thanksgiving and Christmas coming up soon."

Rhonda and I exchanged worried glances.

"We'll work around them and make it happen," I said, unwilling to lose out on the possibility of business like this.

"Jean-Luc and I can handle the wedding meals," said Rhonda. "The hotel is known for its outstanding food."

"That would be wonderful for the wedding day. The rehearsal dinner is something they might want to do off property. I thought I'd go look at a few places in town."

We gave Brenda a send-off with a list of the two or three best restaurants. Then Rhonda and I raced into the office.

"Royalty?" squealed Rhonda. "Can you imagine it, Annie?" She rubbed her hands together. "I'm going to do a little research online to see if I can find out any information about royal engagements."

"I'll check on our little princess here to see how the rest of the day went with her. We don't want Jerry to quit because of Tina's antics. Especially now. We're going to be busy if we want to have everything done in time for a holiday wedding."

"A holiday *royal* wedding," Rhonda amended, grinning.

Jerry answered the door to Tina's suite. Holding a finger to his lips, he led me inside. Tina was settled in front of the television watching movies.

She ignored us as we made our way through the suite,

outside to the patio.

"How's it going?' I asked Jerry.

He shrugged. "We're still waiting for some exercise equipment to be delivered. Tina can do sit-ups and other stuff without it, but she says she'll do better on the equipment."

"Are you getting more rest?" Jerry looked terrible.

He shrugged again.

"I'd better go. I'll check on the training equipment for you."

I left him and headed back to the hotel lobby along the beachside lawn, stopping to greet a couple of our guests lounging by the pool.

One of them, a frequent guest from New York, waved me over. "Who's in that suite you came out of? Whoever she is, she's smoking like a fiend. I thought this was a non-smoking operation, that any smokers had to use the specially designated areas."

"Yes, those are the standard procedures. I'll check on that for you," I said smoothly, irritated that Tina had once more disobeyed the rules. Rhonda had told me she'd spoken to Tina and Jerry about smoking in the room or on the patio.

The woman's husband, sitting next to her, shook his head. "I'm allergic to cigarette smoke." His look of disapproval was penetrating.

My stomach clenched. These were good, repeat customers. "We'll take care of it," I quickly said, though inwardly I wondered how to make someone like Tina follow our rules. If the situation were different, I'd ask her to leave. We couldn't lose the goodwill of valued guests, but we also couldn't turn away good business even if it meant dealing with someone as selfish and spoiled as Tina.

Mumbling under my breath, I trudged back to Tina's suite.

Standing on the patio outside her room, I tapped on the sliding door. Tina got up from the couch and strolled over to me. At the smirk on her face, I drew in a breath and told myself to be patient.

"Yeah? What do you want?"

"May I come in?" I asked nicely.

She opened the door and shrugged. "Okay."

Jerry appeared from his connecting room and gave me a questioning look.

"One of our very strict rules is no smoking on the premises except in special areas we've set up by the garage and at the back of the garden. It's important to the health of some of our guests. I understand Tina has been smoking on the patio and I can certainly smell cigarette smoke here inside this room. Please, don't let it happen again."

"More fucking rules? That's it! I'm leaving!" cried Tina, shaking a finger at me.

Suddenly, it was too much. "Okay, we'll call your agent and tell her it's not working out. Tim can help you make arrangements to get to the airport."

I turned to leave.

A hand met my shoulder. "Wait! You can't do that. You have to keep me here." Unexpected moisture coated Tina's eyes.

"It's too late," I said, telling myself to be firm. "It would've been good if this had worked out, but the situation has become impossible. You're not cooperating. Do you have any idea how much work it's going to take to get this suite back to our standards of clean and fresh? It will take a deep cleaning of all surfaces. It might even mean replacing the carpet, and reupholstering or replacing the furniture, along with the other soft goods."

Tina looked around the room. "I don't see anything wrong with it. The maid can clean it up. I'm not going to."

I bit back an angry response. This discussion was going

nowhere. "It's not working out for us. Good-bye, Tina."

"How about one more chance?" said Tina, surprising me.

I took several deep breaths, wishing we didn't need the business. But we did. I drew a deep breath and slowly let it out. "Okay. But that's it. Just one more chance or out you go. Period."

Tina walked out of the room.

As I told Rhonda later, I had no idea if Tina would obey the rules, but I was at my breaking point with her.

Rhonda often worked in the kitchen with Jean-Luc, preparing dinner meals. In the evenings, I hosted both guests and local residents for meetings and private dinners. The Beach House Hotel served as an upscale, discreet place where people could meet and dine in a setting that anyone would appreciate. These special gatherings were a nice financial boost for us.

I mingled with tonight's private-function guests, making an effort to remember names as I talked individually with them, ensuring they were comfortable.

When it was announced that dinner was about to be served, I led them to the small, private dining room, where Jean-Luc's wife, Sabine, was waiting to supervise the two servers attending them. Everyone on staff knew the danger of letting Jean-Luc's hot food grow cold.

After making sure that all was in order, I went to check on the main dining room.

The happy chatter of dinner guests greeted me. Dining at the hotel had become well-known not only for lunches but for dinners too. Jean-Luc had come from *Chat L'orange*, a well-known restaurant in Boston, but he'd decided total retirement in Florida wasn't for him. Here at the hotel, he loved creating innovative dinners that most of our guests adored. The ones who complained about the food earned a private puff of disgust from him.

His wife Sabine was an unexpected bonus. Cultured and well-acquainted with proper table service, she oversaw the waitstaff, who worked for us on a part-time basis. These staff members learned a whole lot more from her than where to place forks, spoons, and knives. They learned about gracious living, discreet service, and how to take care of guests seamlessly by anticipating their needs.

"Looks like another great evening," I said as I strolled into the kitchen.

"*Mais oui,*" said Jean-Luc, giving Rhonda a side-glance.

"I almost ruined the frickin' hollandaise by not stirring slowly enough," Rhonda confessed, rolling her eyes.

Determined not to be drawn into the bickering between the two of them, I simply nodded. As much as they irritated one another, Jean-Luc and Rhonda had become fast friends who managed to cook together. But a Frenchman and an Italian determined to have her own way would give any kitchen a troubled air, so the other staff in the kitchen were careful to give them space.

Jean-Luc offered me a plate with some broccoli and a couple of slices of roast lamb served with a mustard and wine sauce. I gladly accepted it and sat down at the kitchen table to eat it. Pink, but not too rare, the lamb tempted me to ask for more. But I'd learned to take small amounts, though Jean-Luc's desserts made with heavy cream were a more difficult challenge.

"How's the dinner meeting going?" Rhonda asked, placing a dollop of whipped cream atop a lemony dessert tart on a tray with others.

"Very good. Hmmm. They're going to love that," I said,

staring hungrily at the sweet pastry.

She grinned and glanced at Jean-Luc.

"One of my mother's *Italian* recipes."

I laughed. The blend of French and Italian cooking made our menus fun.

CHAPTER FIVE

I awoke and stretched in bed, intent on making some kind of peace with Tina. She'd been allowed to make everyone else miserable, and it was time to resolve that. Long ago, I'd learned that kids respected boundaries. Though Tina was in her mid-twenties, emotionally, she was about two, possibly three. Perhaps she needed to be approached differently. Besides, I couldn't escape the idea that inside the young woman was a vulnerable girl crying for help, and I wanted to know why.

Dressed in shorts and a T-shirt, I made my way through the hotel to Tina's rooms. Early light filled the sky with possibility. The usual tropical storm season would be coming to a close in a few weeks, but on this particular day, it was showing a reluctance to leave us. Rain was in the forecast, and a restless breeze whirled around me.

The Gulf water reflected the weather. Waves splashed on shore, their grayish color edged with frothy white tips that formed foamy smiles on the sand as the water receded.

I thought of Vaughn and the magical moment I'd shared with him after we first met. Standing quietly on the sand next to him, holding hands as we'd looked out over the water, I'd fallen in love with him then and there. I missed him.

I moved along to Tina's suite, knocked softly on the door, and waited for Jerry to answer.

The door opened.

I stepped back and blinked in surprise. Tina was wearing gym shorts and a tank top, looking as if she'd been up for a while. Her hair was pulled away from her face and formed a single braid that drooped behind her head and onto her shoulders. Without makeup and no attitude marring her face, she looked ... well, adorable.

"Are you ready for your morning walk?" I asked cheerfully.

"Duh." Her lips formed a familiar pout.

Shaking my head, I held my tongue. Tina was back to her obnoxious self. But for a brief moment, I'd seen the girl who could win hearts on a movie screen.

"Okay, let's go," I said, trying not to let Tina's mood ruin my day.

We left the room and went out onto the beach.

I started walking down the sand.

Tina called to me. "Hey, wait! Aren't we going to stop and listen to the waves or whatever you like to do?"

I stopped, not sure if she was teasing me or not.

"Ann, I mean it," said Tina sweetly. "I liked what you showed me yesterday. It was pretty cool."

Not sure where we were going with this, I walked back to her and took hold of her hand. Actors could pretend so many things. Though I'd been a bit leery at the beginning of my relationship with Vaughn, I'd learned to trust what he was saying. With Tina, I wasn't sure.

Facing the water, she turned to me. "Well? I'm waiting."

I drew in a deep breath and drew her closer to the edge of the water. "Okay, breathe deeply and close your eyes. Now listen. Can you hear the waves lapping the shore? The rhythm is so peaceful. Take another deep breath. Hear the cry of the birds? Let your shoulders relax. There. Now be still."

In the silence that followed between us, I could sense a shift in Tina. I cracked my eyes open and stared in surprise. Tears were silently rolling down Tina's cheeks.

Instinctively, I pulled her toward me. "What's wrong?" I

whispered, wrapping my arms around her.

She opened her eyes and jerked away from me. "What are you doing? Are you some kind of pervert?"

At the venom in her voice, I stumbled away from her. "Good God! I don't know what kind of stunt you're pulling, but I think we'd better get you back to your room."

Not caring if she followed or not, I turned on my heel and headed off the beach. Behind me, I heard the sounds of her running to catch up to me.

She grabbed hold of my arm, jerking me to a stop.

"Hey, look, Ann. You're not going to tell anyone about this, are you?"

Through lips gone wooden with anger, I managed to get out the words, "What do you mean by *this*?"

She lowered her head. When she raised it again, tears filled her eyes. "Me, crying like a baby. And then being upset. I don't want anyone else to know."

Trying to understand, I shook my head. "No. I won't tell."

Tina wiped her eyes. "Thank you."

My mind continued to spin as we walked back to her room without exchanging another word. Jerry met us on the patio, where he'd apparently been watching us.

"Everything okay?" he asked, giving us both questioning looks.

I glanced at Tina and nodded. "Thanks."

"See you later?" Tina said, giving me a look that dared me to say anything about our experience.

"Tomorrow. I'll see you tomorrow, Tina." I couldn't wait to get away so I could think about all that had happened.

After breakfast, with our guests happily fed, Rhonda and I met in the office to go over the schedule for the day.

"How did your morning walk with Tina go?" Rhonda asked, pushing away her barely touched cup of coffee.

"Something's off with Tina. Her behavior is so erratic, so emotional. I wonder if she's taking drugs."

"I'll speak to her about it," said Rhonda firmly. "We're not going to have any drugs here, not if I can help it. We don't want any of that kind of publicity. That would kill our business." Her brow knitted with worry. "I think we made a big mistake by having Tina come here."

"Me too." There was a lot more to that girl than most people knew. I didn't know what to think of her.

"How are room reservations coming along?" Rhonda said.

We went over the list. It was a small steady stream of business that I appreciated, but we needed more than that to cover our costs and make a profit.

I sighed. "We have to do better until the high season kicks in." Mid-January through March were peak-season months when we could normally count on a lot of "snowbirds" visiting from the north.

"Let's see what we can do to convince Brenda to have the royal wedding take place here," I added. "At the moment, we can offer her the rooms she needs, but we can't hold onto them forever without a commitment and a deposit."

"I looked online for any information on royal engagements or anything else that might tell us who it is. I found nothing at all about it anywhere on the web." Her eyes gleamed. "But, Annie, I don't care who it is. For us to be able to say that royalty stayed here at the hotel would be a big deal."

"Yes, it would. And the girls would love it."

A shadow crossed Rhonda's face. "Have you heard from Liz recently? I tried to call Angela, but she didn't pick up, and she hasn't called me back. It's not like her."

"Mmm, I had the same problem trying to reach Liz. I

wonder if our dear daughters are up to something." Liz was usually good about calling me back.

"Well, at least Angela will be home for Thanksgiving. She promised me that," said Rhonda. Her eyes filled. "I can't help wishing she'd chosen a college in Florida. Boston seems so far away. I don't even know most of her friends."

"I know how you feel. I'm happy Liz is staying with Nell Sanders in Washington, but it's a life I know little about. I guess I'll find out more at Thanksgiving."

Rhonda beamed at me. "Just think, if Ange and Liz hadn't met in college their freshman year, we wouldn't be here running a hotel together. Life sure is funny sometimes."

We chuckled together. It was a roller coaster ride neither one of us had ever imagined.

I checked my watch. "Brenda's limo should be here shortly. Before she leaves, let's check with her about the wedding plans."

"You bet!" Rhonda jumped up out of her chair and stood a moment, holding onto the edge of her desk. Her face grew pale.

"What's wrong?" I asked. "Are you all right?"

"I think I might have the flu. I feel a little odd." She shot me a mischievous grin. "Maybe Will and I need more sleep."

Shaking my head, I felt my lips curve. Rhonda had confided in me that after years of taking care of his sickly wife Ethel, Will was entranced with the idea of making love with a healthy, lusty woman. I was happy for her. Rhonda deserved that kind of delight after being ridiculed by her ex for her appearance.

We found Brenda with Tim in the front hall, as she was checking out of the hotel.

She noticed us and smiled. "I hoped I would see you again. I've found the perfect spot for the rehearsal dinner. A little

French restaurant where the bridal party can have all the privacy they need."

"René's?" I asked.

"Yes. It's quite a lovely spot."

"He's a friend of Jean-Luc's. After ours, it's the next best in town," said Rhonda proudly. "You'll be happy with it."

At Rhonda's enthusiasm, Brenda's eyes twinkled. "Not as happy as here, but I think it'll do."

"So when will you know if we're selected for the wedding?" I asked, crossing my fingers behind my back.

"And when can you tell us who it is?" said Rhonda.

"I hope to have answers for you within a week or two. In the meantime, are you going ahead with the assumption you'll get it?"

"Yes," I said, "but we'll need a commitment fairly soon, or I'll have to release rooms that come into demand."

Brenda gave us a satisfied smile. "Good. I'm rooting for you. Really, I am. My New York clients are still raving about filming the soap opera here and how well it worked."

Tim took care of her luggage as we walked Brenda out to the limo waiting for her.

Rhonda and I exchanged hugs with her and then stood aside as she climbed into the car.

As we watched the limousine pull out of the front circle, Rhonda said, "They'd better come through for us, Annie. You know how I love weddings. And this one would put us on the map in Europe."

"It would be a great way to grow our business," I said. My body became cold at the idea of failing. Our first months of operation had beaten all our forecasts, but now we needed to make up for some slow weeks. After suddenly having no money and no means to support myself following my divorce, the thought of being in that situation again was something that kept me worrying about the future.

Bruce Taylor, from Tropical Spa Equipment and Supplies, arrived to meet with us and check out the condition of equipment we'd recently installed. A striking man with gray hair and bright blue eyes, whom I guessed to be in his fifties, he was eager to please us.

"Do you know of a good masseuse?" I asked. "The one we've been using is moving to Arizona to one of the big spas there."

Bruce smiled. "As a matter of fact, I do. My son Troy is a trained masseur. Given the right circumstances, you might be able to talk him into leaving his present situation to come and work for you."

After we showed Bruce out, Rhonda said, "Do you mind if I go home? I need to take a nap. Don't worry. I'll be back in time to help with dinner."

I gave her a quizzical look. "You okay?"

"Just sleepy." A wicked smile crossed her face and faded.

I held up my hand. "No, don't tell me."

She laughed and left me in the office to finish up some paperwork.

That night, talking on the phone with Vaughn, I filled him in on the day's activities without getting into my strange experience with Tina. Though it weighed heavily on my mind, I'd promised not to tell anyone else about it. I hadn't and I wouldn't.

Settled among the pillows on my bed, I listened as he told me about the day's filming. I'd learned from watching the filming of the soap opera how tedious the process could be. It was a hurry-up-and-wait sort of thing. Lighting needed to be adjusted, and retakes of scenes due to a number of reasons meant hanging around or doing the same scene over and over. Not quite as exciting as I'd first imagined.

"So no more kissing scenes with Alicia?" I said, smiling.

"Yeah. We're done with that. At least for now. Maybe I'll have to find someone else to kiss. You know, to keep in practice for you."

I laughed. "Better not."

"So where are you right now?" he asked, his voice becoming low, seductive.

"I'm in bed. How about you?"

"About to get up. But I'll take time for you. So ... tell me what you're wearing."

I smiled. "Well, not much," I said, enjoying this game with the man I loved.

CHAPTER SIX

In the light of dawn, I trudged across the hotel's lawn wondering what kind of person I was going to have to deal with this morning. I knew now Tina was very vulnerable; she was also unpredictable and difficult.

When I arrived at her room, Tina was standing outside dressed for our outing. Pleased, I said, "Good morning! Looks like the rain has left us. It should be a nice walk."

She said nothing but acknowledged me with a nod.

"So how're things going?" I said as we crossed the lawn to the sandy beach.

"Terrible. That Jerry won't let me do anything I want." A practiced pout pursed her lips.

"Like what?"

"I've got to have something good to eat, not the stuff you've been giving me. And I can learn my lines in a hurry. No one needs to tell me to do it." She pulled me to a stop. "Can't you order McDonald's for me? Please? I'll pay you a lot of money."

"Don't you want the role in the movie?" I said. "To get it, you have to lose weight. You've already lost a couple of pounds. That's why you're here."

She frowned. "Yeah. So what?"

"Then why aren't you cooperating? Jerry's doing the job we hired him to do. So are we." I gave her a steady look. "We want to help you."

"You want the money," scoffed Tina. "I know how that works."

"We're not desperate, Tina." A little white lie.

"Well, I am," she said. "Desperate for some frickin' decent food."

Sighing, I moved away from her. It wasn't an easy situation for any of us.

Tina caught up to me. Walking beside me, she mumbled under her breath. I ignored her and picked up speed, moving freely along the sandy shore. Surprisingly, Tina stayed beside me. We'd gone a mile or so when I noticed a figure coming toward us.

Brock Goodwin.

"Let's turn around. We've gone far enough," I said. He was the last person I wanted to meet.

Tina noticed him and gave me a knowing look. "It's that guy you don't like. What's up with that?"

I shook my head. "Nothing I'm willing to talk about."

Tina turned and, waving her hand at Brock, called out to him. Before I could stop her, she took off running toward him.

Gritting my teeth, I watched her for a moment and then hurried after her. Brock and Tina together would be disastrous.

As I approached them, I heard Brock telling her, "It's the eighth house down the beach from the hotel. Why? Are you going to come visit me?"

She gave him a coy smile and did a little shimmy with her shoulders. "I just might."

His eyes lit up.

"Or might not," I said, upset by the way Brock was leering at her. Once a slime, always a slime.

"Now, Ann, we're only being friendly," he said petulantly.

My hand itched to slap the smirk off his face, but I refused to say more to him in front of Tina. I had the feeling she'd use it against me in the future.

"Come on, Tina. Let's go."

She made a face but surprised me by joining me and heading down the beach at my side.

Brock caught up to us. "Wait! Ann, why don't you and Rhonda come to the party I'm holding tomorrow night, and bring your friend?" He smiled at Tina and turned to me.

"Thanks, Brock, but we're really busy with the hotel."

"Well, maybe Tina and her boyfriend could come."

Tina's face reflected my astonishment. "Boyfriend?"

Brock clucked his tongue. "Oh, come on! I've seen the guy who hangs around with her. So what do you say?"

"We'll see."

"Guess that's the best I can do." Brock gave us a little salute and trotted ahead of us.

I pulled Tina to a stop. "What's with you and Jerry? Why would he think Jerry's your boyfriend?"

Tina looked away from me and kicked at the sand with a bare foot.

"Well?"

"He must have seen me trying to get Jerry to find me some real food. I was fooling around with him. That's all."

My mind raced, but I remained quiet as I moved along the beach. Vaughn had mentioned to me that Tina seemed more than willing to use her body to get her way. Now that I'd seen the way she was with Brock, a sick feeling came over me.

Tina glanced over at me. "So ... what? You think I'm bad or something?"

"Something."

Tina came to a stop and glared at me. "You don't know what it's like getting roles in movies and dealing with the Hollywood scene," she snarled at me. "You're just a ... a stupid loser. So leave me the fuck alone!"

A gasp of dismay left my throat as she ran ahead.

I took my time catching up with her. Beside me, the slap of

the waves meeting the shore and retreating in a steady pattern soothed me. Tina was more than a "wild child," she was a mess. A part of me wanted her to pack her bags and leave us alone. Another part of me wanted to try to draw her into a hug again, and I wasn't sure why.

After seeing Tina back to her room and preparing for the day, I headed to the hotel. Consuela and Tim were scheduled to be on duty. Having them live on the premises was a blessing for us, but we were careful not to take advantage of them. Though Rhonda or I were on duty every day and most evenings, we were adding staff as we needed them. We'd hired Dave Reynolds, recently retired from the corporate world, to take the night shift, acting as a front desk clerk and night auditor. Newly widowed, he was glad for the opportunity to keep busy during what he called the loneliest hours of any day.

When I entered the hotel, Tim waved me over . "The guests in #203 want to extend their stay through the weekend. Can we do it?"

"Let me check, and I'll get back to you."

I went into the office to go over our reservations and found Rhonda sitting in her chair, resting her head on her desk. At my appearance she lifted her head; her face was noticeably pale.

Alarm raced through my body. Something was wrong. Very wrong. Rhonda was a healthy woman.

"Rhonda, what is it?"

She shook her head. "I ... I ... don't know."

I placed a hand on her shoulder. "This isn't like you at all. I'm worried. I want you to call the doctor right now. I'll wait right here until you do."

"Okay."

My stomach clenched. She'd agreed too easily.

I took a seat at my desk and listened as Rhonda explained to the person on the other end of the call that she'd been feeling sick for some time. And tired. And not like herself.

She hung up and turned to me. "I can see Dr. Benson at eleven o'clock today."

"Good. I'm glad." Relief seeped into my voice. "I need to check reservations. The Brauns in #203 want to extend their stay over the weekend."

"They're the people from Chicago, right?" said Rhonda. "Friends of Jack and Lily Russell?"

"Yes, and we promised Jack to take good care of them. They're important clients of his." Jack Russell was a figure well-known in Chicago legal circles for handling a number of sensitive political issues.

After looking at the reservations chart, I drew a breath. "We're booked because of the golf tournament in town. But why don't we go ahead and let them stay? If we don't have any cancellations, we'll put someone in the Presidential Suite."

"Okay," Rhonda said instantly, "we'll take a chance and do it."

Keeping the hotel full was a tricky business. We didn't want to overbook rooms and have to "walk" people to another property. On the other hand, when people canceled reservations at the last minute, we were stuck with an empty room, and even with our deposit policy, we lost out.

Hours passed in the office without our usual chatter and banter. Unspoken concern hovered in the air. I noticed Rhonda staring at the clock on the wall.

"Do you want me to drive you to the doctor's office?" I asked her.

A look of relief crossed her face. "Will you?"

My heart rate took a dive. Rhonda was usually very independent, not this worried bundle of nerves. Maybe, I thought with dread, she sensed something was terribly wrong with her.

I informed Tim we were going, and then Rhonda and I left the hotel. "Why don't you stay here at the front of the hotel? I'll drive my car around and pick you up."

Again, Rhonda nodded, eager to comply.

I all but flew across the lawn to my house and quickly got into my car. Driving up to the front circle of the hotel, I watched Rhonda make her way toward my car. Her expression was unusually grave.

I waited patiently while she climbed in the car and got settled. Then I took off. My mind whirled at what this doctor's visit might mean—to her, to us, to the hotel.

"Will you come inside with me?" Rhonda asked when I pulled into the medical building's parking lot.

My stomach filled with acid. "Sure."

Inside the doctor's office, the receptionist greeted us with a wide smile. "Hi, Ms. Rutherford! Thank you so much for inviting my boyfriend and me to come to the hotel for lunch. It was delicious. We definitely want to have our wedding reception there."

I smiled. "When you're ready, call the hotel, and if Rhonda and I aren't there, Sabine will be glad to help you. She does a wonderful job with weddings."

She beamed at me and turned to Rhonda.

"Dr. Benson can see you now, Mrs. Grayson."

Rhonda drew a deep breath and gave me a weak smile. "I'll be out as soon as I can."

"Don't worry," I said. "I'll wait right here for you." Nothing would make me leave until I knew she was going to be okay.

While I leafed through one boring magazine after another, several minutes passed. I sat in the waiting room becoming more and more concerned.

The receptionist's voice startled me from my fog of worry. "Ms. Rutherford? Mrs. Grayson would like you to come on back."

I jumped to my feet. "Is everything all right?"

The receptionist's expression gave nothing away. She simply indicated the door leading to the back of the office.

My feet felt leaden as I made my way down the hall past examination rooms.

At the end of the hallway, the door to the doctor's office was partially open. My heart stuttered to a stop when I saw Rhonda crying.

I rushed forward. "Rhonda, what is it?"

She shook her head. "Annie, you won't believe it! It can't be happening to me."

"Oh my God! What is it?"

She swiped at her eyes, and when she looked up at me, her lips curved into a tremulous smile. "I'm almost three months pregnant."

I was so stunned I couldn't think of anything to say for a moment. "Oh, but that's wonderful!" Throwing my arms around Rhonda, I hugged her tight.

Rhonda shook her head. "I can't believe it. Will told me he couldn't have children. What am I going to do? I'm forty-two, and he's fifty-two."

"What are you going to do? You're going to have a baby," I said, tearing up as relief mixed with joy.

Rhonda's eyes filled. "I'm so happy, so scared."

"What did Dr. Benson say?"

A tiny Asian woman approached us, smiling. Ruth Benson, the primary care doctor Rhonda and I both used, was a woman in her fifties who was as smart as she was small. Tiny and efficient, she homed in on symptoms like a bullet to a target, no muss, no fuss. As tough as she was on facts, she was as gentle a soul as one could have when dealing with difficult situations.

The doctor approached, smiling. "Dr. Benson says Rhonda's in good health and should do fine. We'll run our regular tests to make sure, but everything looks fine."

Rhonda's eyes shone. "Will is going to be so happy. He's always regretted not having children." Her smile wavered. "Oh no! What will Angela say when she finds out?"

"She'll be happy for you, I'm sure." Angela was a great girl who loved her mother.

"I'm so relieved," said Rhonda. "I was sure I had some terrible disease. I don't remember feeling like this with Angela." A look of wonder crossed her face. "Maybe it'll be a boy. A boy for Will."

Dr. Benson gave Rhonda a list of instructions and other paperwork, and then we left the office.

"Will you drop me off at Will's office?" Rhonda asked me. "I can't wait to tell him the news."

I grinned. "Sure. I imagine he'll be thrilled."

"What if he isn't?" Rhonda's brow wrinkled with worry.

My smile was confident. "He will be. Trust me."

Rhonda returned to the hotel later that day and pulled me into the office.

"How did it go?" I asked.

She patted a hand on her chest, fighting emotion. "It was one of the sweetest things ever. Annie, he broke down and cried for joy. Like me, he's totally surprised and so very proud and happy. And then he wanted me to sit down and take it easy. He said he's going to take good care of me ... of the baby and me. I told him I'll be fine after I get over being sick."

"He's a very sweet man," I said, meaning it. "And he's going to make a wonderful father."

"He wants me to work fewer hours at the hotel. I told him it wasn't fair to you, but he's not happy with me working late at night."

I wasn't surprised. "We'll add some hours to Dorothy's schedule during the afternoon to give you time to rest, and we'll have Sabine come in every evening instead of part-time. With Jean-Luc working here, I'm sure she won't mind."

"But it's not fair to you," said Rhonda.

"One day at a time, remember?" I could never repay Rhonda for what she'd done for me, and if her being pregnant meant extra work for me, I'd gladly do it.

Rhonda pulled me into a hug. "How did I ever get so lucky? Having you for my best friend is better than winning the lottery."

I laughed. We both knew it wasn't true. If she hadn't won the lottery, there'd never be The Beach House Hotel. Baby or not, I'd make sure to do the best I could to continue to make our hotel a success. I wouldn't; I couldn't fail.

CHAPTER SEVEN

As I stood in the bathroom after taking a shower, I stared at my body. Though I was a couple of years younger than Rhonda, I couldn't imagine bearing another baby. It wasn't a possibility because I'd had a hysterectomy, but the reality of its happening to her sent a frisson of worry through me. Would age make a difference to her and her baby? Would her having a baby destroy our ability to run a hotel as a team? And if so, how could I keep it going by myself?

I caught a glimpse of my reflection in the glass shower door. Blue eyes stared back at me critically. At five-three, and with my shoulder-length black hair hanging straight, I didn't look close to forty, though the big four-o would happen within the year. But the energy I had was more important than age and was brought about by my determination to make the hotel succeed. Losing Rhonda to motherhood even for a short time would be a challenge, but somehow I'd make it work, though the thought of adding to my workload was depressing.

Calmer thoughts prevailed as I dried off. I told myself Rhonda could continue to do a lot of work for the hotel, and after the baby was born, she'd no doubt find a good nanny to help her. Dorothy Stern would be delighted to spend more time in the office taking Rhonda's place when necessary.

Thinking of Dorothy, my lips curved. She was a woman in her sixties, quick witted, and newly retired from a retail business she'd owned. Bright-eyed, even as she peered at the world through the thick lenses of her glasses, she observed things that needed to be done and saw people as they really were. I treasured her. Other members of the staff had proved to be loyal and hardworking as well. We'd all have to pull together.

More confident now, I settled down in bed to read a book from one of my favorite authors. A light-hearted, easy read was exactly what I needed, and having time to do this was a real treat for me. My eyes were beginning to droop when the phone rang. I picked it up, and seeing who it was, I smiled happily. Liz.

"Hi, honey? What's up?" I asked, pleased to be able to connect finally.

"Not much. With me anyway. Angela was here in DC with her boyfriend, and we hung out for a while."

I perked up. "What boyfriend is this?"

"A guy she met at summer camp. He was a financial consultant to the owners of the camp for several weeks while we were there."

"Oh, nice." I waited to hear more, but Liz was uncharacteristically quiet. I knew something else must be on her mind and waited for her to speak.

"I've been thinking I might want to go back to college next semester. I tried talking to Dad about it, but he said the two of you would have to work it out. Will you call him, Mom?"

I gritted my teeth. As part of the divorce settlement, we had set aside a fund for Liz's college education. But in true-Robert fashion, he'd wiggled around the rules and used it to build a fancy house for Kandie and himself—a house he'd subsequently been forced to sell under threat of foreclosure. My lawyer had worked out an agreement with him, but it still stung.

"Mom?"

Still fighting the old anger I felt toward him, I relented. "Okay, Liz, I'll do it. What brought about this change? You insisted you needed time off from school."

"Yeah, well unless you have a college education, you can't find a decent job. Nell helped me get a low-level job in a PR firm, but it doesn't pay much. I want something better than that. Now I want to get a marketing degree."

My lips curved. Building that kind of determination to succeed was worth her taking a semester off from school.

"I've applied for a scholarship at the school, but it won't cover all the costs. The dean said there'd be no problem in my getting back in."

"All right. Let's see what we can do." Only for my daughter would I be in touch with my ex. I was in no position to pay Liz's tuition myself, and I didn't want her loaded down with unnecessary student loans.

"Thanks, Mom! You okay? Anything new with you and Vaughn?"

"I'm fine and so is Vaughn. Nothing new." I bit back any words about Rhonda's baby because I didn't know if Rhonda had talked to Angela yet.

"Okay, talk to you later. Love you."

"Love you too." I clicked off the call with a sigh. I'd tried to talk Liz into staying at BU, but she'd insisted she needed time off and a break from Boston. It would've been so much easier if she'd stayed in school.

Turning off the light, I realized sleep would not come easily. Robert and I weren't good at talking anymore. In truth, we probably never had been very good at it. And now conversations between us turned cruel.

The next morning, after my walk with Tina, I hurried to get ready for work. When I entered the hotel, I checked in with Dave Reynolds and Tim, who were making the transition from night shift to the day shift.

"A cold snap has hit New England," Tim said giving me a wide smile.

We exchanged looks of satisfaction. With people facing the reality of wintertime approaching, more reservations were coming in. But it also meant we were running out of time to learn if we'd be hosting the royal wedding.

In the office, Rhonda was poring over our brochures. "I've thought we should play up our spa. Especially if we hire a new masseur."

"Good idea. We can put together spa packages. Lunch at The Beach House Hotel could include a low-calorie luncheon and afternoon session at the spa."

"Yes! Girlfriends can come together here." She gave me an impish grin. "Or it could be a romantic time for couples."

I laughed. Ever since marrying Will, Rhonda's focus had been on their love life. In someone else, it would be uncouth. With Rhonda and Will, it was endearing.

A few minutes later, the owner of Tropical Spa Equipment and Supplies arrived with a handsome young man. After exchanging greetings with us, Bruce Taylor introduced his son, Troy.

"I'm interested in applying for the job of manager as well as becoming one of the masseurs," said Troy.

I studied him. Tall and broad-shouldered, he looked like he could handle clients of any size. He had dark hair and light blue eyes that shone with kindness. Troy held out a hand.

I shook it eagerly. "That is something we definitely can talk about." With Rhonda contributing less time to running the hotel, it would be great not to have to worry as much about the daily operation of the spa.

I turned to Troy. "Tell us a bit about yourself and what experience you've had running a spa."

Troy grinned boyishly. "Well, since my dad runs a spa-related business, I got interested in them as a young kid. I trained to be a physical therapist but decided, instead, to get my certificate in massage therapy. The cost of schooling was an issue. Through my dad, I've been able to build a good client list."

"You've actually never run a spa?"

He shook his head. "But I've got a lot of good ideas, loyal customers, and can make this small operation work. I know I can because I helped a friend do it."

I blinked in surprise. This quiet-spoken young man was smart and confident. I liked him.

"Okay, put together some of your ideas for Rhonda and me, and we'll talk."

"And give us references," said Rhonda. "I like what I hear, but we've learned to get references. Right, Annie?"

I'd been the one to hire someone too quickly to help with landscaping, and he'd ended up stealing from us.

After Bruce and Troy left, Rhonda said, "I liked Troy. He seemed pretty eager to do the work and yet he wasn't too uptight." She stretched her body. "Oh boy! I'd like him to give me a massage right now."

A new idea came to me. "We can advertise it to expectant mothers who want a little pre-baby vacation. We had quite a few guests celebrating like that last winter. There's no reason we can't make a visit to The Beach House Hotel a year-round gift for new mothers-to-be."

"And I'll be the first to test it out." She wrapped her arms around her body, hugging herself. "Omigod! I can't believe I'm having a baby! It's a miracle!"

I felt a grin spread across my face. It was such a wonderful thing to see her so excited. "Have you told Angela yet?"

Rhonda shook her head. "I'm going to wait until I see her.

I want to tell her in person."

"I talked to Liz last night. She said Angela and her boyfriend visited her in DC last weekend."

Rhonda's eyes widened. "Boyfriend? Did she say who it was? I wonder if that's why I haven't heard from her. It's so not like Angela." She lifted the phone. "I'm going to call her right now."

I waited as Rhonda punched in Angela's number. After a minute or so, Rhonda shook her head. "She's not answering." Worry lines creased her brow. "Oh my God! Maybe she's hurt. Maybe she's been in an accident."

Placing a hand on Rhonda's shoulder, I spoke firmly. "Don't even go there, Rhonda. She's fine or was a few days ago. No doubt she's busy at school. She's always been a good student."

Rhonda drew in a deep breath and let it out. "You're right. Angela's a good girl. She must simply be busy, though I have to tell you, Annie, I don't like it when my baby girl is too busy to call her mother!"

I smiled in agreement. As parents of only children, Rhonda and I understood all too well how hard it was to help your child become more and more independent.

"She'll call soon. I'm sure of it," I said.

CHAPTER EIGHT

I'd just ended a conversation with Vaughn when Rhonda called.

"Hi. I just spoke with Angela. She's agreed to come here this weekend and bring that new boyfriend of hers. She says she's sorry she didn't call me back but, like you said, she's been real busy."

"That's great. I'm glad you two finally connected." In truth, I was a little jealous of the forthcoming visit. I hadn't seen Liz in several months.

"Yeah, well, I'm not sure I'm going to like what's going on with her boyfriend. His name is Reggie Smythe. What kind of freakin' name is that? It's just a fancy way of saying 'Smith.'"

"Now, Rhonda ..." I began.

"I know, I know," she said, "but Angela needs someone down to earth, someone real, someone who will see her as the wonderful girl she is. Apparently, Reggie's from some high-society family in Newport, Rhode Island, and New York."

"He's only a boyfriend, right?"

"Yeah, but what if she's really serious about him? What will I do then?"

"You'll be supportive," I said firmly. "You haven't even met him yet. Give him a chance."

"I know, I know, but there was a certain sound in her voice like I get around Will. You know what I mean?"

"Yes," I said, smiling. Rhonda's voice softened whenever Will was around.

"She wasn't going to come home, but I told her, 'If you're

traveling all over with him, visiting Liz and all, I want to meet him.'"

"So she told you about going to see Liz in DC?"

"Yes," said Rhonda. "It's gotta be serious if they're traveling together. Did Liz say anything about their visit?"

"She only mentioned it in passing because she called to tell me she wants to go back to school. We discussed it, and I've reluctantly agreed to talk to Robert about his need to finance it."

"That rat bastard? He'll probably find an excuse not to do it. Like always."

"That's pretty much what I expect. It's so unfair. But, for Liz, I'll make an effort to talk to him because I can't pay for it, and I don't think it's fair for her to be burdened with student loans when he was supposed to cover those expenses all along."

"Good luck. Listen, I gotta go. I'm meeting with Consuela first thing in the morning to show a new hire the kitchen operation."

After hanging up, I leaned back against my pillow. If, as Rhonda said, Angela and her boyfriend were doing a lot of traveling together, it certainly did seem serious. Next time I talked to Liz, I'd ask her about it. In the meantime, I'd be busy with things at the hotel, but not too busy to stop worrying about putting heads in beds, as it's known in the hotel business. And we hadn't heard from Brenda yet regarding the wedding. A royal wedding would be perfect PR for the hotel.

I awoke to the sound of rain hitting the glass of my bedroom windows with tiny pings. More than anything I wanted to stay in bed until my normal time to get up. But then I thought of Tina and forced myself out of bed. We wouldn't be able to walk on the beach, but maybe I could surprise her by bringing her over to the hotel for a cup of coffee.

After taking a shower and freshening my hair, I put on a pair of slacks, a tank-top, and a summer sweater and headed out.

The rain had stopped, but drops of rainwater continued to slide off the palm fronds above me, dropping to the ground in a steady rhythm. Hibiscus blossoms hung their pink heads like scolded school children.

I hurried across the lawn, leaving footprints on the wet grass.

When I got to Tina's room, all seemed quiet. I knocked on the door and then rang the bell. Several minutes later Tina came to the door dressed in short pajama bottoms and a tank top. She looked terrible.

Stepping inside and drawing closer to her, I inhaled the smell of alcohol coming from her.

"What do you want?" she said, shutting her eyes and clapping a hand to her forehead.

"What's going on? Where's Jerry?" His door to the suite was open, but I saw no sign of him. And looking through the open doorway, I noticed he apparently hadn't slept in his bed.

"He went out last night with friends he met at the gym. He called to say he'd be back this morning."

I hid my surprise. "Get dressed. I have just the thing to help you get over whatever booze you drank last night."

Tina studied me a moment. "You're kidding, right? You're not going to scream at me?"

"Not now," I said, forcing a smile I didn't really feel. "Maybe later, when you're looking and feeling better, we'll talk about it."

"All right. I'll be out in a minute." She staggered into her room and closed the door.

When she returned to the living room, she had dressed in jeans and an over-sized T-shirt. Her hair was knotted on top of her head, and over-sized sunglasses covered her eyes .

"Ready?" I asked.

"I guess. Nobody will see me, right?"

"We'll go in the back entrance of the hotel, directly into the kitchen. Come on."

Tina trotted behind me, moaning now and then.

We entered the back of the hotel and into the kitchen. "Go ahead and have a seat. I'll fix you something for the hangover." Rhonda had come up with a special remedy. Tina wasn't the first guest with a hangover, and she wouldn't be the last.

I went to work putting together a smoothie of mixed berry fruit juice, banana, egg, a touch of lime Gatorade, and a small scoop of vanilla protein powder. While it was being whipped into a frothy mixture, I handed Tina two aspirins and a glass of water. "Better take these."

She swallowed the pills and eyed the mixture I was pouring into a large glass. "What's that?"

"Something some of our guests like. It may help you get rid of your headache and the alcohol in your system. That, and time."

Tina frowned. "Why are you so nice to me?"

"As I said before, you're our guest, and we want to help you."

The look she gave me was full of suspicion, but she drank down the mixture and then laid her head down on the table.

"Here's Consuela. She and Rhonda have been trying to come up with tasty low-calorie meals for you."

Tina lifted her head and studied Consuela. "Thanks."

"This is our guest in #102," I explained to Consuela, amused by her startled expression. At the moment, Tina looked as if she were twelve.

Consuela smiled at Tina and went about putting on an apron. "Rhonda will be here soon. We're showing one of the staffers how she can help me in the kitchen."

"All right, we'll leave you. It's time to get back to the room," I said to Tina. "You probably want to rest."

She nodded and followed me out of the kitchen.

When we returned to her suite, Jerry met us at the door. "Whew! I was worried when I found the suite empty. It's too rainy for a walk."

Tina stumbled into her room, leaving me alone with Jerry.

"I was surprised to find you gone," I said. "We hired you to keep watch on Tina. She obviously did a lot of drinking while you were away."

We studied one another.

I remained quiet, waiting for an explanation.

Finally, Jerry said, "Yeah. I should've stayed here, but I met some friends last night." He looked uncomfortable for a moment then said, "I'm sorry."

"You can't leave Tina alone any time you want. We'll need to work out a schedule, so you have some free time. Until then, you need to do the job we hired you for. Understand?"

"Thanks. I appreciate that."

I'd no sooner returned to the hotel when Tim approached me. "One of the guests is accusing Ana of taking a pair of earrings from her room."

I pressed my lips together. Ana was as honest a person as one could meet. Hardworking, she wouldn't jeopardize her job as a housekeeper by doing something so foolish.

"Which guest are you talking about?"

"Mrs. Pennypacker in #218. She's traveling with her sister. Both swear the earrings were on top of the dresser when they went for breakfast this morning. Now they're gone."

"Have you looked for the earrings yourself?" I said to Tim. He shook his head. "I've been busy with other guests."

"Okay, I'll go up and speak to them," I said, hoping for a quick solution. Along with offering our guests discretion, we wanted them to have complete trust in our staff.

Isobel Pennypacker was a woman in her sixties who loved to come to Sabal every few months to get away from her demanding family in Palm Beach. She and her sister Rosie, a couple of years younger, were an interesting pair. Wealthy, married multiple times, Isobel enjoyed the privacy we offered. She and Rosie could often be seen sitting by the pool in their bikinis. I'd been a little shocked when I'd first seen their exposed bodies, but they didn't seem to care what they looked like. They'd sipped their afternoon tropical drinks, laughing together over the magazine articles they quietly read to one another. In the evenings, the two sisters dressed up for dinner. As Isobel once told me, there weren't many truly upscale places around like ours, places that deserved dressing in proper attire.

Hoping to solve this issue of lost jewelry quickly, I tapped on her door.

Isobel opened the door. "Ah, Ann. It's terrible. I'm frantic. The diamond earrings my latest husband gave me are gone. I'm sure the housekeeper took them. The earrings were here; then they were gone."

"May I come in?" I asked. "I'd like to check for myself."

"Sure, but Rosie and I have looked everywhere."

She waved me inside.

"Let's start at the beginning. When did you last wear those earrings?"

"Last night at dinner. Before going to bed, I put them on the bureau. And after Rosie and I came back from breakfast, I checked, and they were gone. The housekeeper had made the bed and cleaned the room, so I know it was the housekeeper." Her face flushed with indignation.

"Where do you keep the rest of your jewelry?"

"In the safe, like we were told," said Isobel, flashing me a blue-eyed look that barely hid her irritation.

"Okay, let's take a look. Sometimes people automatically place their jewelry there without thinking much about it." Isobel had so many jewels I'd often wondered how she kept track of them.

Isobel scoffed at me. "I'm not *that* old."

"No, of course not," I said, "but let's double-check."

Isobel opened the safe and withdrew a satin, zippered bag.

I held my breath. As certain as I was about Ana not stealing, I knew artful hotel thieves could hide among respectable groups.

Isobel unzipped the bag and spread her collection of jewelry on the bed.

"Oh!" She clapped a hand to her cheek. "They're here!"

"I'm so glad you've found them. I would hate for anyone to accuse our dedicated staff of a crime they didn't commit." I kept my tone friendly, but it was upsetting to think how easily someone like Isobel could blame a hard-working housekeeper for something like this.

Regret washed Isobel's face. "I'm sorry. I really am." Her expression brightened. "I'll be sure to leave an extra big tip for her."

"That would be very nice. Anything else I can help you ladies with?"

"Oh, no," said Rosie. "We're all set. We love staying here, you know."

"And we love having you," I said sincerely, giving them each a hug.

Isobel's smile was sheepish. "Thank you again."

I left them and headed to my office.

As I entered, Rhonda looked up from the paperwork on her desk. "Where were you?

I told her about Isobel Pennypacker and said, "Do you think we need to add more security?"

"No," said Rhonda. "I suspect Isobel is a lot older than she tells her friends and us."

We laughed together.

"How did the trial period for the new hire in the kitchen go?" I asked her.

"I think she's going to be fine. She was respectful of Consuela, and she already has worked with Jean-Luc. If she can work with that frustrating Frenchman, she can work with anyone!"

"We can always find someone to replace Jean-Luc," I teased, lying through my teeth.

Rhonda's eyes widened. "Of course, we can't. Why do you think I let him try to boss me around in the kitchen?"

I chuckled. Rhonda may get in verbal battles with Jean-Luc, but we both knew we could never replace him. And at this point, I didn't want to replace anyone. I was already beginning to wonder what I'd do when Rhonda had her baby, and I had to take on even more responsibilities.

When I got back to the office after having gone home for lunch and a break, I had a message to call Vaughn.

I punched in his number, expecting to receive a voice mail message.

"Hello?" he said in the deep voice that was his alone.

Warmth surged through me. "Hi! What's going on? Where are you?"

"Here," he said. "Or almost."

"Really?" My pulse sprinted with anticipation.

"I'll be there in a few minutes. I landed a short while ago. See if you can take the afternoon off. I'm here for only two days. I had to see you."

"Don't worry. I'll find a way to get out of my commitments," I said happily. "Can't wait to see you!"

I felt like a starry-eyed teen as I raced to find Rhonda.

She was doing an inventory of sheets and towels in an upstairs closet. There was a discrepancy between our count and that of the commercial laundry we were now using.

"Vaughn is here! I need to have the rest of the day off. Can you handle the dinner tonight? Sabine is due to come in, but I was going to help her with a business group."

"He's here?" Rhonda beamed at me. "Sure, honey, I'll cover for you." She threw her arms around me. "It's time you took a break anyhow. I'll call Dorothy and ask her to come in early and to stay late to handle the phones. You go ahead and have fun."

"Thanks!" I turned and made a hasty getaway. I loved it when Vaughn surprised me like this .

Outside, the sun had broken through the morning cloud cover. White puffs of clouds raced across the sky, which had turned the deep blue that normally followed our rainstorms. Drops of water sat like diamonds on the leaves of plants, as bright as the expectation bursting inside me.

I stood at the bottom of the steps and watched with growing excitement as Vaughn drove through the gates and pulled into the front circle.

He came to a stop and climbed out of the rental car.

I ran toward him.

He met me halfway and swung me up into his arms. At six feet two, he was a robust man who had been every housewife's secret love on afternoon television. But now, he was the man I loved like no one else.

"Ahhh, feels so good to be home, so good to have you in my arms." His melodious voice surrounded me as powerfully as his arms.

I looked up at him. Others might see only his handsome features—those dark, knowing eyes of his, the curly dark hair I loved to touch—but I saw beyond them into his heart.

He lowered his lips to mine. I delighted in the taste and feel of them. Desire, as I'd never known with another man, filled my body. I hugged him tighter to me, loving the way we fit. From his reaction, he obviously did too.

Face flushed, he pulled back. A smile curved his lips. "Guess you missed me, huh?"

I grinned. "Oh, yeah."

"Let me pull the car around to your house," Vaughn said. "I've been traveling for hours, and a nice, relaxing swim in your pool sounds great."

"To me also," I said happily. "Let me tell Tim I'll be gone for the rest of the day and then I'll meet you there."

As he climbed into the car, I rushed inside the hotel to talk to Tim.

Moments later, I hurried over to my house, my heart singing with happiness. My man had come home.

Vaughn was unloading his suitcase from the trunk of the car when I got there. I opened the front door and ushered him inside, enjoying his presence as he moved into the master bedroom with me following behind.

He grinned and peeled off his shirt, exposing the planes of his strong, lightly haired chest. "This heat feels good," he said. "It was damp and cold in Ireland."

"Do you have to go back there?"

"A few more scenes there, then I'm off to Hollywood."

"Thank you for coming home, even if it's for only a short time."

He gave me the kind of smile that made my heart pause and then spring forward. Then he pulled me to him.

I laid my head against his bare chest, inhaling the spicy after-shave lotion he wore and listening to the pounding of his heart.

"Any idea how much I wanted to be here while the filming was taking place?" he murmured, rubbing my back.

I looked up at him. "I wanted you here more than you did, believe me."

He grinned. "Playing that game, are we?"

I laughed. "Let me get changed and I'll join you in the pool."

"No need to bother with a bathing suit. You still have the security guards here on duty, don't you?"

"Yes, but ..."

"But nothing. Come on. We don't need suits. We've got all the privacy we want," he said impatiently.

Recalling my humiliation at being caught topless in the pool with him and having it posted everywhere in the press, I hesitated.

He waited.

I pushed thoughts of my proper grandmother away. "Okay, you're on."

As I removed my clothes, I studied his tempting body, free of clothes, and worried about my own. Having a baby changed a woman's body.

As if he knew my hesitancy, Vaughn came over to me. Lifting my chin, he forced me to look into his eyes. "You're beautiful, Ann. Remember, I'm a father, and I know what a mother's body looks like. Besides, I'm sick of looking at twig-thin bodies. I like a woman with curves, and you've got them in all the right places."

I sighed. If I didn't already love him, I would've fallen madly in love with him right then.

We took bottles of water with us out to the pool and then jumped in. The cool water sluiced my body in silky caresses as I swam the length of the pool and back to get warm. Vaughn swam with sure, strong strokes. I sat on the pool steps, content to watch him move easily through the water. I was glad I'd had a pool put in, though it was a bit of extravagance for me.

When Vaughn finished swimming, he sat beside me on the steps, chest-high in water. "That felt great. I think I'm ready to go inside. How about you?"

He was looking at me with an intention I could not miss.

"I thought you'd never ask."

That evening, before going over to the hotel for dinner, Vaughn and I sat on the patio sipping cocktails. When we'd first begun our relationship, we'd stayed away from the hotel. But, in time, we decided guests would have to honor our privacy as much as that of our other guests. After all, the hotel was in many ways my home.

"How's Tina doing here?" Vaughn asked, taking another sip of his vodka and tonic.

"She can be totally obnoxious, but there's something very vulnerable about her that I find disturbing. She reaches out to me, then pushes me away as if she's afraid to reveal too much. What do you know about her background?"

"Her mother is one of those stage-mother types. I met her once. That was one time too many." His lip curled. "She actually tried to proposition me."

I let that thought settle. "I don't keep up with Hollywood

gossip. How long has Tina been a star?"

"She started out as a young kid on a television show, then moved on to another show where she played a willful teenager. I guess she broke into the movies when she was about fifteen. If I remember, *Love on the Rocks* was her first movie. It wasn't well received, but her role of a sexy Lolita-type character got her a lot of notice."

"I imagine Hollywood and all that goes with it can be a pretty ugly scene," I said.

"To do well in that environment, you have to have people with a lot of common sense around you. That's why I was so grateful to Ellen for keeping me grounded." His expression softened. "And now I've got you. Ellen would've liked you, you know."

"And I would've liked her," I said, meaning it. His first wife had died far too young, but she'd helped Vaughn become the sensitive man and expert lover that he was. I'd always be grateful to her for that.

"So what's new at the hotel?" Vaughn said, grabbing a handful of almonds. "You told me about the new masseur. Last year, I could've used a good massage after helping Manny with the landscaping."

It amazed me that Vaughn loved being involved in the landscaping around the hotel grounds. He contended by doing so he was able to produce something beautiful that had nothing to do with his acting job. But I knew it was something to keep him busy during down times between jobs. Nothing more.

After talking for a while longer, we decided to walk over to the hotel for a quick bite of dinner before taking a stroll along the beach.

As we entered the hotel, one of the guests walking by stopped and stared at Vaughn.

"Wow! You look exactly like Vaughn Sanders on that television show *The Sins of the Children.*"

His smile was a little forced. "Well, that's a nice compliment," he said smoothly.

Taking Vaughn's arm, I led him away. "Sorry about that."

He shrugged. "I don't care as long as I'm with you. That's what counts with me. You know the real Vaughn Sanders, not the movie star."

"Indeed, I do." We exchanged smiles.

When we walked into the kitchen, Rhonda rushed over to Vaughn and gave him a big hug. "Glad to see you here. Annie's really missed you. We all have." She turned to me, her eyes glowing. "Did you tell him?"

I shook my head. "I promised you I wouldn't."

"Will's out on the patio. Come with me, Vaughn." She tugged on his hand like an eager child.

He gave me a quizzical look.

"Go. It's important."

I followed as Rhonda led him outside to a corner of the patio free of other guests.

Seeing us, Will rose to his feet and held out a hand to Vaughn.

"Hi, how are you?" Vaughn said, shaking hands with him like the friends they'd become.

Rhonda nudged Will. "Go ahead and tell him, Will."

Color crept to Will's cheeks. He grinned and wrapped an arm around Rhonda. "Great news, Vaughn. Rhonda and I are going to have a baby. Can you imagine that?" A note of awe filled his voice.

Wide-eyed, Vaughn turned to me.

"It's true," I replied, smiling.

Vaughn clapped Will on the back. "Well, old guy, congratulations! I can't think of happier news for you." He hugged Rhonda. "You're a great mom already. I know you'll be good with this one too."

Tears spilled down Rhonda's cheeks. "Can you believe it? Will and me and a new baby?"

I handed her a tissue. "It's wonderful, sweetie."

"I can't believe I'm going to be a father," said Will, looking dazed.

As Vaughn and I left them, I turned back. Rhonda had taken her tissue and was dabbing at Will's eyes.

Their sweetness touched my heart.

CHAPTER NINE

After Vaughn and I had dinner, we left the hotel for our walk.

As we stepped onto the beach, silver beams from the moonlit skies sparkled on the grains of sand. Stars filled the sky, twinkling secret messages to us, making me believe I was in a fairyland. Or maybe I felt that way because happiness had spun a web around me, wrapping me in a cocoon of wonder.

A jarring voice shattered the peaceful moment. "Well, look who's here. Vaughn Sanders."

Vaughn drew me to his side and turned around. "Hello, Valentina. What a nice surprise."

She gave him a devious smile. "The last time we met, you didn't think it was such a nice surprise. Does Ann know about that time? Or any others with all those women?"

My heart stuttered to a stop. I'd had to endure a couple of instances where I was led to believe Vaughn was cheating on me. I'd learned he wasn't the type, but after being rejected by Robert, I was still insecure about such things. And wherever we went, women surrounded Vaughn.

Vaughn's lips thinned in anger. "What are you suggesting, Valentina? If you want to talk about it, I'm more than willing to let Ann know how you and your mother came to me on the set one night, offering so-called 'services' in exchange for a recommendation that you star in the next movie."

Tina gasped. "Liar! I already had been named the star."

Vaughn shook his head. "Not until you visited another trailer. I know how you and that mother of yours operate."

I stared at Vaughn, unable to remember when I'd seen him so angry. Turning to Tina, I said, "I don't know what you're doing, but if you're trying to ruin the relationship between Vaughn and me, it won't work." I noticed she was alone. "Where's Jerry?"

"With his friends, what else?"

"I'll see you in the morning, Tina."

She turned and ran down the beach.

I took hold of Vaughn's hand. "Walk with me?"

He nodded, though he still clenched his jaw .

We walked in silence. What had seemed a magical scene a few moments ago had turned ugly. The thought of a mother using her daughter that way kept bile rising in my throat.

Down the beach, in a public area, a couple of benches had been placed on the edge of the sand. I dropped down onto one of them, too disillusioned to go on.

Vaughn sat beside me. "Are you okay, Ann?"

Shaking my head, I turned to him. "It's all true, isn't it? Tina and her mother?"

"Hollywood can be pretty damn twisted. Especially for those wanting to break into movies. You've heard stories like theirs before, haven't you?"

I swallowed hard. "Yes, but this hits me hard. I'm pretty sure this is a big reason for Tina's behavior. What kind of monster is her mother?"

"A greedy, pushy, stage mother of the worst kind." He exhaled a long breath. "I should've reported her or done something."

"Tina was over eighteen when this happened. Right?"

At his nod, my hands knotted into fists. "Then I'm not sure you or anyone could do much about it. But know what? I'm going to try."

Vaughn turned to me. "Be careful, Ann. This girl isn't like

Liz. She can hurt you."

"I know," I said softly, afraid of what Tina could do to the reputation of the hotel if she chose to be that cruel.

Lying in bed with Vaughn, I leaned my head against his chest, listening to the strong beat of his heart. The clean, spicy smell of him filled my nostrils. It seemed so right to have him next to me.

"Thanks, Ann," he murmured.

I gazed up at him. "For what?"

"For not quizzing me on the things Tina said. It means a lot to me. Especially after all the business with Lily Dorio and the way she set me up to make everyone believe something was going on between us."

I squeezed him. "I trust you, Vaughn. In your line of business, temptations are great, but I know the kind of man you are. You've proved it to me."

He pulled me even closer to him. "I love you more than you'll ever know," he murmured, lowering his lips to mine.

At their softness, the taste of him, pleasure soared through me. This man, this wonderful man, was mine. And he was about to make me his.

After a restless night of tossing and turning, I awoke to a bright morning. The sun was already up and showing itself. I left Vaughn sleeping in bed and quietly put on a pair of shorts and a T-shirt and slipped sandals onto my feet. After quickly brushing my teeth and washing my face, I ran a brush through my hair. In the mirror, my eyes lit with determination. I'd worried about Tina all night.

But now I had a plan.

I left a note for Vaughn on the kitchen counter and slipped unnoticed out of the house.

As I jogged across the front lawn of the hotel, I silently enumerated the steps I was about to take to try and make things better for everyone.

I tapped on Tina's door and waited impatiently for someone to answer.

Jerry opened the door sleepily. The reek of alcohol and cigarette smoke surrounded him like a gray cloud of neglect.

"Hi. May I come in?" I said, more determined than ever to follow through on my plan.

"Sure," said Jerry. "You here for Tina? She's still sleeping."

"I'm here to tell you that you're fired, Jerry. We're going to do things differently. I'm sorry hiring you didn't work out the way we thought it would."

"Fired? Really?" His surprise was genuine, which told me he hadn't taken our last conversation seriously.

Tina came out of the room wearing an oversized T-shirt. "I heard you. He's fired?"

"Yes," I said calmly. "Better get dressed. You're coming with me. We're going into town."

The pout that had formed on her lips disappeared.

A moment later, she poked her head out of her room and gave me a quizzical look. "Town?"

"Hurry," I said.

"Am I being fired because of being with my friends?" Jerry asked.

"You're being fired because you didn't do your job. I'm sorry, but it's not working out."

Jerry and I exchanged steady looks.

Then Jerry said, "Guess I'd better go pack."

Tina appeared, her manner subdued. "Are you sending me back to California?"

"No, we're not. After Vaughn leaves, you're going to move in with me."

She placed her hands on her hips and glared at me. "What if I don't want to live with you?"

"Then you'll have to go home," I said. "You get to choose. It's up to you."

Tina's eyes widened. "Up to me? Really?"

"If you want the role in the movie, you're going to have to work for it. Not me, not our staff, not Jerry. You."

Her brow creased, and I observed a silent debate going on in her mind. "Is this about last night on the beach with you and Vaughn?"

"Not really," I said. "It's about you taking charge of yourself with a little help from us."

Her frown grew deeper, but she remained quiet.

"Okay, let's go, Tina. Jerry, we'll work out a final payment for you. Now, if you'll let Tim at the front desk know when you're ready to check out, he can help you."

I held out my hand. "Thank you, Jerry. I realize it wasn't an easy job."

"An understatement," he all but growled as he shook my hand.

Leaving Tina's room, I knew I was acting abruptly, but I figured it was the only way to make Tina understand she had no choice but to go along with the new plan.

"Where are we going?" Tina asked, hurrying to catch up with me as I crossed the front lawn with purpose and headed to the gates.

"Downtown. From now on you'll be hiding out in plain view. I suggest you do something to your hair. And while we're at it, new clothes might be a consideration. They would provide a better disguise. You're a good enough actor to take care of the rest."

A smile spread across Tina's face. "So I don't have to be treated like a prisoner anymore?"

I shook my head. "Nope. It's all up to you."

"Okay. Where do I get my hair done?"

"Hair Designs is just the place. Malinda does my hair, and she owes me a favor. I'm sure she'll squeeze you in. That'll be our first stop."

Now that I'd come up with my plan, I was excited about it. Rhonda and I and the hotel staff wouldn't have to worry if Tina didn't do what she was supposed to do. And if she decided to eat everything in sight, it wouldn't be our problem. I'd let her agent know about the change in plans and Tina could decide for herself if she wanted to continue.

Hair Designs was a full-service hair salon. Tucked in at the end of Palm Avenue, it was the source of service for many of the residents who disguised their true hair color and wanted upscale styling. Malinda was one of the co-owners and my favorite.

I tapped on the glass door, catching Malinda's attention. Smiling, she headed our way. Though it was before normal hours, she had the habit of coming in early to do the books and other administrative work before the salon opened. A tall, curvy woman, she loved to play with her own hair color. Today her tousled style was in a bright hue that matched the green in her eyes.

"Cool," said Tina softly, taking in Malinda's appearance.

"Disguise, remember?"

She frowned at me. "How about blond?"

I shrugged. "Let's see what Malinda says."

An hour later, Tina left the salon with me in a new, shorter hairdo in tastefully streaked blond tones. Seeing her like this, with a smile on her face, I was once more reminded of how pretty she was.

"I like it," I said.

Her eyes sparkled. "Me too."

"Okay, next stop. Styles."

"What's that? A clothing store? It better not be where you shop. I don't want to dress like an old lady."

I ignored her remark and kept walking.

Tina hurried to catch up to me. "Sorry. I'm only doing this, you know, so I can keep on staying here."

I shrugged. "You can do whatever you choose as long as you are kind and considerate to everyone around you."

"What if I decide to go on a dessert binge? Huh? What then?"

I stopped and faced her. "Then you go home. It's all very simple," I said, knowing it wasn't simple at all. Even though she'd put up a fight at the beginning, she'd made good progress. And although she was technically an adult, emotionally, she was very young, very vulnerable, and very hurt. We'd talk about some of that later. Now we were going shopping.

Styles had barely opened when we walked in. Christine, my favorite clerk, greeted me with a smile. "You here for some of our latest fashions?"

I shook my head. "Tina is here for some basic items. She's visiting for a while and needs some suitable things to wear around the hotel."

As Christine took a good, long look at Tina, I held my breath. But there was no flicker of recognition.

"Well, Tina," said Christine. "This is going to be fun. You have a lovely figure and we have some things I think you'll really like." She turned to me. "By the way, how's Liz? She's such a doll. I was so glad to be able to help her get ready for her wonderful new job in DC."

"Liz is great. She should be here for Thanksgiving. I'm sure she'll find time to pay you a visit."

"Okay, Tina. Let's get started." Christine took another long look at her. "I'm guessing you're a size 4 or 6. Come this way."

I was pleased. Tina was a larger size than that when she'd first arrived. She needed to be a size 2. She rolled her eyes at me but followed Christine to the back of the store to the dressing rooms.

I took a seat on a couch by Tina's dressing room and watched as Christine moved back and forth between various racks of clothing and the dressing room, carrying an assortment of items.

Occasionally, Tina emerged to show me what she was wearing. She looked great in everything she tried on.

It took less time than I'd thought to choose a number of basic pieces of casual clothing, along with two dressier outfits to wear at the hotel for dinner. I charged them to my account, but would put it on Tina's hotel account when we got back.

As we left the store, Tina wore one of her new outfits—a short skirt that tastefully showed off her legs and a V-neck knit top that was both sexy and stylish. She'd deny it if I called her on it, but with her new hairstyle and classier outfit, she acted more ladylike. I knew it wouldn't last, but I took a moment to say, "You look really nice."

She forced a frown, but I'd already seen the look of pleasure on her face.

At the hotel, I ushered Tina into the kitchen. "Rhonda, we have a special guest here."

Rhonda studied Tina and then grinned. "Well, whaddya know. You look great, honey." She turned to me. "What's going on?"

"Let's go into the office and I'll fill you in." I turned to

Consuela. "Tina can have whatever she wants. Will you fix it for her, please?"

"*Si*, Annie."

Rhonda blinked in surprise. "Really? You're going to let Tina do that?"

"*We're* going to let her do that. I'll explain all of it to you. But first I need a cup of coffee."

Consuela handed me a fresh cup.

I took a grateful sip of the hot liquid and carried it into the office.

"Where's Vaughn?" Rhonda asked when we got settled in our chairs.

"At my house. He knows I'm with Tina, but I need to go to him. I've ignored him for too long. First, I want to tell you what I've done. I hope you approve."

I started by telling Rhonda about the exchange between Tina and Vaughn, what I'd learned about Tina's upbringing and what I'd done about Jerry.

Rhonda's eyebrows drew down into an angry V. She knotted her hands into fists. "I could wring that woman's neck for doing that to her daughter."

"I agree. Tina's more a wounded child than a young woman her age, but I think we can help her. After Vaughn leaves, she can move in with me. We'll let her be in charge. Only she can decide if she wants the role in the movie enough to lose the weight. We can't do it for her. And if she can't be kind and considerate to others, she's out."

Rhonda gave me a worried look. "But we'll suggest certain meals for her. Right?"

"Of course. And she can choose whether to eat them or not."

Rhonda sat back in her chair and thought for a moment. "I like it. We're not really giving up on helping her and we're sorta keeping our promise to her agent. Right?"

"That's the way I see it. But we're not having her locked up like a prisoner anymore."

"Okay. That's what we'll do. And we can use her two rooms for regular guests after we scrub and clean the hell out of them. We'll put the gym equipment we ordered for her in our workout room. She can use it there." Rhonda shook her head. "I have to tell ya, Annie, she better shape up and mix in or she's gone. We don't need her kind of behavior around here."

"I have the odd feeling she's going to give this new way of doing things a sincere try. If you mention going home to her, she all but blanches."

"What a mess. I'll talk to Tina myself and make sure Jerry's room is cleared out so we can send the housekeepers in. Good job, Annie." She waved me out of the room. "Now get back to Vaughn."

"Thanks." Vaughn was a good guy but it wasn't always fair to him for me to be so tied up in the hotel business. "He's flying out tonight and I want to spend as much time with him as I can."

Rhonda gave me a sly look and a thumbs up sign.

CHAPTER TEN

As I walked into my house, I heard Vaughn moving about in the kitchen.

"Hello!" I called out.

He appeared in the doorway, a scowl on his face. "Where were you? I'd about given up on you. It's almost lunch time."

I hurried over to him. "Oh, Vaughn, I'm sorry. Dealing with Tina took longer than I'd thought. What have you been doing while I've been gone?"

"I met with Manny for a while and now I'm hungry. I'm making ham and Swiss cheese sandwiches. Want one?"

"Sounds good. Tina and I didn't have a real breakfast."

"What were the two of you doing?" he asked with a bit of irritation still in his voice.

I followed him into the kitchen, and while we sat and ate our sandwiches, I told him about my morning.

"It sounds like a good idea. Then if she doesn't lose the weight, she can't blame you." He leaned over and gave me a kiss. "Smart woman."

"Thanks. I'm not at all sure the plan is going to work, but I knew I had to try something different to help Tina. It was becoming an issue at the hotel. My duties at the hotel are pulling me in deeper and deeper. Sometimes, with all the goings-on there, it feels like I'm walking in quicksand full of problems."

Vaughn stood and gave me a sexy smile. "I've got a way to get your mind off the problems at the hotel. Come with me."

I smiled. "You're on."

###

Later, after making delicious love, we lazed in the pool and talked idly about our children. His son Ty lived in San Francisco and was in a relationship with a nice Chinese girl who worked at the same computer company as he. I'd met him once and liked him a lot. He had the same kind of quiet strength as his father. Nell, his daughter, was like a second daughter to me. We'd connected from the first time we met when she'd come to the hotel to visit Vaughn during the filming of *The Sins of the Children*. She'd already promised to come for Christmas.

"Liz is going back to school next semester. She's got everything in place but the financing." I made a face. "She made me promise to call Robert to ask him to pay for it like he was supposed to do."

"You mean to pay back the dollars he stole from her?" scoffed Vaughn. He had yet to meet Robert and wasn't in any hurry to do so.

"You're right. The education fund was hers all along. I'll call him, but not until tomorrow. I don't want to ruin my time with you." Sitting with him in the pool, talking freely, was such a treat. Robert hadn't had the patience to relax and enjoy simple things with me. More than that, conversation with him wasn't fun. He liked to correct whatever I had to say.

Vaughn pulled me into deeper water and wrapped his arms around me. "I hate the thought of leaving."

"Me too. When do you think you'll be back?"

"It depends on how fast we can wrap up the film. The weather has been working against us."

I said nothing, determined not to make his departure more difficult. Falling in love with someone like him had its trials. I was a planner, someone who liked to know what was going to happen and when. Not knowing when I'd see him again was hard for me.

Too soon the time came for Vaughn to leave. He was driving back to Miami. From there, he'd fly to Dublin.

Packed and ready, Vaughn stood with me outside.

I swallowed hard, wondering how I could bear to let him go. He filled my life with a deep-seated joy I'd never known.

"I'll be in touch," he said leaning down to kiss me Good-bye.

I closed my eyes, storing the taste and touch of him in my mind for me to pull out and savor on lonely nights.

"Love you, Ann," he murmured, pulling away.

"Love you too. Be safe." Sadness seeped through me as I watched him climb into his rental car. The door closed, and he settled behind the wheel. Determined to be better about spending quality time with him, I waved long after his car had left my driveway, already feeling empty and alone.

As I returned to the house, I was well aware I couldn't put off a call to Robert any longer. In my office, I stood by the window looking out at the tropical plantings, fighting the idea of talking to him. The waving of palm fronds playing in the breeze calmed me enough to pick up the phone.

Liz had talked about applying for a scholarship, but it wouldn't be enough. And as Vaughn had mentioned, Robert had stolen the money we'd set aside for Liz. The fact that his business had taken a deep hit was not my problem. If he'd listened to me and the other board members, it might not have happened.

I drew a deep breath. I had to talk to him. There was no way I could pay for Liz's tuition. Not with all that was going on at the hotel.

I reluctantly punched in his private office number and waited for several rings for him to pick up.

"Hi, Ann. What is it?" he snapped without even a courteous hello. As Rhonda had assured me many times over the last months, Robert was a jackass.

"Hello, Robert. I'm calling because Liz asked me to talk to you about her going back to school. She needs the money we'd set aside for her education to pay for her tuition. With the sale of your house, you must have enough money to pay for it. It's only fair."

"What isn't fair is that my business is struggling. That's why I had to sell the house I was building for Kandie and our boys."

"Boys? Are you having another child?"

"We're trying. Every boy needs a brother, but then you wouldn't know about that."

His words pierced me, and he knew it. Tears blurred my vision. I'd wanted a lot of children, but it hadn't happened. After several miscarriages, my doctor had told me it was harming my health to keep trying.

Holding back a seething retort, I managed to say, "Your daughter needs what is rightly hers. I don't care how you come up with it, Robert. It's your responsibility. I'm asking you to abide by our agreement."

"What don't you understand?" he snarled. "I need the money for my new family."

"I really don't want to call my lawyer, but I will if you don't follow through. You and I both know what you did was criminal."

"What has happened to you, Ann? Is it all that success at the hotel or that movie star that's made you think you're better than you are?"

His demeaning way of talking to me struck a nerve. I'd lived with it at one time, but I wouldn't allow any more. I clicked off the call and screamed with frustration.

"What's going on?"

I whirled around. Tina stood before me with a frightened look on her face.

Adrenaline left my body, making me feel weak. I sank onto my office chair. "It's a personal issue. What's up?"

"Rhonda is clearing out my room. She said to come to your house. I've brought some of my things."

"Okay. Give me a minute and I'll help you get settled."

I took a couple of deep breaths, telling myself not to let Robert's words destroy my happiness.

"Are you okay?" Tina asked, eying me curiously.

I nodded and rose, unwilling to give any more of my time to worrying about Robert.

We walked into the living room.

Tina gazed all around, her eyes wide with curiosity. "I didn't know you had a pool and everything."

"It's small but nice," I said, allowing a sense of pride to enter my voice. After all that Robert had done to hurt me financially during the divorce, I was very proud of what I'd accomplished.

"Where do you want my things?" Tina asked.

"I'm going to put you in Liz's room. She won't be home until Thanksgiving."

Tina followed me into the room Liz had helped me decorate. Pale yellow washed the walls. A green floral bedspread with a multitude of pillows added a tropical touch to the room and was duplicated by the greenery outside the windows. A number of framed certificates on the walls announced Liz's success in swimming.

"Make yourself at home. Liz tells me the bed is very comfortable." I went over to the closet and pushed clothing aside to make room for Tina's things.

Tina stepped back. "This is so not me. It's all so perfect.

And those certificates. I've never had anything like that. I've been too busy working."

"Anyone home?" came a voice from the front entry.

Manny's nephew Paul met me in the hallway. "Here's the rest of Tina's things."

"Thanks. Let's take them right into her room." I took a small bag from his arms, and he rolled a large suitcase into the room.

I turned to Paul. "Thank you."

He bobbed his head and left.

"If you like, I'll help you unpack," I said to Tina.

She remained unusually quiet as I helped her hang up her clothes and rearrange clothing in the bureau to give her things space.

"What?" I finally asked when she continued to stare at me.

She shrugged. "Why are you being so nice to me?"

I blinked in surprise. "In what way?"

"You know, helping me get settled here."

It struck me then. "Your mother never did this with you?"

"I can take care of myself," she said defensively. "I don't need you or anyone else to help me."

"Oh, okay." Wondering at her change in attitude, I left the room and headed into my office. I was about to call Rhonda when I saw her approaching my house. I went outside to greet her.

"Thought I'd better come over to check on Tina," said Rhonda. "I've got the housekeepers cleaning her suite. It's a freakin' disaster. I'm worried she's going to make a mess here. We need to talk to her about it."

"The rooms were that bad?"

"It burns my butt that someone like Tina can be such a slob. In order to get rid of the smell of cigarettes, we're going to have to recover the furniture or replace it, along with the carpet. And, Annie, I think we should repaint the walls."

I couldn't help sighing. It was an expense we didn't need.

Rhonda and I entered the house to find Tina lounging outside by the pool. Wearing a bikini that hid nothing, she smiled up at us. "This is much nicer than staying in my room."

I sat down on a chair beside her and Rhonda pulled up another chair. "That's the point of being here," I said. "But it comes with a price."

She snorted. "I've got plenty of money."

"You don't understand," I said. "The cost has nothing to do with money. It's all about your cooperation."

Tina sat up. "What do you mean?"

"We mean you can't be a slob in this house," said Rhonda. "Do you have any idea what it will cost us to make your suite available to other guests? You broke our no smoking rule and otherwise trashed the rooms."

"Yeah? So what?"

Rhonda's face turned bright red. I held up a hand to stop Rhonda from saying anything else and turned to Tina. "That selfish attitude won't work here at the hotel or in my house. It may seem impossible to you, Tina, but the world doesn't revolve around you. You're only one person here. And rules are set up to help everyone."

Tina lifted her sunglasses and rolled her eyes at me. "So now you're going to treat me like a baby?"

"Noooo," I said slowly. "We're going to treat you like an adult. If it doesn't work out, our problem will be over. You'll be gone."

Tina jumped to her feet and scowled at us. "Maybe I'll go now."

"Okay. I'll help you pack."

Tina stamped her foot. "You make me so fucking mad!"

Rhonda hefted herself to her feet. "Annie, this isn't going

to work. I'm going to call her agent. With everything else that's going on, we don't have time for this."

"You wouldn't do that!" Tina said. "You can't!"

Rhonda placed her hands on her hips and glared at Tina. "Yeah, I can. Trust me."

Tina sank down on the lounge chair. "Okay. What do I have to do to stay at this frickin' place?"

"The rules are simple," I began, feeling as if I were talking to an eight-year-old. "Keep yourself and the room neat and tidy. No smoking. No alcohol here at the house without permission. And if I ever hear you talk to any of the staff disrespectfully, you're out. Understand?"

"And I can eat anything I want?"

"Yep. If you want to regain the weight you've lost, there's nothing I can do. It's up to you as to whether you lose and keep off the weight for the movie."

"Yeah," said Rhonda. "You decide."

After a short hesitation, Tina nodded. "Okay. I guess I'll stay. I don't want to go back home."

Rhonda and I exchanged meaningful glances.

"Okay, that's settled," I said. "I'm going to be working here for a while and then I'll go over to the hotel. We have a small dinner party tonight that I have to oversee."

"What'll I do?" said Tina in a voice that held a whine.

I shrugged. "You could learn your lines, exercise, watch television or come to the hotel. It's up to you."

She looked down meekly.

I realized then that she was used to being programmed and wondered if by leaving her on her own, we were about to create a nicer person or a monster.

CHAPTER ELEVEN

Rhonda paced the office. "One more hour! I can't wait to see Angela. What am I going to do if I can't stand her boyfriend? He sounds so awful!"

"Don't prejudge," I said, remembering how I'd wrongly judged Rhonda for being so demanding, so sure of herself, so crude. Now I knew she was one of the best friends I ever could have.

Her cheeks flushed prettily. "I wonder what she'll say about the baby?"

"I'm sure she'll be delighted." Rhonda's excitement was contagious. She glanced at the clock. "I can't wait any longer to go to the airport. You'll come with me, won't you? Ange told me that Reggie is very proper and she wants me to make a good impression on him. With Will at an investment meeting, I need you to be there with me."

At the idea of Rhonda striving to be "very proper", I hid a smile. Rhonda was Rhonda, and she was fine as she was.

"Sure. I'll go with you." I was pretty anxious to meet Reggie Smythe myself.

As we drove to the airport, Rhonda chatted nervously about the baby. "I can't decide what I want to name a girl. If it's a boy, naturally he'll be a William Junior. Both Will and I agree on that. Though I wouldn't want to call him Bill. Will and Bill? That's too awkward. But Will's middle name is Andrew so we'll probably call him Andy. What do you think?"

"Andy Grayson? I like it. Has a good strong sound to it."

"Thanks." Rhonda's eyes lit with excitement. "I can't wait

to tell Angela. She's wanted a baby brother or sister for years. Who knew she'd get one now? Not me."

I chuckled. "It's quite a surprise, all right."

We parked the car at the airport and went inside to wait for the plane's arrival. Dressed in a light blue caftan, Rhonda's pacing reminded me of a bluebird flitting about.

I placed a hand on her arm. "Settle down. She'll be here soon. The plane is at the gate."

"You're right. Let's go sit. I told her I'd meet her in baggage claim, but I can't leave this spot. This is where they'll enter the terminal."

We took seats in a row of chairs that faced the hallway that led from the gates. I ignored Rhonda's restless movements and let my mind settle on my recent conversation with Liz. Was there another reason she hadn't said much about Angela's visit?

The sound of a group of passengers heading toward us ended my musing. I got to my feet and stood by as Rhonda scanned the crowd. "There she is!" Rhonda cried, waving her arms enthusiastically.

Angela noticed her mother and frowned. The young man beside her asked Angela something. Looking miserable, Angela nodded.

Rhonda didn't seem to notice. She continued waving and calling out to Angela.

As Angela and her boyfriend drew closer, Rhonda rushed forward and pulled Angela to her for a bosomy hug. "Oh, baby girl. I've missed you so much!"

A smile crossed Angela's face and then she stepped back. "Mom, I want you to meet Reggie Smythe. Reggie, this is my mother and," she turned to me, "Ann Rutherford, my mother's business partner."

"Very nice to meet you," Rhonda said in a quiet polite voice, unlike her usual exuberant manner. She glanced at me.

"Yes," I said, "It's so nice you could make a visit."

"Thanks," he said, eying Rhonda with an expression of surprise.

As Angela and her mother chatted about Will's absence, I studied Reggie. With his hair slicked back, horn-rimmed glasses and preppy clothes, he looked more like a thirty-five-year-old than the young man I knew to be a senior in college.

"How's business?" Reggie asked me. "Before I came here, I read up on The Beach House Hotel. It looks nice."

"Thank you. I think you'll be impressed. Our guests love it."

"Love what?" said Rhonda.

"I was just saying our guests love the hotel."

Rhonda elbowed Reggie. "Wait 'til you see it. It's a bit fancy, but we're real proud of it. Aren't we, Annie?"

"Oh, yes," I said, wondering at the look of distress on Angela's face. As we headed out for the parking garage, I held Angela back. "Hey, are you okay?"

She frowned. "Mom sometimes embarrasses me."

"I can't believe you said that. There's nothing to be embarrassed about. Your mother is one of the nicest people I know."

"I just want Reggie to like her," Angela said, looking distressed.

Reggie turned back to us.

As Angela hurried to catch up to him, I had no time to follow up with more discussion. But I was disturbed by Angela's reaction. It wasn't like her. Rhonda being Rhonda had never been a problem for her daughter before. Had being with Reggie changed her?

On the ride back to the hotel I tried to keep the conversation going.

"So tell us about yourself, Reggie," I said. "You're a senior at BU. What's your major?"

"I'm taking business courses," he said. "Someday I want to go into business with my father. He's with an investment banking firm in New York."

"Oh," said Rhonda. "Will does investment work too. They probably have a lot in common."

"I doubt it," said Reggie. "My father's in international investment banking."

At Rhonda's look of dismay, I said, "Financial consultants today are well aware of international markets. That's how it works."

"Of course. But my father's firm is considered one of the best in the world."

"So, do you live in New York?" I asked.

"My parents have a large penthouse there. But I like to spend time in Newport. We have a summer cottage there."

"It's no cottage," said Angela. "It's almost the size of The Beach House. We went there for a weekend."

Rhonda glanced at her daughter through the rear-view mirror. "Sounds to me like you're doing a lot of traveling. You're not forgetting your schoolwork, are you, Angela?"

"Oh, Mom. I work hard during the week. Don't I, Reg?"

"She's a good student."

Angela grinned at him. "I got a better grade than you in the Business Relations course we took together."

He laughed. "Like I said, you're a good student."

Some of the tension inside the car eased.

By the time we arrived at the hotel, I decided Reggie wasn't as stuffy as I'd first thought. Angela seemed to bring out a warmer side to him.

As we pulled into the front circle of the hotel, Tina came down the steps toward us. Seeing me in the front passenger seat, she waved and went on her way.

"That looked like Valentina Marquis?" said Angela. "Is she here?"

"Wow!" said Reggie. "She's hot!"

I turned around and faced Reggie. "I don't know if Angela told you about our privacy policy, but our guests are asked to refrain from addressing well-known persons without being asked. Lots of famous people come and go here for that kind of anonymity."

"Okay," he said agreeably.

"She's staying with me for a few weeks," I said, following our rule of not giving out any particulars.

I climbed out of the car. "Thanks, Rhonda. See you later, after the kids are settled at your house."

"I'll be back," she said.

I waved Rhonda off and went inside to check for messages.

Tim and his new assistant were working together at the front desk computer. He looked up. "I'm teaching Julie the reservations system."

"Good. As things get busier, we all need to be able to know what's going on. Any messages?"

He handed me a piece of paper.

At the name on it, my heart sped up. "Thanks!"

I hurried into the office and closed the door. After punching in the number, I waited nervously for Brenda to pick up the call.

She greeted me with a cheery, "Hello".

Blood pulsed through me in anxious beats.

"Hi, Brenda. I hope you called us with good news."

"As a matter of fact, I did. I've heard back from the family regarding the wedding and they've chosen The Beach House Hotel as the place for their small private wedding. For political reasons, they don't want to make a big splash of the marriage."

I sank down in my chair with a sigh of relief. Having the

wedding at the hotel would mean a lot to our bottom line.

"That's wonderful news," I said. "Can you tell us about the family?"

"As you might know, the monarchy of Bavaria was abolished in the early twentieth century. Though there have been movements through the years to re-establish a monarchy, that has never really happened. But there has been a succession of pretenders to the throne and the royal family is well-respected. A cousin once removed to one of them claims a certain royal status. That's who I've been working for—Joseph and Charlotte Hassel. Their youngest daughter Katrina is marrying a young man from New York. The Hassels are not happy with their daughter's choice, but have chosen to go along with it, preferring to give an older daughter the more public wedding they want for her."

"How soon is this quiet wedding to take place?"

"They'd like to plan the wedding for January 5th, Epiphany Eve. In Germany, it is traditionally a time to drink to the health and luck of family and friends in the coming year. They'll want to come here a couple of days early, of course, and leave a day or two after the wedding.

"They plan to arrive on January 3rd and will need the Presidential Suite, the Bridal Suite, and at least eight other rooms. Can you arrange that?"

"Yes," I said, relieved it hadn't been planned before Christmas or New Year's Eve and that they wanted fewer rooms than we'd thought. To make things even easier, Tina would be gone by then.

"As I did before, I'll send you a list of requirements. The bride has very definite ideas about what she wants. I'm afraid she's somewhat of a bridezilla."

I held back a groan. "Thanks so much, Brenda. We'll take good care of both the bride's family and the groom's."

Her voice held a smile. "I know I can count on you. Talk to you soon."

As soon as I clicked off the call, I phoned Rhonda.

"Yay! I knew it!" she shrieked into my ear. "I'm on my way back to the hotel. I'm bringing the kids with me so Angela can show Reggie around." She lowered her voice. "I'm trying, Annie. I'm really trying to understand what Angela sees in him."

"Good work. See you soon."

I was in the office, working on rearranging reservations for the week following New Year's when Rhonda burst into the office. She grabbed my hands, pulled me out of my chair and had me do a little dance with her.

"I knew it! Royalty at The Beach House Hotel. Perfect!"

"Whoa! It's not exactly the happiest occasion apparently. We'll have to be careful about announcing it." I passed along the information Brenda had given me.

"Sounds like a typical family, huh?" Her expression grew grim. "Annie, that Reggie is a regular little prick. How dare he say Will and his father would have nothing in common? I'm glad Will didn't hear that."

"Have you told Angela about the baby?"

"Not yet. I'm waiting for Will to be there when I do." Rhonda shook her head. "I don't know what's going on with her. She's acting so quiet, so strange. She agrees with everything Reggie says. I don't like it."

"She may be nervous. It's the first time she's brought home a boy from college. Take it one day at a time."

"Yeah, maybe you're right. I'll give them both a chance to mellow a bit."

Angela appeared at the office door with Reggie. "And this is where all the decisions are made." She indicated our office with a flourish.

"Nice," Reggie answered.

"We're going for a swim before going back home and getting ready for dinner. We're eating here tonight, right?" said Angela.

"Jean-Luc and I are preparing a special meal. Annie is going to join us for dinner in the private dining room."

"Too bad Vaughn couldn't be here," said Angela, smiling at me.

"I wish he could, but he's gone back to Ireland to do more filming."

Reggie's eyes widened. "Vaughn? Vaughn Sanders?"

"I told you about him," Angela said, elbowing him playfully.

"I thought you were joking. First Valentina and now Vaughn. This place is a lot ... well, different than I thought it'd be."

At the stern look that Rhonda gave him, the smile on Reggie's face evaporated.

"Come on. Let's go take a swim," said Angela.

As they left the room, Angela turned around and frowned at her mother with disapproval.

Rhonda plopped down in a chair. "See what I mean? It's different between Ange and me. It's almost as if she doesn't like me."

"It must be nerves," I said.

The family reunion Rhonda had hoped for was off to a shaky start, and I had the awful feeling that it wasn't about to improve.

CHAPTER TWELVE

Dinner in our small, private dining room was always special. Tonight I sat at the long, linen-covered table and silently monitored the dining staff serving our first course. Three Oysters Rockefeller sat on a bed of rock salt atop a small glass plate. I could hardly wait to taste the lemony hollandaise sauce that had been dabbed on top of the baked oysters. In deference to her pregnancy, Rhonda was having only one.

"My favorite," said Will, waiting for Rhonda to pick up her seafood fork so we could begin. When she did, the rest of us dug into the appetizer eagerly. All but Reggie, that is. He sat silently while we ate ours.

"You don't like oysters?" Rhonda asked.

He shook his head. "I'm allergic to shellfish."

"Oh, I'm sorry. I didn't know," said Rhonda. "May we serve you something else?"

"No, that's fine," Reggie said agreeably. "I'll wait for the main course."

"I think you're really going to like it." Rhonda smiled at him. "Veal Parmesan is one of my specialties. It's actually one of my mother's recipes. I make it with her famous tomato sauce."

A look of distress crossed Reggie's face. He turned to Angela, sitting next to him.

"Reg doesn't like tomatoes," Angela said. "They make his skin itch."

I knew Rhonda well enough to know what a blow that was to her. But, to her credit, she spoke in a soft, controlled voice.

"What can we get you for dinner then?"

"Can you serve him the veal without the sauce?" Angela said, giving her mother a pleading look.

"Sure. Excuse me while I go talk to Jean-Luc." Rhonda rose from her chair and left the room, her back straight.

Reggie gave us all a weak smile. "Pretty funny, huh? Being with an Italian family and not liking tomatoes."

I returned his smile, but it was a bigger problem than he knew. Rhonda was a fabulous cook and a full-blown foodie who came from a family that showed and reciprocated love by providing one another with good Italian food.

Rhonda returned. "It's all been taken care of," she said, avoiding Angela's gaze.

During the main course, Will gently prodded Angela and Reggie to talk about themselves and how they met. Reggie told of his weeks at the camp in New Hampshire offering financial advice to the owners of the camp as an internship project. Angela and Liz had spent two summers there as counselors.

"You should have seen Angela the first time a snake crawled toward her," said Reggie, shaking his head. "She was screaming like crazy."

Angela gave him a wide smile. "But you saved me. I'll never forget it."

The look he gave her could've steamed his glasses.

I couldn't help smiling. They were adorable together.

Rhonda's eyebrows lifted. "So why haven't I heard more about the two of you being together?"

Reggie shifted in his seat. "At the end of the summer, we decided to break up."

"Yeah, we thought it was a summer romance sort of thing, but then we decided we wanted to be together. Right, Reg?"

He smiled at her. "Yeah, I couldn't break up with you, after all."

Dessert was served. After we'd eaten our fruit tarts and finished our coffee, Angela got to her feet. "Thanks for a nice meal. May Reggie and I be excused?"

"Sure," Rhonda said. "See you later. Don't be too late, okay?"

Angela glanced at Reggie and grinned. "Well, not too, too late."

Reggie laughed, and they left together.

Alone in the room, the three of us looked at each other and sighed.

"Young love. I'd forgotten how fresh and new that is," I said.

Rhonda shook her head. "It'll never work. How can Angela be serious about someone like that? He doesn't even like my food! What is that all about?"

"Now, Rhonda," said Will, "the boy has allergies."

Rhonda placed her napkin on the tablecloth with a little slap. "Angela has grown up with good food all her life. Good Italian food. How is she going to get by without it? And before Reggie came here for dinner, I heard them talking. Every time Angela said something, he corrected her as if she didn't know anything."

"What were they talking about?" I asked.

"Some course they were taking together." Rhonda's jaw jutted out. "My Angela is a smart girl. She doesn't need anyone making her think she's dumb."

"Was Angela upset by it?" Will said.

Rhonda shook her head. "No, of course not. She thinks he's wonderful. Absolutely wonderful."

"Then what's your problem?" I said.

"I don't want Ange to get hurt. He's from another world. Not ours."

Will placed an arm around Rhonda. "Let things unfold

naturally, honey. Like you said, Angela is a smart girl. She'll figure it all out."

Rhonda dabbed at her eyes with her napkin. "It's these hormones racing through me." She shook her head. "But I really am worried about her. She's been so upset with me, so distant, I haven't even told her about the new baby."

"All in good time," Will said. "Why don't we get you home so you can rest?"

Rhonda gave him a loving smile. "Guess that would help. I'm so tired. Do you mind, Annie?"

"No, Tim and Julie will handle things here. And I'll make sure Jean-Luc and Sabine are set for the rest of the evening."

Will and Rhonda left, and I wandered out to the kitchen where I found Tina eating a plate of spaghetti.

She glanced up at me and ducked her head.

"Is it good?" I asked.

"Yes, and I'm eating all of it. So there." She shot me a challenging look.

I shrugged. "Your choice. Remember?"

She slammed down her fork and stomped out of the room.

I was sitting in my office when Tina came in. She sat down in Rhonda's chair and crossed her arms. "I want to go home."

"Fine. Call your agent and tell her. We can make arrangements to get you to the airport anytime."

She pounded a fist on the desk. "Why are you doing this to me?"

I gave her a steady look. "Doing what? Making you responsible for yourself?"

She let out a long breath and got to her feet. "I'll let you know when I'm leaving."

"Okay. See you at my house. I'll be there soon."

Tina left, and I leaned back in my chair. Mothers and daughters. Women and girls. I had to admit, it was sometimes a crazy world.

Seeing my house lit in the dark, a warm feeling went through me. Tina had turned on the outside light for me. Maybe, I thought, beneath the bratty exterior was a heart that was kinder and softer than I knew.

I stepped inside the house and called out, "Tina, are you here?"

She came out of the bedroom, holding a notebook.

"What's that?"

She sighed. "The script."

"Oh? How's it going?"

She shrugged. "Okay, I guess. I'm not going home yet. I'll wait a few more days and then decide."

"Okay. It's such a pleasant evening, do you want to sit outside with a cup of coffee or tea?"

"I guess so. Coffee sounds nice." She gave me an impish grin. "With a lot of sugar."

"I'll get the coffee ready. You add what you want."

She frowned. "You're no fun!"

Determined not to get sucked into her game, I said, "Some people don't agree with you."

"You mean Vaughn Sanders? How'd *you* ever land him?"

I gave her a warning look. "Nice. Remember?"

She rolled her eyes. "All right then. How'd you two meet?"

"Let's get our coffee and I'll tell you all about it."

A few minutes later, I led Tina out to the lanai. We took seats facing one another. The cooler night air was refreshing after the heat of the day. My shoulders relaxed. All was going smoothly at the hotel. I swallowed the hot liquid and sighed with contentment. It was one of my favorite times of the day.

Tina took a sip of her black coffee and leaned back in her

chair. "So tell me about Vaughn. No matter what happened with my mom and me, I still think he's a cool guy."

I told her about filming *The Sins of the Children* at the hotel and how I'd met his children. I explained that after some time, the two of us decided we'd try to make our relationship work, even with his crazy schedule and appearances and my commitment to the hotel.

"That's real nice," said Tina. "I never knew my father."

I knew I might be treading in dangerous territory but I felt compelled to say, "Has your mother always been part of your stage life? Did you go to regular school? Was she always pushing you?"

Tina's body grew stiff, and I wondered if I'd gone too far.

Then Tina pulled her feet up onto the chair, wrapped her arms around her knees and lowered her face to them.

I watched silently, unsure what if anything I should do or say.

When Tina lifted her head, I saw something like despair on her face and waited for her to say something.

"My mother's the one who wanted to be a star. I was happy to be just a kid, but my mother told me I had to bring in money, that she couldn't do it." She scoffed. "My mother can't act on screen, but she sure can put on an act with men, lots of men."

"So then she made you help with that too?" The thought turned the coffee I'd swallowed into acid.

Tina looked away from me.

"There are people you can talk to," I said gently.

Tina jumped up so fast the little metal table next to her chair flipped on its side, shattering her coffee mug into sharp pieces that scattered across the floor.

"Damn you!" I watched the play of muscles in her throat as she worked to swallow. "Why would I want to talk to anyone about it?" Tina shouted. Without waiting for an answer, she ran into the house.

I rose and followed her to Liz's room. "Look, I'm sorry. I didn't mean to upset you."

Tina pulled her suitcase out from under the bed.

"What are you doing?" I asked.

"I'm going home. You can't stop me."

"You do what you want. I'll help you in any way I can."

She looked at me with such sadness I automatically reached for her.

Tina stepped back from me and then rushed forward into my arms.

Tears rolled down my cheeks as I held her shaking body close.

After a few moments, Tina pushed me away. "I'll decide later when I'm going home."

"I hope you'll stay," I said, my voice breaking with emotion.

She turned her back to me. "I will. For a while longer. Now I need to be alone."

I shut the bedroom door behind me and leaned against it. The sigh that escaped me held such pain that I moaned.

CHAPTER THIRTEEN

The sky was a soft gray when I awoke. Pink fingers of sunlight grasped the day with uncertainty, appearing and then hiding behind clouds in a game of peekaboo.

I climbed out of bed and went to check on Tina. She was sound asleep, sprawled across the bed like a little girl.

I shook her gently. "Hey, sleepyhead, do you want to go for a walk?"

She rolled over and groaned. "Don't you ever give up?"

"Just checking," I said, injecting a cheerful tone to my voice. "I'm leaving in a few minutes. If you want to join me, better get up."

She groaned again but climbed out of bed.

I left her to get dressed. Tina had to make her own choices, but that didn't mean I wouldn't try to make it obvious for her. Exercise would make it easier to lose the additional weight she needed to shed.

In the kitchen, I looked out at the patio and pool. I'd cleaned up the mess of her broken coffee mug, but in my mind, I still saw the pain on Tina's face. I wouldn't mention speaking to a professional again, but I was glad I had at least planted the seed of that idea in her head.

As we headed out to the beach, the wind sent a stormy message. I realized I hadn't heard any weather news for a few hours and wondered about Nancy, the latest hurricane to form. Last I heard she was down in the Caribbean near Puerto Rico.

We stepped onto the sand and watched as the waves

washed onto shore for a quick kiss and rolled back to reach for more. Gulls cried and soared in the air , letting the wind carry them in whirling circles of white.

"Ready?" I said. We wouldn't walk too far. I wanted to get to the hotel early.

Our feet pounded the beach as we walked at a steady pace. The vigorous exercise felt good to my desk-bound muscles.

Tina walked beside me lost in her thoughts.

I stopped and stood to look at the water playing with the wind. Tina moved to my side and nudged me with her elbow.

"Here's that Brock guy, coming our way."

"Crap," I muttered.

She gazed at me with curiosity. "Why don't you like him? He's good-looking and rich. So what's the problem?"

"We'll talk about it on the way back to the hotel," I said, bracing myself to greet Brock. He was trotting toward us, blocking our way back to the hotel.

"Hey, there! Why didn't you come to my party, Ann?" He eyed Tina. "I thought you were going to be neighborly. What happened?"

"It's been real busy at the hotel," I said. "In fact, we have to be going now. I'm worried about the weather."

"Guess that Hurricane Nancy is going to pay us a visit, after all. They thought it would die down, but it hasn't."

Sensing my dislike of him, Tina tugged on my hand. "C'mon, Ann. We have to go."

We entered the hotel through the kitchen. I grabbed a cup of coffee and went into my office to see what I could find out about the storm on my computer. The whirling mass of gray on the computer screen looked alarming. And as Brock had said, it was heading our way. Rhonda and I would have to put a safety plan in motion. Uneasy, I left Tina in the kitchen with Consuela and trotted back home to change.

###

"Bad news! Hurricane Nancy is heading our way," I said, returning to the office. At the sight of Rhonda's red-rimmed eyes, I came to a halt. "What's the matter? Are you okay?"

Rhonda shook her head. "I'm dealing with a storm of my own." A sob escaped her. "Oh, Annie, it's awful. Angela is furious about the baby. Do you know what she said when Will and I told her?" Rhonda took in a deep breath and then in a shaky voice she continued, "She said, 'You and Will? A baby? At your age? How could you?' I tried to speak to her, but she left the room before I could stop her. Will said to let her be, but, Annie, you know that's not like Ange."

"Yes, I do. What's the matter with her?"

"Will you speak to her, try to find out what's going on? She'll listen to you." Rhonda blew her nose. "It's all Reggie's fault. I just know it."

"We can't be sure of that," I said calmly, though I couldn't think of another reason for Angela's reaction. "If she and Reggie come to the hotel, I'll try to find out what I can."

"Good, because I can't talk to her, not with a broken heart."

I went over to Rhonda and hugged her . "I'm sorry, Rhonda. I really am."

She dabbed at her eyes with a tissue and then sighed sadly. "Maybe if I keep my focus on the hotel, it won't hurt so much. What did you say about a storm?"

"Have you checked a weather forecast lately? They're saying Hurricane Nancy is heading for Cuba and the Gulf of Mexico."

"The last one was pretty bad," said Rhonda. "Guess we need to check all the lanterns and go over emergency procedures with the staff."

"Yes, and lay in a supply of water and dry food items in case we need them."

The phone rang.

Rhonda picked it up. "Oh, hi!" A look of panic crossed her face. She waved me over to her side. "Yes, Tina is doing fine."

"She's exercising and studying the script," I prompted.

Rhonda relayed that information and listened for a few minutes. Then I heard her say, "No, I don't know why she isn't picking up. She might be busy. Yes, I'll ask her to give you a call."

She replaced the phone. "Wow, is Tina's mother pissed. She sounds like a real tough broad. No wonder Tina's the way she is. Her mother is really harsh." She gave me a worried look. "So, how's it going with Tina at your house? Getting better?"

I shrugged. "She's threatened to leave a couple of times, but at least she started studying her lines. That's a good sign."

Later, as I was checking on supplies we'd stored, I noticed Angela and Reggie lying out by the pool. Remembering my promise to Rhonda, I crossed the Oriental carpet in the lobby and went out to the pool deck to Angela.

She looked up at me and frowned.

"Can we talk a minute?" I said to her.

Her lips thinned. "My mother sent you, didn't she?"

"She's upset, and I wanted to talk to you anyway. I haven't seen you for a couple of months, and I've missed you."

"All right, we'll talk, but not here." She got to her feet and turned to Reggie, stretched out in a chair next to hers. "I'll be back in a few minutes."

"Okay." He waved her off.

We walked over to the wooden deck under the palm trees next to the beach and took seats in a couple of the chairs we kept there. No other guests were around.

I studied Angela a moment. "What's going on with you,

Angela? You seem so cross with your mother. You've hurt her feelings."

She slid her sunglasses to the top of her head so she could see me clearly. "Oh, Ann, I'm so sorry. I love my mother, but I'm very confused." Her eyes teared up. "I love Reggie so much. It's never happened to me before. Not like this."

"Why would that make you upset with your mother?" I said, trying to understand.

"It's *his* mother. She's so proper, nothing at all like Mom. Reggie and I want the parents to meet. In fact, I was going to ask Mom if they could come to the hotel for Thanksgiving. I think Reggie's mother would like it. They're always traveling some place, but they haven't been here."

"It's a busy time at the hotel, but I'm sure we could work something out. Why would your mother's being pregnant be a problem? It sometimes happens between two loving people, you know."

Angela made a face. "Reggie's parents would never have a baby at their age. His mother would think it's gross."

I hid my surprise. "How old are they?"

"About the same age as Will. They don't understand how it is between Reggie and me. They told him to be careful, that I wasn't meant for him. We're trying to change their minds about me."

A thread of apprehension wove through my body and knotted in my stomach. I studied the pain on her sweet, dear face. "They don't think you're good enough for him?"

She shook her head. "Not really."

"What does Reggie say about this?"

"He told me to forget them. He doesn't care what they think. They've never been that close as a family."

"Oh, Angela." I grabbed hold of her hands. "Life isn't that simple, honey."

Tears filled her eyes. "It's got to be. I think I might be pregnant. I haven't told anyone else. Not even Reggie knows. I'm very irregular, so it could be just nerves. The test wasn't positive, but I was so upset I'm not sure I did it right before I was interrupted."

My breath released in a drawn-out sigh. "Oh, my! Maybe we'd better plan that Thanksgiving weekend."

"Promise you won't tell? I can't let my mother know until I'm sure. Especially now."

I stared at Angela's pleading look and reluctantly nodded. "Okay, but now you have to do a favor for me. You need to talk to your mother. It's one of the most exciting times of her life, and whether Reggie's parents would approve or not is of no consequence. It's none of their damn business. Understand?"

Tears spilled down Angela's cheeks. "You're right. I'll go talk to Mom now."

She left.

I stared out at the water, wondering how life could be so unpredictable, so wonderful, so painful.

Knowing all of that and more lay ahead, I prayed I'd be able to help my dearest friend.

CHAPTER FOURTEEN

"What did you say to Angela?" Rhonda asked when I met up with her in the kitchen. "She's more like her old self. Guess I surprised her with the baby news, huh? She says she didn't mean to be so awful, but she was totally shocked." Rhonda chuckled. "Not as much as Will and me, of course."

I gave Rhonda a hug, happy she and Angela had worked out a few things. But I couldn't help wondering how Rhonda would feel if it turned out that Angela was pregnant too. I hated being forced to keep such news secret.

After a busy morning, I headed to my house, needing some time alone to think. I'd made a call to the interior designer who'd helped us with the renovations of The Beach House. Now that the idea had come to me, I thought turning Tina's two-room-suite into an upscale, bridal suite would be a very good marketing tool. But, naturally, I wanted to work on figures to see what the payoff could be.

As I walked into my house, I saw Tina out by the pool, talking on the phone. I went out to the patio to let her know I was home and heard her say, "Okay, Brock, you win. I'll see you tonight."

The blood left my face. "Tina, what are you doing?"

At the sound of my voice, she whirled around. "What are *you* doing, sneaking up on me like that?"

"I didn't mean to scare you, and I didn't mean to overhear your conversation. But, Tina, what are you doing with Brock?"

"Not that it's any of your business, I'm meeting him for dinner. He's taking me to a fancy hotel down the beach." At my look of dismay, she shook her head. "You can't stop me!"

I forced a deep breath in and out, trying to control the anger I felt for Brock's calling her at the house.

"You may not like him, but he's not so bad. It's been a long time since I've had a man drool over me like that. I'm bored. I want to get dressed up and go out."

"But Brock is no gentleman," I protested. "He's a pig who'll do anything to get his own way."

Tina shook her head. "They're all pigs, but I need a night of fun."

"Listen to me. He's more than a pig. He tried to force himself on me. Understand? You have to make your own choices, but when you place yourself in a dangerous situation, I can't sit by idly and watch that happen. I'm sorry, Tina, but if you choose to go out with him after all I've told you about him, you'll have to leave my house."

She stamped a bare foot on the hard surface. "But you said everything would be up to me, that I could choose what I ate and whether I stayed or not."

"That's right. You can choose whether to stay here or not."

"Why are you doing this? I only want to have a little fun with the guy."

"Didn't your mother ever make it clear that you deserve some respect? That you don't need to go out with someone like Brock, even if he has money and thinks he's a bigshot?"

Tina's face flushed a pink that might have been pretty in another situation. Tears filled her eyes. "No! Dammit! My mother taught me to use men for pleasure! Screw them and leave them with a promise of something better! But then you wouldn't know anything about that kind of life, would you?"

I started to reach for her but she pushed me away so hard I tumbled to the ground.

Tina ran into Liz's bedroom and slammed the door.

I slowly got to my feet. Tina's behavior was unacceptable, but I knew now the reasons behind it, and I wouldn't give up on her now. Limping slightly, I made my way into my office. As I got to my desk, my cell phone rang. I picked it up and clicked onto the call.

At the sound of Vaughn's sweet hello, tears flooded my eyes. "H-h-hello."

"Hey, what's wrong, honey?" he said.

"Just about everything. Tina, Angela, a storm named Nancy, a boy named Reggie and secrets that are choking me."

"Whoa," said Vaughn. "This doesn't sound like Ann Rutherford, warrior at heart."

"Ann Rutherford needs you," I said, meaning it with my whole being.

"I'm here, Ann. With you in spirit. Remember that."

I swiped at my eyes. I'd take what I could because there were times I didn't like being strong and determined—times I wanted to be babied and cuddled.

Later, soothed by my phone call with Vaughn, I decided to let Tina be by herself for a while.

I was working on the figures for the bridal suite when she came into my office.

"Hi, Tina," I said calmly. "What have you decided?"

Wearing a troubled expression, she took a seat in a chair and faced me. "You called me a whore."

I shook my head. "I never said that, Tina."

"But that's what you implied. Is that what you think of me?"

I took a moment to find the right words.

"I think your behavior is something no mother should encourage. I'm not sure what she's looking for. You have a nice career and what I would imagine is a nice income. Isn't that enough for her?"

"Nothing's ever enough for her!" Tina's shout startled me. "I can never do enough for her!" she continued in angry, slicing tones. "She doesn't care about me. It's all about her."

"I'm sorry to hear that, Tina," I said, barely controlling the rising anger I felt toward her mother. "We've been talking about choices. Maybe it's time for you to make some of those choices on your own."

"I've got a little brother I have to help," Tina said. "He goes to a private school for students who need special attention. I can't let him down."

"Maybe you can talk to someone who will help you sort all these issues out. Someone more knowledgeable than I."

"What?" she sneered. "Now you think I'm crazy!"

"That's not what I said or meant," I said, injecting a calmness into my voice I didn't feel. "These things are confusing. It might be easier for you if you have someone help you."

She sighed. "I called Brock and told him I couldn't meet him tonight. He was really pissed about it. You were right, Ann, he's an asshole. He called me all kinds of names."

"I'm glad you got out of the date. That was a good choice."

Tina made a face. "He wasn't that hot anyway."

"So what shall we have for supper?" I said, trying for a safer topic. "We can have a quiet meal right here tonight. Then how about watching a movie?"

Tina gave me an incredulous stare. "I gave up a nice evening out for something like this?"

My heart warmed at the smile beginning to form on her face. "It's not the Ritz, but it's damn close!"

We laughed together.

As I told Rhonda later, Tina and I were taking baby steps forward and giant leaps back. The worst part was never knowing what kind of reaction I might get from her.

CHAPTER FIFTEEN

I stood with Rhonda by the front steps of the hotel watching Angela and Reggie climb into one of our limos. Paul was driving them to the airport. Rhonda had opted not to go with them, confessing she'd only make a fool of herself saying goodbye to Angela in front of Reggie, that she already had the feeling she was losing her daughter for more than the few weeks until the Thanksgiving break.

Beside me now, she was blubbering like a baby and waving goodbye even as they passed through the hotel's gates.

After the limo had disappeared, she turned to me. "I told Angela and Reggie that I would be happy to have his parents come for a visit, even though I'm not. Will you help me write the invitation to them? They wanted me to go ahead and send an email because his parents are traveling."

"Sure. We'll make it nice and even send a follow-up letter, which could include a brochure of the hotel. They might turn out to be good customers of ours."

Rhonda curled her lip. "I doubt it. I wish Angela would pick out someone more fun. But she says she loves Reggie. Funny, I'd never imagined her going for someone like him."

"He loves her, Rhonda. They were so cute together. He's not what we expected, that's all. Let's go into the office. I want to tell you what I've come up with for the bridal suite for Katrina Hassel."

"Okay, and then we'll put together the stuff for the Smythes."

In the office, we looked over the sketches I'd made. They

showed a king-size bed, huge closet, and large bathroom with plenty of mirror space above counters on which we could place perfumes, make-up, and other cosmetics for those last-minute touches. A lounge-area sketch showed several couches and chairs for bridesmaids, a second television, and a mini kitchen with snack-bar seating.

Rhonda grinned. "I like it. We were going to have to refurbish Tina's suite anyway, and those rooms are perfect, off to one end like they are, giving them privacy."

"I think we can turn this into a moneymaker," I said, happy for her support.

"I sure like that idea. I have a feeling this wedding party isn't going to be easy."

"Me too." We were still waiting for Brenda's list of requirements.

We wrote and refined the letter and email for Arthur and Katherine Smythe. After we sent off the email, Rhonda placed the letter and brochure in an envelope, sealed it, and gave it a little pat. "Guess I'll take this down to the post office. I don't want the storm to delay it."

"I'd better get back to Tina. She's going through a rough time. I'll do my usual financial work there."

When I got to my house, Tina was nowhere in sight. I checked the bedroom. Her things were still there. In the kitchen, I noticed a slip of paper tucked under the pepper mill and picked it up. It read: *Gone on errands. Will be back later. VM*

At the signature, my eyebrows lifted. What did it mean?

I was in the kitchen, checking supplies for the coming storm when Tina came in.

"Hi!" I said, holding back on the many questions I had.

Tina plunked down into a kitchen chair. She propped her chin on a hand and sat, staring into space.

"What's up?" I asked. "Did you go downtown?"

"Uh, huh. I went to see Will."

"Will? Our Will?"

"Yeah. After you left, my mother called me. We had a terrible fight. I told her I didn't want to do this movie, that I didn't like the role. She blew up and threatened all kinds of things."

"Oh? And so you went to Will because ..."

"Because I need to protect my money. I'm old enough to have my own accounts, but I need to put it with someone I trust. I know Will enough to feel sure he'd never try to cheat me."

"Absolutely," I quickly agreed. "He's as honest as they come."

"We did a lot of talking. He helped me transfer some of my money into various funds we both liked. It's enough that my brother will always be taken care of."

I swallowed hard. "So what are you doing about your career?"

"I'm taking a break. I need to think things through. Maybe I'll never go back to making a movie. After talking to you, I realize how unhappy I've been."

Alarm dried my throat. "But, Tina, I never wanted you to quit the movies. I only wanted you to be more thoughtful of others and especially yourself. I wanted you to be safe."

"Well, I've already told my agent I'm not doing it. It was the kind of role *you* wouldn't let *your* daughter do." Tina's dark eyes shone with tears. "Maybe I don't want to be called a slut anymore. Maybe I want to be normal, like your daughter. I've seen all those certificates in her room, the clothing in her closet, the kind of life she has. Maybe I want it too."

"What do your mother and agent think about all this?"

"My mother doesn't know, but she'll find out soon enough.

She and my agent are a real team. They'll start hounding me. Wait and see."

My mind spun. "If they can't reach you, they'll probably try to call the hotel. I'll leave word that my number is not to be given out for any reason."

"I've turned my cell off," said Tina. "I can't deal with them anymore."

I took a seat at the kitchen table and faced her. "Maybe you should talk to a professional about how best to handle them and your new life." I raised my hand to stop her. "And before you think I'm talking about you being crazy, I'm not. But, Tina, you've got a big fight ahead of you. A fight you want to win."

"Do you know of anyone?" Tina asked me, apparently resigned to doing it.

"Yes, it's someone one of our guests used. Let me get the phone number for you. She's a lovely woman who's become a social friend of mine. Her name is Barbara Holmes."

I went to the office to find Barbara's business card. When I returned, I found Tina curled up on one of the patio chairs.

"Here's the information." I handed Tina the card and noticed the first rays of a sunset streaking through the sky. I grabbed her hand. "Hurry! Come with me!"

She scrambled to her feet. "Where are we going?"

"To find the green flash," I said, grinning.

She frowned. "What are you talking about?"

"Just come with me."

As we hurried across the hotel's lawn toward the beach, I explained it. "It's fun to look for it, even if it's rare for anyone to see it." We joined a few other guests on the wooden deck by the beach. Though a hurricane was threatening to come our way and puffy clouds raced in the sky, the horizon was clear for the moment.

"Watch," I said.

The large, orange globe of the sun continued its descent, sending shards of light into the surrounding sky. But before it could get down to the horizon, clouds obscured it.

A murmur of disappointment came from the guests around us.

"Sorry," I said to Tina as we walked back to the house. "It's something we can look for again. Hopefully, before you leave, we'll see it."

Tina pulled me to a stop. "I don't have anywhere else to go. Can I stay here for a while? At least until I make some decisions about the future?"

"Let's see how things go, Tina. Everything is happening too fast for you to make more big decisions quickly. Talk to Barbara. She'll help you."

Tina looked down at the ground and kicked her foot despondently.

"Hey, let's go home," I said gently. "It'll all work out."

At home, I enjoyed a glass of wine and put together a large, green, leafy salad, topped with cooked shrimp from the hotel, bits of hard-boiled eggs, and a few capers in a lemony dressing.

Tina sipped a glass of iced tea and watched me. "My mother hates to cook."

"Do you cook?"

"I like it. Trouble is, I like all the stuff I'm not supposed to eat."

I couldn't help myself. I said, "Okay, after dinner we're going to the Green Cow for some frozen yogurt."

Tina's eyes lit with mischief. "You're fun after all, Ann."

I grinned. "After this, I'm not going to lead you astray. Film or no film."

She held up her hand for a high-five, and I clapped it. There was peace between us for the moment, but I knew it wouldn't last. Tina's issues were larger than anyone could easily handle.

"What's going on?" Rhonda said, bursting into our office. "I got a call at home late last night from Dave during his night shift at the desk saying someone named Skye Marks phoned the hotel, threatening to expose us for the corruption of her daughter."

I frowned. "You'd better sit down. The reason he couldn't get hold of me was that I was out with Tina. We went to get a frozen yogurt and then to see a late movie. By the time we returned home, and I saw his message, he'd already called you. I didn't want to disturb you again."

After she took a seat, I noticed her cradling her stomach. "Are you okay?"

She looked down at her hands and laughed. "I love this baby already. Know what I mean?"

"Yes. I can't wait to see him or her."

"I don't care what any test may say, this is a little boy. For Will." Her expression grew serious. "So what's going on? This woman is Tina's mother. Right?"

"Afraid so. Tina's quit the movie and has hired Will as her financial manager."

Rhonda's eyes widened. "So that's what he couldn't tell me! I'll be damned."

"There's going to be a big fight. I suggested she see Barbara Holmes for counseling, and Tina said she'd call her."

"Wow! You never know about people, do you?" said Rhonda. "We have our share of strange ones here, but I swear Tina is one of the most surprising."

"Do you think her mother is going to try to ruin the hotel's reputation?" My stomach knotted at the idea. I'd overextended myself to buy into the hotel. If it failed, I didn't know what I'd do. I'd never ask Rhonda or Vaughn for money. I couldn't live with myself for doing something like that. My grandmother had drilled it into my head that no one else owed me a thing, that I had to make my own way.

Rhonda drew herself up with indignation. "She can try to ruin us, but it won't work. We already have an excellent reputation. She's a crazy lady who should be thrown in jail for what she's done to her daughter. It's one screwed-up family. We should never have said we'd take Tina."

"Well, it's too late," I said, shaking my head. "She's here now, and she doesn't want to leave."

CHAPTER SIXTEEN

A couple of days later, Hurricane Nancy, irrepressible storm that she was, made her way through the Caribbean toward Cuba, threatening to do some damage. A Category 4 hurricane, she sent shivers of fear through us. Dorothy and Dave joined the day staff in the dining room to review emergency procedures. Both had promised to be on hand at the hotel should we need them.

"The lanterns we'd set aside for each room have fresh batteries, and I've distributed extra bottles of water to the rooms," Tim reported.

"If we should lose electricity, our generator will kick in automatically, providing emergency lighting throughout the hotel and keeping the refrigerators and freezers in the kitchen going," I said to the staff in the meeting. "Even the office equipment will be kept going. But the safety of our guests will be the most important issue. We need to be aware of that."

"What about all the windows and sliding glass doors?" asked Dorothy.

"Manny and Paul are trying to round up as much plywood as they can to board up the windows. Apparently, there's a shortage."

"Consuela and I are preparing some easy meals ahead of time," said Rhonda.

"How many guests do we have scheduled in?" said Julie.

"Twenty-four at last count," I said. "Those numbers may decrease as people realize the hurricane will hit us. In fact, as much as it hurts us to do so, we're suggesting guests delay their visit for a day or two." I drew a deep breath. "We need to warn our current guests about the storm. They might want to travel inland while they can."

After answering a few more questions, Rhonda and I led the staff on a tour of the property, explaining what lights would be lit and what areas of the hotel were of most concern. Tim was assigned the task of clearing off the poolside deck and patio furniture to be stored in the garage. During the last storm, we'd lost some furniture and all the umbrellas. This time, we hoped not to have to replace anything.

At home, I reviewed safety plans with Tina. The more she listened, the more concerned she became. "Ann, you're making this sound really scary."

"It can be. But chances are by the time the storm gets here, it'll be a lot of wind and rain, not the severe hit that Cuba will probably take. Besides, you'll be safe here as long as you stay away from the windows and glass doors." Lacking plywood, the hotel staff had taped my windows.

"I talked to Barbara today. I like her, Ann." Tina gave me a shy smile. "I think she likes me, too."

"I'm glad. *I* think *I* like you too."

We smiled at one another. "Why don't we go to the hotel for an early dinner? The storm shouldn't reach us until sometime during the night."

Jean-Luc was in the kitchen when we arrived there. He glanced at Tina. "Are we eating real food tonight?"

Tina played along. *"Oui, mais un petit seulement."*

Jean-Luc lifted his eyebrows. *"Parlez-vous français?"*

Tina laughed. "Not really. I had to learn a little French for a movie." She glanced at me. "One of the ones you wouldn't like."

"We're serving a chicken and mushroom special. I think you'll like that," said Sabine, joining us. "Perhaps it will suit the two of you?"

"Sounds delicious," I said. "Thank you for coming in early. We're suggesting to our guests that they eat early."

"Yes," said Sabine. "Maria and Paul are already serving appetizers and drinks to them in the living room."

"Good," I said. "Relaxing a bit might soothe the jitters of some of our guests."

While Tina and Sabine chatted in the kitchen, I walked into the living room. A number of guests were sitting and talking to one another. Light from outside was constricted by the large X's of tape placed on the double sliding glass doors. The smaller windows facing the Gulf were boarded up, but we'd run out of wood. Now I wished we'd gone ahead with the installation of hurricane shutters that we'd decided we couldn't afford.

The breeze picked up. Palm trees swayed in the wind, their fronds grasping the air with narrow strands like fingers reaching for something. Gray clouds raced across the darkening skies. The Gulf waves slapped against the sand like angry hands.

I turned away from the view outside to spend time chatting with each of the guests. We had to make sure they had what they needed to get through a stormy night.

A guest, a woman from Canada, caught hold of my hand. "I've never been in such a storm. I have to confess I'm nervous about it."

"If things get bad, we'll gather in the library where there are no windows. Our staff and I will be here to help you."

Moving along, I spoke to another couple—honeymooners. The bride, a sweet-looking young girl, beamed at me. "This is so exciting. It'll make our honeymoon so special." She gazed lovingly at her groom.

I couldn't help thinking of Angela and Reggie. His parents

had sent a message, agreeing to come for Thanksgiving, but I wasn't at all confident it would be a happy visit.

Tina and I ate dinner at the kitchen table, out of the way of the staff, who were working smoothly to prepare the meal before heading home to care for their families.

Later, I walked Tina over to my house. I'd stay there with her as long as I could, but as the storm got closer, I'd move over to the hotel to help our guests.

I checked my lanai. The hotel staff had put my outdoor furniture into the pool, where it would be safe. But my larger potted plants were still sitting on rolling trollies. I rolled the largest ones against the wall of the house. Tina and I carried smaller plants and decorative items into the house. Hopefully, the screen cage around the pool would stay intact. I'd already repaired it once, due to another storm.

We turned on the television in the living room. Tina sat beside me on the couch, looking more and more worried as reports came in that Nancy would hit the southwest coast of Florida. There was no point in going to bed. Not with news like that.

I checked the large flashlights and lanterns I kept on hand and found them to be fine. Nevertheless, I pulled out a bag of batteries and placed them on the counter.

"All set," I announced to Tina. "We might as well watch a movie. I don't think either one of us is going to sleep for a while. Why don't you choose something?"

"How about this?" Tina indicated an animated family feature.

"Sure, that would be great. I haven't seen something like this in ages."

She laughed. "Neither have I. My mother wasn't one to sit around and watch movies with me. But this is one of my brother's favorites."

"So you and your brother are close?" I said, probing for information.

"Yeah, we are. He has Down syndrome. My mother tried to put him in an acting program, but he didn't like it. He had too much trouble memorizing lines. But he goes to a special school, and he likes that." She shook her head and sighed. "My mother doesn't have much patience with either him or me, so it's not great. I've been thinking about him. Maybe someday he can move in with me."

"That would be a nice, generous thing," I said. "But how would your mother feel about that?"

Tina's scoff was telling. "She'd love it. Believe me."

Sitting side by side, we watched the antics of little toys in the movie, laughing together. It was a nice time, but I missed my daughter. When the movie was over, I went into the kitchen to call her.

Liz answered right away. "Hi, Mom! I saw on television that Hurricane Nancy is headed your way. Are you all right? Are you prepared?"

"We're as ready as we can be," I said. "We don't yet know what the impact will be on us after the storm crosses Cuba. There's a chance it could be downgraded to a tropical storm. We have to wait and see. By the way, Angela's boyfriend was here, and his parents are coming for Thanksgiving. It will be good to have you here for that. I'm sure Angela would like your support."

"Uh, there's something I have to tell you," said Liz. There was an uneasiness to her voice that I recognized. "Dad called me. He's going to come up with a lot of the money for my tuition. The only problem is, he made me promise to go there for Thanksgiving."

"Whaaat! He knows I was counting on seeing you. You live in the same area. You can visit him anytime. Why is he insisting on a Thanksgiving visit?"

"You know Dad. There's always a twist. But under the circumstances, how could I refuse? I need that money."

"Oh, honey, I wish I were in a position to give it to you. But at the moment, I'm not. We're upgrading a couple of rooms in anticipation of a good season, including an important wedding."

"Mom, don't worry about it. Dad owes me that money. Even if I have to spend time with Kandie to make him pay up, I'll do it. Besides, little Robbie is a cutie."

"Well, I guess that's the way it'll be," I said, unable to hide my disappointment.

"Love you, Mom," said Liz. "I'll definitely be there for Christmas. What did you think of Reggie?"

"I liked him. You know Rhonda. It'll take her a while to get over Angela's dating someone who doesn't like her cooking. He's allergic to shellfish, and tomatoes make his skin itch."

Liz laughed. "I can hear Rhonda now. How's she feeling? Angela told me about the baby."

"Rhonda's looking much better and is over that early morning sickness. But she's nervous as can be about meeting Reggie's parents. I don't blame her. They don't sound like easy people to get along with."

"Yeah," said Liz. "They're not happy about Reggie dating Angela."

Worry pinched my gut. Angela was a sweet, nice girl. I'd hate for anyone to hurt her or the baby she might be having.

"Call me tomorrow when you get a chance," said Liz. "I want to know you're all right."

"Sure, sweetie. Love you. I'd better go."

"Wow!" said Tina, startling me. I'd forgotten she was close enough to hear my conversation with Liz. "That was your daughter? You guys do seem close."

"We are. At her age, she's more like a friend than my daughter."

Tina shook her head. "That's never going to happen between my mother and me."

I let her comment go. I didn't see that happening either.

A while later, the television weather crew reported the mountains of Cuba had weakened the hurricane, which had then been downgraded to a tropical storm, but it was still on track to head right for us. They suggested everyone hunker down until it had passed. Rain had already started ahead of the storm, and now the wind was picking up.

"I'd better get over to the hotel," I said to Tina. "I wish you would come with me."

Tina glanced at the weather outside and shook her head. "I'll stay here. I don't want to go outside in that wind, and I feel safe here."

"Okay, then. Keep the lantern by you, in case you need it. Otherwise, you know what to do. If it gets bad, stay inside the guest bathroom where there are no windows. Stay there until the wind dies down." Impulsively, I gave her a quick hug. "I'd rather stay here too, but I can't leave our guests. See you in the morning."

I put on a rain parka and stepped outside.

The wind grabbed the breath from my throat. I stood a moment, trying to draw in air, gasping like a fish out of the water. My hair whipped around in the wind, stinging my cheeks. No wonder Tina didn't want to be outside, I thought, ducking my head and running through the rain as fast as I could toward the hotel.

By the time I reached the double front doors, my hair was hanging down in strings, and my feet were wet. I entered the lobby and hurried into the kitchen hallway to grab a towel and do my best to dry off.

I took off my wet sandals and wiggled my toes. So much for formality, I thought and quickly assessed the situation. Rhonda had handled the dinner shift and left, along with Jean-Luc and Sabine. Dave had not yet arrived for the night shift.

In the living room, guests lounged on chairs and couches, focused on the television screen. It was almost a party atmosphere as strangers talked, becoming friends who were sharing an adventure together. I refilled the coffee pot that had been placed on a side table and brought out a fresh platter of cookies.

Tim came over to me. "Looks like it might not be too bad."

"I hope not.."

As soon as the words were out of my mouth, the lights went out.

"Uh-oh," he said.

A cry went up from the living room.

"Stay calm, everyone," I announced. "The generator has kicked on, and emergency lighting is available at the exits and in the halls. For those of you who forgot to keep flashlights or lanterns with you, we've got extras at the front desk."

I was returning to the lobby when my cell rang. I checked caller ID and picked up the call.

"Hi, Tina. What's up?"

"I'm scared," she said. "I should've come to the hotel with you."

"You'd better stay inside right there. Heaven knows what's happening outside. The wind is howling. It could be dangerous."

"I know. That's why I want to be with you," Tina said.

"When the eye of the storm hits, things will slow down. Maybe you can try to get here then," I said. "Look, I've got to go. One of our guests is calling for help."

I hung up and headed upstairs. Alice Wentworth, an older woman traveling with her husband Marv, was standing in the hallway. "We heard a loud crack, and something hit the building right where our room is. My husband is checking on it now."

I went into their room and waved my flashlight all around, checking the window and the sliding glass door leading to the balcony. A huge palm frond was lying on the balcony. Relieved it hadn't broken any of the taped glass, I turned to them.

"We'll get that cleaned up tomorrow morning. You'd better come downstairs with me."

I led them downstairs to the library and left them to check on things in the kitchen.

As I was passing the front door of the hotel, I heard what sounded like some kind of creature howling. Confused, I cracked the door open. The outside lights, dimly lit by the generator, displayed a body sprawled on the front circle. A large palm branch lay nearby.

"Tim!" I screamed. "Help me!"

He came running.

"Someone's hurt," I said, "or worse. Come on!"

Together we ran outside.

As I got closer to the body, I realized who it was.

"Tina!" I shrieked. "Are you okay?"

"Owww!" she cried. "It hurts!"

Struggling a bit, Tim lifted the palm branch off her leg.

I knelt in the soggy grass beside her. "What happened? Where does it hurt?"

"My leg! My leg!" she screamed.

Staring at the way her leg was twisted, I knew it must be broken. "Tim, call 911 and get someone here right away. And then bring blankets to us."

He sprinted to the hotel.

I grabbed hold of Tina's hand and huddled over her, trying to protect her from the stinging rain. "Okay, hon, we're getting help for you. I'll stay right here beside you. It looks like your leg might be broken."

She laid her head on the ground and moaned. "It freaking hurts."

"I'm sure it does. Hold on. They'll be here soon." I prayed they'd be able to come to our aid quickly. I was certain the howling wind and the driving rain meant more than one emergency call.

It seemed to take forever for an ambulance to show up. But then things happened quickly. One EMT checked her over while another made quick work of splinting the leg. Then carefully they lifted her onto a collapsible gurney and rolled it into the ambulance.

"May I go with her?" I asked. "She's living with me."

The EMTs exchanged glances, and then one of them nodded. "Okay, we'll take it nice and easy. I'll help you get in."

The hospital wasn't far away, so it was a short ride. They kept the sirens off.

Once there, the EMTs moved with efficiency. I watched as they wheeled Tina into the emergency room. In the reception area, I gave what information I could to the emergency room triage nurse and then sat to wait to be called to Tina's bedside.

After what seemed a lifetime, a nurse appeared. "Ann Rutherford?"

"Yes." I stood, acutely aware I was in bare feet and soaking clothes.

"You may come back now," the nurse said. "Follow me."

She led me to a curtained bed and slid open the curtain on one side. "Tina. Your friend Ann is here."

Tina looked up at me drowsily. "Hi."

I took hold of her hand, careful to avoid the IV the nurses

had inserted.

A young man in a white coat appeared. "Hello, I'm Dr. John Wilson. I understand this patient, Tina Marks, is living with you."

"Glad to meet you. I'm Ann Rutherford. What injuries does she have?"

"Unfortunately, she has displaced fractures of the tibia and fibula. We'll prepare her for surgery. The X-rays shows pretty clean breaks, so I'm not anticipating any real problems. We'll put in plates and screws where necessary."

"And then what happens?" I said. Did it mean that no matter what she finally decided, the next movie was out for Tina?

"A good recovery normally takes several weeks. And then there will be some physical therapy needed to build back strength."

I glanced over at Tina. She was dozing, no doubt from the medication they'd given her.

"Ms. Marks has signed the papers for surgery. As I've explained to her, she should be back to an almost normal existence in a couple of months. There was no compound fracture, which makes things a bit easier."

"Thank you, Doctor. When is the surgery taking place?"

"We'll have a room in another twenty minutes or so." He glanced at me. "Enough time, I should think, for you to go home and change before coming back."

I brushed back my wet hair from my face. "Thanks. I think I'll do that."

"See you soon," I whispered to Tina, leaning over and placing a kiss on her cheek.

She stirred, opened her eyes, gave me a weak smile and drifted back to sleep.

CHAPTER SEVENTEEN

Tim picked me up at the hospital in the hotel van. Driving back to the hotel I was able to distinguish debris on the lawns we passed by in the dark. Trees were obviously down in some areas.

"How are things at the hotel?" I asked him, trying not to shiver in the air-conditioned van. We couldn't turn it off; the windshield was fogged up from the change in temperature even as rain continued to blur the view.

Tim turned to me with an unhappy expression. "Things in the lobby are pretty bad where debris blown by the wind broke the glass, and the rain got in."

"My God! How many windows got broken?"

"Hard to tell until we get a good look. All the windows that were boarded up seem to be fine, from what I could tell."

I collapsed against the seat of the van. More problems.

When she heard what had happened, Rhonda insisted on coming to the hotel to maintain control there while I went back to the hospital to be with Tina. The quick-moving storm had spent most of its energy, though electricity was still out. With daylight, we'd know more about property damage.

Will arrived at the hotel with Rhonda. After dropping her off, he drove me to the hospital.

"Thanks, Will," I said, stepping out of the car. I knew he was anxious to get back to Rhonda. It was cute to see how protective he'd become of her.

"I'll call the hotel when I'm ready to be picked up," I told him and hurried inside.

A nurse directed me to the surgical waiting room. Sitting with other anxious people, I wondered what these broken bones would do to Tina's career. She'd boldly stated she didn't want to do the movie. Now she wouldn't be able to. Would she be upset the choice had been taken away from her? "Tina Marks?" said a nurse wearing blue scrubs.

I held up my hand.

The nurse came over to me. "She's come through the surgery just fine. The doctor was able to do a smooth reduction, lining up the bones and making sure they will stay in place. You can come back and see her. She's ready to leave the recovery room. She'll stay the rest of the night and be released tomorrow."

I followed the nurse back to a room with curtained sections and to Tina's bed.

"Hi, honey," I said, taking hold of her hand.

"See why I don't like the wind?" Tina said drowsily.

"You scared me, you know. I thought you were dead." Tears unexpectedly stung my eyes. I blinked them back. "But you're going to be fine. You came through the surgery well."

"Guess I won't be doing my usual moves, huh?"

"We'll talk about all that later. They're going to put you in a room. Then tomorrow you'll come back to the hotel with me."

"Home sweet home," she said, barely able to move her lips. "Water. I need some water."

I called the nurse, and she brought a glass of water and a straw. "Sip slowly," she instructed.

After Tina had taken a few small sips, the nurse turned to me. "Looks like she'll be in room #316. Why don't you meet us there?"

"Okay. See you in a few minutes, Tina." I turned to go.

"Ann?"

I turned back. "Yes?"

"Thanks for being here. It wouldn't have happened if I didn't feel safer with you than anyone else."

This time, the tears that stung my eyes couldn't be blinked away. I took hold of her hand again and squeezed it. "You'll always be safe with me. I promise."

"Thanks. No one's ever said that to me before."

When I turned away this time, I let the tears that had filled my eyes overflow. Life was sometimes so sad.

I left Tina with the promise to pick her up later that day.

Dawn was making a valiant effort to break through the cloud cover as Tim drove me back to the hotel. Pink and orange mingled with gray above us while branches covered lawns in an array of ghostly shapes and, in a few instances, spread across roads. Hibiscus and other blossoms hung their heads on bushes, drooping with an abundance of wetness, their colors muted.

As he drove through the gates of the hotel, Tim slowed to assess the damage. The electricity was back on. We, like others, had branches and palm fronds strewn about and unhappy, wilted flowers, but no severe tree damage.

Tim dropped me off in my driveway. I thanked him and walked around to the back of my house.

The pool cage screen was coated with water, giving it a glass-like appearance, but it stood tall and unbent. Thankful my house hadn't been damaged like the hotel, tears of relief stung my eyes. My house, my precious little house, was in good condition.

In the kitchen, I made a cup of coffee and then went about straightening up. When I opened the door to Liz's room, I expected to find a mess. But it was surprisingly tidy. Even the bedcovers had been pulled up hastily before Tina left for the hotel. I shook my head. She was a person of such contradictions.

After moving patio articles and plants back outside, I headed to work. I'd get some rest after I made sure things were in good shape there.

At the hotel, I saw that the staff had cordoned off the lobby area, where a housekeeper was sweeping up broken glass along the sliders leading out to the patio and swimming area. The carpet inside was wet. One of the women was trying to soak some of the wetness up with towels. Another was wiping down furniture.

I found Consuela and Rhonda busy in the kitchen preparing breakfast. Paul had arrived and was about to go out and help Manny with the landscape issues. Guests were eating in the dining room.

"Hi," said Rhonda. "You saw what happened to the lobby?"

"Any other damage?" I asked.

"We'll need to replace a few other windows, but everything else seems fine at first glance. I thought the sliders would be protected where they sat beneath the overhang. We'll have to think about those hurricane shutters."

My mind spun with figures. Another expense we didn't need.

"How is Tina?" Rhonda said to me. "And is everything okay at your place?"

"I can't believe it. My house survived without any real damage. And Tina came through the surgery very well. I'll pick her up this afternoon."

Rhonda gave me a worried look. "Does this mean she'll stay with you until she recovers? That could be months."

"I'm not sure what's going to happen. I don't see how Tina can be in the movie now, even if she wanted to change her mind." I sighed. "We'll have to wait and see. I found out Liz isn't coming home for Thanksgiving, so I've got the space for Tina until Christmas, when Liz will be here."

Rhonda frowned. "What do you mean Liz isn't coming home for Thanksgiving? She always comes here."

"Robert made a deal with her. In exchange for paying her tuition, she had to agree to go there for Thanksgiving." The words left a bitter taste in my mouth.

"That bastard," muttered Rhonda. "He's such a jerk."

"Don't I know it," I agreed.

"Aw, don't worry, Annie. At least she'll be here for Christmas. Say, why don't we put Tina here in the hotel? That way she'll have help whenever she needs it."

"Good idea. Being here at the hotel might be safer for her. There'd always be someone around to protect her. Her agent wasn't happy when she found out the movie Tina was supposed to be in was no longer a consideration. Heaven knows what her mother will say."

Turning to the work at hand, I met with Ana and the other housekeepers. Now that the storm had moved north, we were left with the clean-up. Staff needed to remove all the tape from windows and doors, and then they'd have to sweep off outside patios and balconies before they could restore furniture to them.

Manny and Paul were working outside taking down the window boards and installing them over the broken sliders in the lobby before cleaning up the yard and hauling away debris. Unfortunately, it would take a while to replace the glass that had been broken in the sliders. Tim was collecting lanterns and storing them to be used for the next storm, and then he'd help move the furniture outside.

Later, I went to check on the spa. Troy came over to me. "Everything came through in good shape here."

"Great. I think I have your first client. Tina fractured her leg. She'll be needing some physical therapy and massages."

He smiled. "Any more news on that important wedding?"

"The wedding is going to be January 5th. So the week following New Year's Day will be very busy here. I suspect a few soothing massages will help everyone."

By then, I'd need a massage of my own.

When I picked up Tina from the hospital, it became apparent she'd need special care. Wearing an adjustable splint on her leg, she struggled with the crutches she'd been given. With help from the nurse's aide, I got her into my car. She leaned back against the passenger's seat and let out a long sigh. "I'm so tired."

"Rhonda and I have set aside a room for you at the hotel— the room closest to our office. That way, if you need anything at any time of day or night, you'll have it."

Tina gave me such a stricken look, I flinched.

"But I want to be with you," she said.

"I honestly think you'll be more comfortable at the hotel. It's where I spend most of my time."

The disappointment on Tina's face disappeared. "Okay, I can do that."

I pulled up to the front of the hotel.

"Do you want a wheelchair?" I asked Tina, helping her out of the car.

"No, I want to do this myself," Tina said.

Rhonda met us at the front of the hotel, next to the discreet ramp beside the front steps.

As Tina inched her way up the ramp, Rhonda and I walked on either side of her. Once through the front entrance, Tina sat for a moment in the lobby area to catch her breath. Then she headed to the room we'd set aside for her.

By the time she made it to her room, Tina's face had gone pale.

"You rest here," I said sympathetically, helping her to lie down on the bed.

"What can I bring you?" asked Rhonda.

"How about a Diet Coke and a hamburger?" Tina said, giving us a look of defiance. "It doesn't matter now. No movie. No diet. I'm done with all that."

"Does your agent know?" Rhonda said.

"No, but I'm about to tell her my decision is final, that I'm not reconsidering it like she asked."

Rhonda and I exchanged glances, and then I said, "Okay, we'll send in a tray. Anything else we can do?"

"Yes. Ann, will you stay here while I talk to my agent? She sometimes scares me."

"Sure," I said, finding her remark very telling. No wonder Tina felt so bullied. Both her agent and her mother were apparent monsters, thinking only of themselves.

Tina took out her phone from the purse I'd carried inside for her. Giving me a worried glance, she punched in the number and waited for a response.

I studied her. The pain medicine had softened her features, making her appear even more vulnerable.

As Tina told her agent about the accident, I listened carefully.

"No, I'm not going to be in this movie," said Tina firmly. "They'll have to find someone else. No, I don't care who they get. In fact, I don't care if I'm ever in a movie again."

Through the phone, I could hear the agent's angry shouts.

"What's happened to me?" said Tina. "I'm getting a life of my own. Not the one you want me to have or the one my mother wants me to have. But the one I want for myself."

More shouting from the agent echoed around Tina.

"The owners? Ann and Rhonda have done a wonderful job here. Don't you go badmouthing them or the hotel, or I'll tell everyone about some of the crap you put me through. Goodbye."

She clicked off the phone and buried her face in her hands.

I went to her and put an arm around her shaking shoulders. "Are you going to be all right?"

She lifted a tear-streaked face. "I think so. But, Ann, my agent is really mad. She says she should never have sent me here, that I've changed."

I sat down on the bed next to Tina. "So she doesn't like the fact you've changed. How do you feel about that?"

All anguish left Tina's face. "I think being here might have saved my life, being with people who care and talking to someone like Barbara."

"Good, I'm glad," I said. "We won't worry about the rest right now."

"But, Ann, she told me she's going to make you pay by telling everyone not to come here."

I caught my breath. "She wants to give us some bad press?"

"Yeah, but she won't. She did some really bad stuff to boost my career. She knows I could ruin her."

I forced a calmness into my voice. "All right. We'll let it go for now. Let's concentrate on getting you well. I'm going to leave you so you can get some rest. If you need anything, call the front desk, and we'll take care of it."

When I went to find her, Rhonda was in the kitchen talking to Jean-Luc. I signaled her to follow me to the office.

She groaned as she sat down. Patting her stomach, she said, "I think this baby is going to be big. I can't imagine waiting another five months for him to arrive." There was a glow to Rhonda that was charming. "So, what's up, Annie?"

I filled her in on Tina's conversation with her agent.

"It's her mother I'm worried about," said Rhonda. "Who knows what she'll say about all this. She's already threatened us."

The phone rang. As if we'd called her forth from an Ouija board, caller ID identified someone named Marks with a California number.

"I'll take it," said Rhonda. "We're not putting up with any bullshit from her."

I listened as they exchanged greetings . Then I watched outrage paint Rhonda's face in bold strokes. She handed me the phone. "You talk to her, Annie, or else I'm going to lose it. She's trying to blame us for everything."

"This is Ann Rutherford speaking. May I help you?"

Tina's mother went into a tirade filled with expletives.

When I was finally able to break into the conversation, I was as angry as I'd ever been.

"Stop right now," I said in a barely controlled voice. "Your daughter defied our instructions to stay inside during the storm. If she had listened to us, she might not be in this position. What arrangements she may or may not make concerning the movie is of no concern to us. She's an adult who can make her own choices."

But Tina's mother wasn't ready to give up. "I'm going to sue your hotel and take out ads in all the papers to expose you for ruining my daughter's career."

Through clenched teeth, I said, "I wouldn't do that if I were you. We know too much about your ruining your daughter's life to make it worth your while to threaten us or try to smear the hotel's reputation. Believe me, if you went forward with a plan like this, you would not be happy."

"We'll see about that," Tina's mother said and abruptly ended the call.

I hung up and turned to Rhonda. "Do you think she could actually hurt our business?"

Rhonda shrugged. "But remember, she's not the only one in Hollywood who knows this hotel. Vaughn's reputation is much better than hers. He can help us if any problems come up."

I unclasped my hands. "You're right. But it's important for us to keep the hotel's reputation intact. It's how we built our business."

Rhonda shook her head. "I'm tellin' you, Annie, if that broad does anything to hurt us, I'm going to report her to the authorities. How any mother could treat her daughter the way she does is beyond me. It's criminal. That's what it is."

"Absolutely," I said, unable to shake the image of a girl's innocence being shattered.

CHAPTER EIGHTEEN

Two nights later, at the end of a long evening watching over local guests at a birthday celebration in the small private dining room, I went to Tina's room to check on her.

She was propped up in bed watching television and munching on cookies that we offered to guests at night. She glanced at me and turned her attention back to the television.

"How are you doing?" I said.

Tina sighed. "My mother called. She told me I could sue you for a lot of money. She said you should have trimmed those palm trees. She said you should be waiting on me hand and foot and that she's going to tell everyone not to come here."

I blinked in surprise. "Sue us? Trim the trees? Wait a minute! You were asked to stay inside my house until the storm calmed down, which you didn't do. And you know very well, Tina, we've welcomed you here and given you good service even at the most difficult times."

Tina's face crumpled. "I don't want to sue you. It's my mother. God! She gets me so uptight with all her demands."

I placed a hand on her shoulder. "Listen, I know you're upset. Why don't you get some more rest, and I'll see you in the morning? We can talk then. Dave is on night duty at the front desk. If you need him, he's here for you."

Tina gave me an apologetic look. "Ann? I'm sorry."

"Yeah, me too," I replied, still shaken by how quickly Tina's whole demeanor could flip.

And I wondered how far her mother would go to sue us.

When I returned to my house, it seemed eerily empty. I decided to soak in the tub to try and loosen the tension in my shoulders. It had been a helluva day.

I was drying off when my phone rang. Vaughn.

"Hi, sweetheart," he said in the deep, sexy voice his viewers and I loved so much.

I smiled, wrapped my towel around me, and took a seat on the side of the spa tub. "Hi, darling. I miss you a whole lot."

"Yeah, miss you too. But, Ann, I'm not going to make it to the hotel for Thanksgiving. Ty has asked me to come to San Francisco. He's going to propose to June, and he wants me to meet the Changs."

"Oh no! I was counting on seeing you!" I took a moment. "But I'm happy for him and I liked June when I met her." My tone was hollow with disappointment. First Liz, now Vaughn opting out for the holiday. After all that was going on, it seemed too much.

"Wish you could go there with me," said Vaughn.

"Me too, but I can't leave the hotel at the busy holiday time. Besides, I've already promised Rhonda I'd be here to help entertain the parents of Angela's boyfriend. I have a feeling both Rhonda and Angela are going to need all the help they can get."

I explained what I meant, and then I told him about the storm and Tina's injury.

"You know Tina's mother," I said. "Do you think she could hurt our business? She told Tina to sue us. And she's threatened to spread rumors about us."

"Tina's mother is well-known in the business as the kind of conniving person she is, so I don't think anyone of substance will take her seriously. Besides," Vaughn said, "a number of stars have come to the hotel and loved it."

"You're right," I said. "I should have more faith in the reputation Rhonda and I have worked so hard to create for the hotel."

We chatted for a while longer. I treasured this time with him. But after we hung up, a flood of disappointment surged through me. Sometimes running our small hotel seemed overwhelming. My time wasn't my own. I was forced to give up things I really wanted to do. More than that, I was constantly worried about succeeding.

A chill hung in the air when I went out to the beach for my early morning walk. I zipped up my lightweight jacket and headed down the sandy stretch, letting the movement of my body warm me.

The sun rose like a smiling face. Optimism filled me. The worry that had trailed me evaporated, making me feel better about things. Ty's asking his father to be present in his life now seemed sweet. And Tina's becoming upset at her mother's pushiness seemed helpful. Still troublesome was the upcoming visit of Reggie's parents. I headed back to the hotel with a fresh determination to protect Rhonda from being hurt.

Before checking on Tina, I went to the spa where Troy was supervising final arrangements with the young girl he'd signed up to do manicures and pedicures.

There was a clean, tropical feeling to the space. A citrus odor filled the air. In a back corner, two massage rooms were set up. A bathroom, complete with shower sat between them. And in another private area at the opposite end of the space, two chairs with spa tubs and tables for doing nails were in place. There, Tammi, the girlfriend of one of our part-time waiters, was opening boxes of polishes and gels. She looked up at me and waved me over.

"This is so nice! My customers can't wait to come to the hotel to get their nails done."

"Great. Remember, they will be eligible for a discount on our lunch menu." Dorothy Stern had suggested it, and Rhonda and I liked the idea.

Before leaving, I spoke to Troy about Tina. He agreed to work with her on becoming better adjusted to crutches and to talk to her about keeping her body active during recovery.

When I went to check on Tina, the room was empty. I found her in the dining room, eating a healthy, low-calorie breakfast.

"How are you?" I asked, taking a seat at her table.

"Much better. I talked to Barbara. I'm going to have a session with her this morning. I need someone to drive me there."

"Of course. Paul or Tim will be happy to do so," I said, pleased with her attitude. "Troy is going to work with you on handling your crutches and keeping your body healthy while you heal."

"Okay," Tina said agreeably.

"And if you'd like a pedicure, Tammi is dying to get started at the spa," I added.

Tina's face brightened. "That would be great!"

I entered the office feeling good about all that was happening. Seated at my desk, I waited for Rhonda to join me. She was working with Maria and Ana on the rooms cleaning schedule—making sure all would be ready for guests checking in.

I was in the middle of reviewing the daily report when I heard a commotion outside. I rose.

A woman who looked vaguely familiar burst through the doorway, followed by Tim.

"Sorry, Ann. I tried to stop her ..." said Tim.

"You're one of the owners? I'm here to see my daughter. Where is she?"

Tim gave me an apologetic look. "I tried to explain that Tina wasn't in her room, that she had an appointment downtown."

"Thanks, Tim. I'll take care of this." Gazing at the brightly painted woman whose clothing was embarrassingly youthful for a woman her age, the anger I felt toward her made my words sharp. "You're Tina's mother?"

"Yeah, so?"

"We don't appreciate being threatened. Your daughter's accident was through no fault of ours."

"Where is she? I want to see that for myself."

"As you've been told, she's off the premises. I'm not certain when she'll return. Though she's a guest here, we don't oversee her schedule."

"Well, I do." Tina's mother glared at me. "And she should be preparing for her next movie."

"You do understand she's fractured her leg, don't you?"

Tina's mother shook her head with disgust. "That's no excuse. She can still act with a broken leg."

The door opened, and Rhonda stomped into the room. "So this is Tina's mother." Rhonda faced the woman with an angry expression that would make any person cringe.

"You talk about suing us?" Rhonda's dark eyes snapped with furor. "You could be put in prison for what you did to your daughter! Get out!"

Aware this confrontation was only going to get worse, I stepped between them. "I'll escort you out, or Tim will."

Tina's mother jerked her arm from my grasp. "I'll do it on my own, but you're going to be sorry. The only thing I was trying to do was to look in on my daughter. Any mother would want to do that."

"Yeah?" said Rhonda behind me. "No mother should pimp her daughter for a role in a movie."

Tina's mother gave a scornful laugh. "Is that what she told you? Little liar."

"If you hurt her in any way, you'll answer to me or Annie here," warned Rhonda.

"It's time for you to go," I said, taking hold of the woman's elbow. Rhonda's temper was only going to get worse.

"I'll make you pay for this," Tina's mother shrieked. "Tina has to support me and her brother. She knows that."

Though I wanted to slap the woman silly, I forced myself to reply in as calm a voice as I could muster, "Leave now, or I'm calling the police."

This time, she didn't resist.

As quickly as I could, I walked her through the hotel. We'd reached the bottom of the outside stairway when the hotel's limo pulled through the gates.

I urged Tina's mother toward the small car in the front circle she'd indicated was hers. I'd just opened the car door so she could climb inside when she turned around. Paul was helping Tina out of the limo.

Her mother pulled away from me and ran toward them, screaming, "There you are, you little liar."

Paul stepped in front of Tina to protect her, but Tina's mother kept trying to push him away.

"What are you doing here, Tina? You need to go back to California with me and get ready for that movie."

Tina's mother grabbed hold of Tina's arm and pulled her.

"Ow!" Tina teetered on her good foot.

I rushed over and steadied her.

"Stop it right now," I cried, glaring at Tina's mother.

"Hello, Mother," Tina said in such icy tones it would chill any soul. "It's so nice you're concerned about my well-being."

The sarcasm in her voice would have made a normal mother wince, but Tina's mother simply stared at her.

"Get your things. We're leaving," her mother said, reaching for her arm.

Tina leaned away from her and then straightened. "No, I'm not leaving. *You* are. And if you don't, I'm going to press charges. You're no longer in charge of my career. I've hired someone to handle my finances, and if I decide to get back into movies, I will do it on my own, with a different agent."

"You can't do that!" her mother cried.

"I can, and I did," said Tina.

Her mother gave her a steady glare full of disgust. "What's happened to you? Look at you! You look ... look ... so ordinary! You'll never be able to make it in the movies like that. You don't have enough talent."

My insides shriveled at the cruelty of those words. Instinctively, I put my arm around Tina. But I couldn't erase the pain on her face. "Let's go inside. Paul, please see that this woman leaves the property."

I helped Tina inside and ushered her to a seat in the lobby. From behind the front desk, Tim covered his hand over the phone receiver and looked over at us. "What's all the shouting about?"

Struggling to control the anger that still pounded through me, I took a trembling breath. "Tim, I need you to call the police and report that someone is harassing one of our guests. Paul will see that she leaves the property, but I want to make a formal report."

Beside me, Tina was quietly sobbing. I put an arm around her shaking shoulders. "I'm so sorry, Tina. I'd hoped she'd be gone before you got back. What can I do to help you?"

She took hold of my hands. "Please, let me stay with you for a few more weeks until I can get things sorted out."

"Sure, I can do that." There was no way I'd let her go back to her old life in California. I tried for an encouraging smile. "You can be my family for Thanksgiving."

Her lips formed a shaky grin that crossed her face and quickly disappeared. "Barbara agreed I'd eventually have to break ties with my mother, at least professionally. Neither one of us knew it was going to happen like this."

"No matter when it happened, I'm sure it wouldn't be easy."

Tina shook her head. "I hate her, you know."

I didn't say a word. How could I?

CHAPTER NINETEEN

Thanksgiving approached in a flurry of pre-holiday business. The new spa packages received good reviews from the guests who took advantage of them. I waited and watched for any sign of retaliation from Tina's mother, but nobody served us legal papers, and nothing showed up in the news about Tina's accident.

Tina moved back into my house and was much more comfortable getting around. Troy was helping her, giving her exercises to strengthen her body and massaging sore muscles when she overdid it.

As Thanksgiving grew closer, Angela kept reminding us that everything had to be perfect for Reggie's parents. Rhonda and I decided to put them in the Presidential Suite.

"They'd better like this," grumbled Rhonda as she walked through the suite with Ana and me, checking its condition.

"I'm sure they will." Even the fussiest of guests fell in love with this space.

"You've got Reggie's room set aside?" Rhonda snorted with irritation. "Don't know why he can't stay at my house. They're all but living together at school."

"His mother insisted that he have his own room. I told her I'd take care of it." They hadn't even arrived at the hotel, and I was already feeling their demanding presence.

Angela and Reggie arrived on the Tuesday before Thanksgiving. After picking them up at the airport, Rhonda dropped them off at the hotel.

I noticed them by the pool sunning themselves in the unusually warm temperatures and went outside to say hello.

"How are you?" I asked Reggie.

He sat up to greet me. "Good, thanks. Glad to be away from the cold in Boston."

Angela smiled at me. "Hi, Ann. We can't wait for his parents to see how nice the hotel is."

Reggie reached for Angela's hand, and they exchanged happy smiles.

"We're going to do our best to give them a good time," I said, dreading the visit.

Later, when Angela came inside alone, I took her aside. "What's going on with you? The last time we talked alone, you were worried about something personal."

She glanced around the empty hallway before facing me. "I redid the test, and it turns out I am pregnant, after all. But I haven't told anyone," she whispered. "I'm not that far along, and up 'til now, I haven't been really sick. I'm not saying anything to anybody including Reggie until I know what the situation is with Reggie and me. I'd never want to force him into marrying me."

I hugged her. I knew very well how unsatisfactory a forced marriage could be. Robert might never have married me if I hadn't gotten pregnant.

When I went into the office, Rhonda beamed at me. "Doesn't Angela look wonderful? It's so good to see her. And Reggie's been real nice to me."

"I'm glad," I said. Whether Rhonda liked it or not, Reggie might soon be part of her family.

"I'm fixing Veal Piccata for dinner. He told me he could eat that." Rhonda grinned. "Maybe there's hope for him yet!"

I laughed. Nothing meant more to Rhonda than feeding

people who loved her cooking. Will had always been one of her biggest fans.

I hung around the hotel until dinner time was over, making sure all was going smoothly. The hotel was three-quarters full. Tomorrow it would be completely booked.

Tina came into the office and sat down.

"What's up?" I asked her.

She shrugged. "I miss my little brother. My mother won't let me talk to him. I'm afraid he'll think I don't care about him anymore."

"Is there anyone who can help you with this situation" Tina had shown me pictures of a teenaged boy with a guileless smile.

"I tried talking to the babysitter about it, but she was afraid that if my mother found out, she'd lose her job."

"How about someone at the school?"

Tina's face brightened. "That might work. They know I love my brother. Thanks, Ann. I hadn't thought of that."

She rose to leave.

"Any news about your plans?"

She sighed and sat back down. "I've talked to a couple of agents. The one I like told me if I quit now, it'll be hard to come back. And if I want to change the kind of roles I've had in the past, it would be even harder. She told me she'd help me if I want her to, but only if I studied the craft. There are a couple of acting coaches I could work with, but I don't know what I want to do."

"Well, you've got time to think about it while your leg heals."

She smiled. "I might even stay in Florida and do something entirely different. Right now, I need to make sure my brother is okay."

As she made her way out of the office, I thought about the

changes in her. I'd thought she might want to go back to her old ways, dressing inappropriately, acting entitled. But her mother's mean remarks to her had apparently served as encouragement to keep her appearance more modest. She certainly wasn't the same girl who'd arrived at the hotel a couple of months ago.

Standing beside Rhonda at the top of the hotel's front stairway, I could almost feel her anxious palpitations. She smoothed her rose-colored caftan again and again with nervous swipes of her hands. Her colorful blond curls were pulled back into a bun at the back of her neck. Diamonds sparkled on her ear lobes and winked on a heavy gold necklace that offset her tan. She'd reduced the amount of mascara she normally wore, giving her eyes a softer look.

"I don't think I've ever felt so insecure in my life," grumbled Rhonda. "Angela made me change my clothes, re-fix my hair and do my makeup differently." She shook her head. "I think this whole thing has all but made her sick. She barely ate breakfast this morning."

"You look fine," I said in a reassuring voice, as the limo with Reggie's parents pulled through the gates of the hotel.

Rhonda grabbed my hand. "Stay with me, partner. I'm scared to death of these people."

I hid my own nervousness. "Rhonda, they're no better or worse than we are. Remember that."

She drew a deep breath and tugged on my hand. "Okay. Here we go."

We descended the stairs with practiced smiles and waited for our driver to assist Katherine Smythe out of the limousine.

Tall and thin, she straightened and gave us a smile that held a chill. Her beige suit and tailored blouse seemed out-of-place in warm, sunny Florida. I recalled Rhonda once telling me not to be so beige and silently prayed she'd say nothing to Katherine.

"Welcome to The Beach House Hotel," Rhonda and I said together.

Confused, Katherine said, "Which one of you is Angela's mother?"

"I am," said Rhonda proudly, "and this is my business partner, Ann Rutherford."

"How do you do?" Katherine shook Rhonda's hand and then mine. "Reginald was anxious for us all to meet. I think it's appropriate that we do."

Rhonda smiled. "Angela and Reggie are really happy together. It took me a while to get used to the idea, but I get it now."

Katherine stiffened. "I see we have a lot to talk about."

It struck me then. With her long legs, sharp nose, and narrow neck, Katherine reminded me of a blue heron on the hunt, about to pluck a fish out of the water. I shook off my fanciful thoughts and turned to Arthur Smythe.

Surprisingly short, he seemed to cower under Katherine's watchful stare. Arthur's full head of hair formed a cloud of gray around his head. His eyes, a bright hazel, sparkled with interest.

"Hello, I'm Arthur Smythe, Reggie's father." He shook hands with Rhonda and then me. A frown creased his broad brow. "I thought Reggie would be here to greet us."

"He and Angela will be along soon. They've been staying at my house," said Rhonda.

"But surely Reggie will have his own room here," said Katherine, turning to me. "You mentioned that when I called to confirm."

"Yes, of course," I said. "It's all been arranged."

"Won't you please come in? We have your suite ready for you," said Rhonda. "I think you'll be pleased. Our guests really like the hotel. Right, Annie?"

"Indeed. We're so happy to have you here," I said trying to conquer my own nerves at their imperious behavior.

Katherine silently followed Rhonda into the hotel. I stayed behind to make sure Arthur had all their things gathered from the inside of the limo.

"Paul will get your suitcases," I told him. "Come with me."

As I turned to go inside, Arthur stopped me. "Any chance of sending up a bottle of Chivas Regal scotch to the room?"

"Sure. We'll be glad to take care of it. Anything else? We've provided fruit and cheese and crackers for your room, along with a small dish of nuts."

"That will be fine," he said.

I waved Tim over and quietly asked him to get the scotch.

I led Arthur inside and up to the second-floor wing which housed the Presidential Suite. As he followed behind me, I had the uncomfortable feeling he was staring at my bum.

When we stepped into the living room of the suite, I overheard Katherine telling Rhonda they would be leaving on Friday morning, not on Sunday as they'd originally planned.

"We have friends in Palm Beach we must visit," Katherine explained to us. "Their daughter is coming out in December, and Reginald will be accompanying her."

"Coming out?" said Rhonda. "You're celebrating that?"

Katherine's "tsk-tsk" was so condescending my cheeks grew hot at her snobbery.

"I mean as a debutante at the International Ball in New York," said Katherine. "It's a tradition, you know, for the best of families to take part in it. Unfortunately, we don't have a daughter, so Reginald will have to represent the family."

"Now, Katherine ..." Arthur began.

"I don't imagine your Angela is involved in anything like that," Katherine said to Rhonda.

Rhonda's cheeks grew bright red. I braced myself for whatever she might say.

Her smile was as fake as Katherine's. "Yeah, I don't believe in all that bullshit to prove to the world that I've got a whole lot of money. I'd rather spend it on people who need it."

Katherine's jaw dropped. "Well, I ... it's a tradition in the best circles ..."

"We'll leave you to get settled," I said smoothly, taking Rhonda's arm and leading her away. Though I could sense her angry resistance, Rhonda allowed me to usher her out of the suite.

We'd begun to descend the stairs when Arthur caught up to us. "Hey, I'm sorry about all that. We have only the one son, and Katherine is overly protective. She doesn't mean to be that way. She's simply worried about Reggie committing to anything too serious at this stage in his life."

He gave us an anxious look. "How about that bottle of scotch I ordered?"

"We'll send it up right away," I said.

"It's on the house," said Rhonda. "You must really need it."

Without waiting for me, she headed on down the stairs.

"Maybe you can help smooth things over," Arthur said to me. "I promised Reggie I'd keep an eye on his mother. He's not like her at all."

"We'll work together to keep things nice. But, Arthur, there's no need for this kind of thing. Nerves or not."

"I agree," he said. "I love my boy and would do anything for him, believe me."

"Then don't hurt him or Angela," I warned him. "And don't make it a contest. I assure you Rhonda has many friends in high places because of all her involvement in charities."

Tim headed toward us carrying a bottle. I knew from the label it was one of our most expensive brands.

Arthur held out his hand. "Thanks, I'll take that, young man."

Still disturbed by the exchange between Katherine and Rhonda, I headed downstairs to the office. Angela's pregnancy would be devastating to Reggie's mother. An unkind person, she'd make Angela's life miserable.

Rhonda was pacing the office when I entered it. She glanced at me. "That woman is a total snob! I bet I have more money than they do, as if that makes a person high society. I'm tellin' ya, Annie, I'm going to pull Angela aside and make it clear that she's to have nothing to do with Reggie. It's a bad situation."

"Let's let things evolve. Arthur told me Reggie isn't like his mother, so let's be fair to him." I wished I could tell her Angela's secret. That would put a very different spin on the situation.

Rhonda clenched her fists and glared at me. "If that boy hurts my Ange, he's going to pay for it big time!"

"Okay, in the meantime we've got to get through the next two days. And, Rhonda, we're going to do it nicely. Agreed?"

She shook her head. "No promises. Like I said, if Angela is hurt in any way, nice is out of the question."

I drew a big breath and let it out slowly. I loved Rhonda, but I never knew what she'd do next.

The office door opened and Angela came into the room. "Hi! How did it go? Are they nice?"

Rhonda and I exchanged glances.

"We're just getting to know each other," Rhonda said tersely.

Angela swung a worried glance to me.

I swallowed hard. "Reggie's father seemed very nice. His

mother is a little ... stiff."

"Oh," Angela said, sinking down into one of the chairs. "That bad?"

"She's a snob," scoffed Rhonda. Her eyes filled, but she quickly blinked evidence of tears away.

Angela noticed and got to her feet. "Did they hurt your feelings, Mom?"

"Never mind me," Rhonda said. "It's you I'm worried about. I don't want any of them to hurt you." She put her arms around Angela and hugged her close.

"So we're off to a bad start," I said, forcing a brightness to my voice. "Let's turn things around and make it pleasant for everyone."

A sigh escaped Angela's lips. "I told Reggie I'd go on up to his parents' room."

"Then you'd better go," I said.

Rhonda clasped her hands together. "Do you want me to go with you, sweetie?"

Angela laughed. "Thanks anyway, Mom. I have to do this on my own."

"You'll be fine," I said. "Go!"

"Hold your head up high, Ange. Don't let anyone treat you badly," said Rhonda.

After Angela left, Rhonda and I gave one another worried looks.

We were still in the office when Angela returned with Reggie.

"How'd it go?" Rhonda asked Angela.

Angela shrugged. "Reggie's dad was real nice, but I don't think I'm going to get along with his mother."

Reggie looked down at the floor and kicked at the carpet with a sneakered foot. When he looked up, he wore a troubled expression. "My mother wants me to marry one of her friend's daughters. I've told her that's never going to happen. But she won't listen."

"That's something you two have to decide for yourselves," I said.

He shook his head. "My mother doesn't think so."

"We're stuck with her until Friday morning," Rhonda said, trying to smile. "So let's make the best of it."

Lunch at The Beach House Hotel was considered a very desirable occasion to celebrate any number of events for both guests and local residents. In fact, our reputation for wonderful lunch offerings had helped our growth tremendously. A broad selection of sandwiches both dainty and hearty accompanied Consuela's array of soups and salads . Specials of the day were prepared by Jean-Luc's sous chef, Carl Lamond.

The large dining room, which was kept casual during breakfast, dressed up nicely with colorful table cloths for lunch and crisp white linens for dinner.

Rhonda insisted I join them for lunch. Curious to see how Angela would do with Reggie's parents, I quickly accepted.

Sabine kept a careful watch on us as we took our seats.

"Isn't this nice?" Reggie said, indicating the room.

His mother smiled. "Yes, it's very pleasant. It reminds me of our home in Newport."

"I like it better," said Reggie with a stubbornness I admired.

"It certainly is pleasant after the rainy days we've had in New England," said Arthur agreeably.

The conversation continued harmlessly until Sabine came over to me. "Ann, Mr. Sanders is on the phone for you."

"Vaughn?" I quickly got to my feet. "Thanks. I'll take it in the office." I turned to the others. "Excuse me, but I need to take a call."

"Say hello to him for me," said Rhonda. "Wish he could be here, but I know he had personal business to tend to with his son."

"Are you talking about Vaughn Sanders, the movie star?" said Katherine in a voice that almost squeaked with excitement.

"He's Annie's fiancé," said Rhonda. "Or all but. They're getting married; only they don't know when."

Different emotions flashed across Katherine's face. "He's coming here?"

"I hope so. He's visiting his son in San Francisco, and then we'll see."

"I'd love to meet him sometime." A flush crept up Katherine's cheeks, softening her features. She glanced at Arthur and then back to me.

I hid a smile. So she was human after all.

Hurrying to my office, I filled with hope. Maybe Vaughn had decided to try and make it home after all.

"Hey, sweetheart," I said cheerfully. "Where are you?"

"San Francisco. I've met the Changs, and all is going well. They're great people, and they like Ty."

"Wonderful. All very different from what's going on here."

After I gave him the details of what was going on, I said, "I wish you could be here."

"What? You want me there to charm Katherine Smythe?"

"No, silly, I want you here to charm me."

We laughed together, comfortable with the idea of exactly what I meant by charming me.

"Actually, I'm on a friend's private jet now. Should be there in time for dinner. The family engagement party went well, and though Ty and June invited me to one of their young friend's for Thanksgiving, I bowed out."

"Ty didn't mind?"

"No, he knows how rarely we can be together."

"He's so sweet! I'll send him my thanks, and I'll see you sometime later."

I hung up relieved. Vaughn's presence not only would mean the world to me but would be appreciated by all of us.

Later, while Rhonda and I were doing an inventory of food for Thanksgiving weekend, Rhonda said, "What do you think, Annie? Is there any hope for Angela and Reggie? Whenever I try to talk to Angela about it, she shuts me down."

"Let's see how the rest of the weekend goes. Having Will at dinner tonight will be a big help. He and Arthur will be able to talk business. And when he arrives, Vaughn can charm Katherine."

Rhonda shook her head. "I don't think anyone can charm that woman."

I sat beside Tina in the small dining room with Rhonda's family and the Smythes, feeling as if some sort of contest was going on. Every time Will said something about business, Arthur had to top it with a story of his own or tell a fact of his own making. Gentle, sweet Will was becoming more and more agitated.

I turned to Katherine, sitting on the other side of me. "What do you do with your time?"

"Well, since I don't have to work, I do a lot of things for charity. It seems only right."

"Yes, I agree." Maybe, I thought, Katherine wasn't so bad. But her husband was becoming a gigantic ass.

Angela and Reggie were sitting opposite Tina. The three of them seemed to be getting along, chatting easily with each other. But then everyone but Arthur was trying very hard to be agreeable.

Sabine served the main course of filets of beef with a bordelaise sauce.

Rhonda stood and held up her glass of sparkling water. "I'd like to make a toast to my daughter, a beautiful girl who has her whole life before her. We love you, honey."

I lifted my glass of cabernet. "Hear! Hear!"

Katherine hesitated for a moment and then lifted her glass, followed by the rest of us.

Arthur rose. "And I like to toast my son, a young man soon to embark on a new career and a new life with me in New York."

Again, glasses were raised. This time with less enthusiasm.

Reggie got to his feet. "I'd like to toast Angela, a girl who's opened my eyes to so many things."

It was several seconds before glasses were raised. All four parents wore unhappy expressions.

Afraid the entire evening might be ruined by the conflicting toasts, I quickly rose to my feet. "Here's to all of us. Health and happiness!"

This time, all glasses were lifted.

Vaughn chose that moment to walk into the room.

CHAPTER TWENTY

Vaughn's presence changed the atmosphere in the room. He came right over to me and gave me a long sweet kiss. Then he turned to Katherine. "Who's this beautiful young woman?"

Eyes shining, she smiled coyly at him and gave him her name.

He returned her smile, sending color into her cheeks. Then he introduced himself to Arthur. After shaking hands with him, Vaughn took a seat next to Katherine.

"So glad you could come," said Rhonda, giving him a broad smile. "You're family, Vaughn, you know that."

"Yes. Glad to be here. Thanks for having me." Vaughn leaned aside so one of the waiters could serve him his meal, the same as we were having. "Speaking of family, how're you and that baby of yours doing?"

Rhonda's cheeks turned a pretty pink. "He and I are doing fine." She turned to Will. "It's a boy. Right, honey?"

His indulgent smile was sweet. He wrapped an arm around her and pulled her close.

"You're having a baby?" Katherine said to Rhonda, clearly shocked. "At your age?"

"Yes, she is," said Will. "And we're thrilled."

Katherine stared thoughtfully at Rhonda.

The conversation turned to other things. Arthur told about an upcoming trip he and Katherine were taking to Europe. Then Katherine, smiling prettily, asked Vaughn questions about his career, and he regaled us with stories of his latest film. I wondered if Tina would mention her experiences in the movie business, but she remained silent, hiding her identity.

After dinner and before everyone left the dining room, Vaughn made a point of walking over to Angela. He hugged her and spoke to Reggie in a clear voice. "This girl is a golden treasure, young man. Don't you dare do anything to hurt her."

Reggie looked up at Vaughn. "No, sir, I won't."

Katherine joined them and put a hand on Reggie's shoulder. "My son is good to his friends. Friends like Angela. Friends like Laurel Larkin."

The silence that followed was filled with pulsing tension.

I waited for Reggie to say something, anything, but he simply stared at his mother and shook his head.

"I think I'm going to go home," said Angela, breaking into the awkwardness. "I'm tired."

"Want me to come with you?" asked Reggie hopefully.

Angela let out a sigh that spoke volumes. "No."

"Wait!" cried Rhonda, but Angela had already turned and was hurrying out of the room.

Reggie started to go after her, but Arthur held him back.

"She's tired, son. Let her go."

Katherine turned to Rhonda. "Well, thank you for dinner. I'm going to head on up to our room. It's been a full day."

Rhonda's eyes were unusually shiny, a sure sign she was trying not to cry. "Yes, indeed, it's been a full day." She sank down into a dining room chair.

Will wrapped an arm around Rhonda. "Let's get you home."

Katherine turned to Reggie. "Don't stay up late. Remember, we have a busy weekend coming up with the Larkins."

Katherine, Arthur, and Reggie left the room together. I turned to Rhonda. "I'm so sorry. I know how disappointed you must be. Reggie's parents are so difficult."

"Yeah, they're the worst. Poor Angela, she'd better get over her fascination with Reggie because it's going nowhere."

I swallowed hard. The parents might think the relationship was dying, but I knew that no matter how everyone else felt, it was far from over.

Tina took me aside, interrupting my dismal thoughts. "While Vaughn is here, I'm going to stay at the hotel. When I heard he was coming, Tim and I arranged it before dinner."

"Oh, how ... sweet," I said. My house was small, and a guest in the house would offer little privacy to Vaughn and me.

"Thank you, Tina," said Vaughn, studying her a moment. "I like the new look and the new person you're becoming. Ann has told me all about it."

A tinge of pink crept up Tina's cheeks. "I'm trying. Dinner tonight was a real test of my acting because those people are stuck-up jerks."

"I think we all had a bit of acting to do to get through the evening. Tomorrow might be easier because everyone will have some free time waiting for our private Thanksgiving dinner. And Rhonda and I will be busy doing hotel stuff for the Thanksgiving celebration."

Vaughn wrapped an arm around my shoulder. "But not too busy for me, I hope."

Tina looked from me to Vaughn and back again. "So this is how it is between the two of you. It seems so, so normal."

I smiled up at Vaughn. "It seems like a fairy tale to me."

"Ugh. You guys are disgusting," teased Tina. "See you tomorrow."

"Let's go home," he said, taking my elbow.

As we were leaving the hotel, we found Reggie sitting on the front steps, head in his hands, like a lost little boy.

We stopped beside him. "What's going on?"

His long sigh trembled in the air, a woeful note. "I love Angela, but it's never going to work. Not with my parents like they are."

"Are you going to let them dictate your life?" I asked. It was a question that had no easy answer.

He shrugged. "I dunno."

Frustrated by his response, I placed a hand on his shoulder and gave him a steady look. "You two need to talk."

"The thing is, Angela's mother isn't too happy with me either."

"She loves her daughter."

"I know. I know," he said. "Guess I'd better go to my room and watch television or something like that. Angela doesn't want me around."

"Oh, I wouldn't be too sure of that. See you later."

Vaughn took my hand. As we walked away I thought of all the reasons I should tell someone what I knew, but I couldn't break a promise to Angela. I needed to give her time to work things out her way.

After dreaming of it so often, having Vaughn beside me seemed like a miracle. I snuggled up to him, loving the weight of him, the length of him in my bed. He pulled me closer and then onto his body. I lay on top of him, looking down at the face that others viewed on a screen but I saw as my lover come home to me.

I cupped his face in my hands and lowered my lips to his, reveling in the taste of them and inhaling the male flavor that was his alone. His hands moved down my back to my bare buttocks. Pressing me closer to him, he shifted and moved until he was inside me. I gasped with pleasure and then joined him in a rhythmic dance.

Sated, and with my head on his chest, I traced the hairs on his chest, sighing softly.

"I love you, Ann," he whispered. "Don't you think it's time we got married?"

I lifted my head and smiled at him. I'd been thinking the same thing. "How about next June? I've always thought a June wedding would be nice, and that would be good timing with my duties at the hotel."

"You want to wait that long?" He grinned at me. "I think you like living in sin, you naughty girl."

I laughed, admitting to myself there was a bit of truth to it. My life with him, so different from what I'd always thought, was much more fun than I'd ever dreamed.

I opened my eyes. Six o'clock. I lay still, enjoying the luxury of having Vaughn there with me. Thanksgiving day at The Beach House Hotel would always be special to me. Two years ago, I'd spent my first Thanksgiving at The Beach House, when it was simply Rhonda's home. Wounded from my divorce, scared for the future, not sure how I felt about Rhonda, I wondered then what my life would become. Taking chances, I'd learned, can sometimes bring good things.

I glanced at Vaughn, pleased I'd taken a chance on him. Carefully, so as not to disturb him, I climbed out of bed and headed into the bathroom. Running a hotel with Rhonda was the biggest challenge of all, but I was thrilled to have been given the opportunity. Without it, I'd no doubt be struggling in Boston, trying to make ends meet while Robert taunted me with his new family.

Dressed for the day, I left Vaughn sleeping and headed over to the hotel. As I was crossing the front lawn, I heard the sound of a car behind me. Turning, I observed Angela driving her little white BMW convertible through the gates of the hotel. Reggie was seated beside her.

Angela waved and pulled to a stop in the front circle.

I approached them. "Everything all right?"

Angela beamed at me. "Don't mention it to anyone, but Reggie spent the night."

"So all is well between you two?"

Angela nodded and turned to Reggie.

"My mother can be a pain in the ass," he said. "I'm sorry she was so rude."

I waited for a word, a sign that he knew anything about a baby.

Angela touched my hand and shook her head at me meaningfully.

I left them to say goodbye to one another and hurried into the hotel. Those kids might think all was settled between them, but I had the horrible feeling that things were about to get worse.

The kitchen was already a scene of activity when I entered it. Consuela was taking a couple of batches of cinnamon rolls out of the oven. A staff member was chopping onions and mushrooms to add to the huge bowl of bread cubes that would form the bulk of stuffing for the turkeys. Another member of the kitchen staff was pouring a pumpkin mixture into pie shells.

I grabbed a cup of coffee and went into the office to check messages. Keeping all tables full for a meal like this was as difficult as keeping all rooms filled. I was at my desk when Tim knocked on the office door and entered.

He looked unusually flustered.

"What's up?" I asked, wondering at his state. Tim wasn't

one to get easily upset.

"It's the Smythes. I just got a call. They're checking out. Aren't they supposed to stay here for Thanksgiving dinner with Rhonda?"

"Checking out?" I rose to my feet with a sense of dread. Their leaving would be the final blow to Rhonda. She prided herself on providing this meal to her holiday guests.

"Did they say when they are leaving?" I checked the clock. Eight a.m.

"Mrs. Smythe said she ordered a limo to pick them up immediately. I know Rhonda will be hurt. And Angela too." He gave me a worried look.

"Let me call Katherine Smythe, and I'll get back to you. But, Tim, I have the awful feeling she's not going to change her mind."

"Me too." He shook his head. "She's not a very nice person."

As he left, I picked up the phone. Drawing a deep breath, I told myself to remain calm, pleasant and helpful—all those qualities we constantly drilled into our staff.

Arthur answered the phone. "Good morning," he said, echoing my greeting.

"I understand you might be leaving the hotel? We'd planned a special dinnertime event for you and Katherine, and I would hate for you to miss it."

"Yes, me too," Arthur said tersely. "But Katherine is adamant. We discovered earlier that Reggie spent the night at Rhonda's house with Angela."

His voice faded as another voice said, "Ann? This is Katherine. I cannot and will not allow such things to go on. Rhonda knew how I felt about Reggie and Angela being together. She should have respected my wishes. She should have sent him home."

"She might not have known he was there," I said. "She's

pregnant, and last night she left here tired. I imagine she was sleeping. She trusts Angela to do the right thing." I cringed at the thought of Angela's pregnancy. Katherine would, no doubt, blame that entire situation on Angela. But I knew it wasn't her fault alone. I'd seen the look of adoration on Reggie's face when he gazed at Angela. He loved her.

"We're leaving. Nothing you can say will change my mind," said Katherine. "And Rhonda having a baby at her age, when she has a child in college? Totally unseemly."

"Your judging Rhonda and Will that way is uncalled for. They're in love and thrilled with a chance, a second chance if you will, to make a family of their own," I said hotly.

"The limo will be here shortly. I have to go. I've asked the front desk clerk to check Reggie and us out of our rooms. Thank you."

Katherine hung up the phone with a finality I knew I couldn't change. I sat back in my desk chair, wondering how I could soften the blow to Rhonda.

Several minutes later, Rhonda entered the office and slammed the door behind her. "That bitch! She's ruined everything!" Tears shone in Rhonda's eyes. "I could kill her! And Angela's hysterical."

"What happened?"

"Angela got a call from Reggie to tell her that his parents are insisting that he leave with them. He said he had no choice but to go with them. They've threatened to cut him off if he doesn't." She slapped a hand on the desk. "They hurt my baby, they pay. Somehow, I'll see that they do."

"Have a seat, Rhonda, and we'll talk about it." An alarming red hue was creeping up her cheeks. "Remain calm for the baby's sake."

"Oh, yeah, I forgot," said Rhonda, promptly sitting in her chair. "But, Annie, it breaks my heart to see Angela so devastated. After the call, she was distraught."

I nodded, well able to imagine how upset she was. As far as I knew, no one else was aware of her pregnancy. I told myself it wasn't up to me to make that private announcement, but I wished I could.

"Have they gone already?" I asked.

"They were getting into the limo when I arrived." She lowered her head into her hands and took several deep breaths. "I tried to tell Angela it was for the best, but she screamed at me that I didn't know anything about love." She lifted her face. "What in the hell does that mean? Doesn't she see how Will and I are together? And if that isn't true love, what is?"

"She sees you as the old folks, not the young lovers they are."

"They *were*, you mean. I never want to see that young punk with her again."

I drew a long breath in and let the air escape slowly. "In the end, it's their choice. Not yours, or Katherine's, or anyone else's."

"Angela's a pretty smart girl," said Rhonda. "I know she'll cut it off."

I didn't say a word. Time would tell who'd win this war of hearts.

Rhonda lifted herself out of the chair, and we turned our attention to the day's activities. Hotel guests had to be taken care of along with the locals who'd made dinner reservations. A lot of hotel guests, knowing what was coming, opted for a light breakfast. As the bulk of our guests went on to other activities, I talked to the dining room staff about the buffet, which would start at noon.

Sabine stood beside me, and after my pep talk, she quietly informed the staff that today's service had to be superb. "One of the travel reporters from Miami is going to be here with his family. This is an opportunity for us to shine. Please remember all the little things I've taught you about quiet, efficient service." Said in her French accent, it was charming.

Rhonda was busy in the kitchen with Jean-Luc. I waved to her. "I'll be back shortly. I want to check on Vaughn."

She winked at me. "Take your time."

I grinned, happy to see her sense of humor return.

On my way out of the hotel, I noticed Angela talking to Manny.

She saw me and rushed over.

"Ann, you heard?" Tears swam in her eyes. Their brown depth held sadness I'd seldom seen in her.

I nodded. "I'm so sorry. What are you going to do now?"

She shook her head. "I'm not sure. Reggie doesn't know about the baby. I may not even tell him."

Alarm pulsed through me in nervous beats. "Are you going to keep the baby?"

She shrugged sadly. "Probably. I can't get rid of it. But I may give it up for adoption. Reggie and I have broken up for good." A sob escaped her throat. "It's clear his mother is going to get her way. Reggie needs his parents' support to get the job he wants in New York—a job that was supposed to support us in the style he wanted for me. And the family they're going to visit is the family whose daughter his parents want Reggie to marry."

Tears rolled down her cheeks.

I hugged her to me. "I'm so sorry, sweetie. Don't you think you'd better talk to your mother? First of all, she'd be crushed, totally crushed, if you placed your baby up for adoption. And then Reggie has rights too. Your baby would have a lot more love than most staying right here in our little family. Remember, you're not alone. We'll all be here to help you."

Angela wiped at her eyes with a tissue. "I'm counting on that. Ann, I don't want you to say a word to anyone else. I need to figure things out. Please. Promise me."

I gave her a defeated sigh. "I haven't told anyone and I won't. But, Angela, I think your mother should know. It's unfair not to tell her."

Shaking her head firmly, Angela said, "I can't tell her. You know my mother. She'd fly up to New York and punch Reggie in the nose and then pull Katherine's hair out strand by strand. And his father? My mother would teach him words he doesn't know."

Though our hearts were breaking, we couldn't help smiling at one another.

"Okay, Angela. But by the New Year, you're going to have to make a lot of decisions about the baby and your life going forward."

Her face became a map of unhappiness, from the wrinkles that creased her brow to the downward slope of her lips. "I know." Her whisper spoke louder than a shout.

Wishing I could make her life easier, I wrapped my arms around her. But my wishes would not change the difficult position she was in.

We said goodbye, and I went on to my house.

Vaughn looked up from the newspaper he was reading. He wore a pair of blue jeans without shoes or shirt. He looked ... well, yummy.

He stood, and I went into his arms, so grateful he'd decided to come home for the holiday. He was such a steadying force for me.

I leaned into his embrace and drew a deep breath.

"What's wrong?" He tipped my chin up and studied me.

"It's Angela. Reggie's parents left this morning, taking him with them. Katherine was furious when she found out Reggie had spent the night at Rhonda's with Angela. They're now on their way to see a friend's family in Palm Beach. Reggie's parents want him to marry their daughter."

"Well, that doesn't always work!" The disgust in Vaughn's voice was satisfying to me. "Reggie is a young adult who should make his own choices."

"He's been told if he doesn't listen to them, he won't get the job in New York. Angela says it's a job he wanted so he could take care of her."

Vaughn shook his head. "What a mess. Angela is too sweet a girl to stay with him."

"But she loves him. She's heartbroken he left."

"Well, let's hope it all works out. Meantime, our daughters called. Nell is having dinner today with a friend of hers. A boyfriend, I gather. I'm trying not to jump to conclusions, but I think it may be serious."

"And?"

"And next time I'm home, I'm going to try to meet him."

I laughed. "You already look like you don't approve of him." Shaking my head, I continued. "It's hard to see your children make choices you might not like. But Nell is a steady girl. So tell me, what did Liz have to say?"

"She was happy to know I'd made it here. She says she's barely surviving her father and Kandie, and she'll call you on your cell later after the crowd leaves."

"Thanks. How about some breakfast?"

He grinned. "Already beat you to it."

"My! How handy you are to have around," I teased.

He pulled me to him, giving me the lopsided grin that made some women all but swoon. "You haven't experienced me at my best today."

At his words and the sexy look he was giving me, my heartbeat pranced like a thoroughbred pony. I checked the clock in the kitchen and grinned, eager to put him to the test. He'd be gone too quickly. Unless I went for it, I'd be left with a missed opportunity.

"Okay, Mister Wonderful. You're on."

His chuckle was a little smug as we walked out of the kitchen, but I didn't care. I knew what lay ahead.

CHAPTER TWENTY-ONE

At the hotel, I found Tina sitting on the patio outside her room with a book.

"What are you reading?" I asked, surprised.

She gave me a sheepish look and held up the book. "Something Troy gave me. A mystery. It's light and easy. Barbara told me to stay busy to keep my mind off my mother and my career."

"Good idea. I wanted to thank you again for arranging to stay here at the hotel. It's been nice having Vaughn home."

"Yeah, yeah," she said, brushing away my thanks.

"Will you join us for dinner?" I asked.

"Can Troy be my date? He's been just great with me."

"Sure." As much as I was dying to know if it was more than a client relationship, I kept quiet. I'd learned to hold back with Tina as much as possible. She was like a deep river that hid dangerous undercurrents, ready to pull you under when you least expected it.

I left her and went back to the kitchen. Rhonda looked up at me with a questioning look.

Laughing, I waved away her curiosity. What Vaughn and I did privately was no one else's concern.

In the dining room, Sabine was overseeing the waitstaff dressing the tables for the Thanksgiving meal. Off to one side of the room were long buffet tables. One, I knew, would hold the turkeys, hams, and ribs of beef; another would hold the side dishes. A third would display the apple, pumpkin, and pecan pies, along with the other pastries and sweets Jean-

Luc's sous chef, Carl, was becoming known for.

I helped place slender crystal vases containing a mixture of mums on each table. Each vase of flowers was accented with a pheasant's tail feather, adding a unique touch to the small fall arrangement.

As I stood back to admire the effect of the crisp white linens on the tables, the sparkling crystal, the gleam of silver, I filled with a sense of satisfaction. Our guests were, for the most part, sophisticated people used to the finer things in life. Each added touch that made them appreciate our hotel was well worth it.

Rhonda came up to me and wrapped an arm around my shoulders. "Whaddya think, Annie? Look good enough for you?"

Smiling, I said, "It's hard to believe it'll be our third Thanksgiving together."

"Yeah, and our second Thanksgiving as a hotel. A lot has happened to us in that time, huh?" She rubbed her small baby bump. "Sure didn't expect this little guy."

I glanced over at her. "Are you feeling better about Angela?"

She lifted her shoulders and let them drop. "The honest truth? I'm worried sick about her. There's something going on with her that I don't like. We have none of the cozy girl-talks like we used to have." Her eyes flashed with indignation. "Probably a good thing those people have left. They obviously didn't like Ange or me. Arthur was a jerk to Will, but that was because Will knew a lot more about what Arthur was up to than most people."

I tried for a positive outlook. "Maybe it was a good thing they didn't stay. At least now we can enjoy our guests without worrying about them."

"Yeah, and pigs fly," said Rhonda. "I'll worry about them

hurting Angela until she's back to her old self."

Unable to tell her the secret I'd been forced to keep, I merely nodded. Nothing was ever going to be the same again.

During a lull between early diners and those who chose to eat in the evening, I sat with Vaughn and the others in our family circle in the small private dining room. Looking around the table, I was struck once more by how much my life had changed. Rhonda and Will had become my best friends. Red-eyed, heartbroken Angela was someone I loved like my own daughter. Tina and Troy were new to the family table, but watching them tentatively reach out to one another, I thought they made a nice addition. I missed Liz terribly. And not having Nell with us was disappointing for both Vaughn and me. Though I was pleased Ty was happy with June, I missed getting to know him better. He and Vaughn were close, and that mattered a lot to me.

Sabine and Rosita served us, taking care to be sure everything was nicely done. Later, they'd do the same for the mayor and his wife, who were hosting a small group in this same dining room.

After our dinner, Rhonda, who'd been standing on her feet most of the day, went home for a rest, promising to return to help handle the evening rush. Vaughn and I decided to use the last of my free time to take a walk. I checked in with Tim, and then we left the hotel.

As we walked onto the sandy stretch of beach, an onshore breeze ruffled Vaughn's dark curls. Observing him out of the corner of my eye, I wondered whether he'd acquiesce and continue in his role in *The Sins of the Children* as the producers were now begging him to do. If he did do it, they'd simply say that over the past several months, the mayor of his little fictional town had been recovering from the gunshot wound, which everyone thought had killed him.

I hoped he'd go back to the soap opera. A regular schedule would be more suitable to me. But I also knew how much Vaughn enjoyed his more creative roles in movies.

"What are you thinking about, Ann?" he asked me now.

I gazed up at him. "I believe I'm going to like being married to you."

He smiled. "Good. With the kids on their own, I want to settle down with you. And I guess commuting from New York won't be too bad. Easier than traveling all over the world. And when I'm here, I like puttering around the place. Gets me ready to go back to the hustle and bustle of my life there."

It was a good plan. He might talk about liking to putter around the hotel, but it didn't take long before he became restless to get back to his acting jobs.

As we usually did when we were on the beach, we took a moment to stand side by side, looking out at the water. Listening to the movement of the blue water was soothing. A trio of brown pelicans flew low over the water. Skimming the waves, their triangle of bodies glided as one, like planes in a Blue Angels air show.

We were interrupted by the sound of someone calling my name. I turned to find Troy helping Tina cross the sand to us.

"Hi." Tina's smile hovered near shyness. "I wanted to show Troy what you and I used to do on our walks, Ann."

Vaughn gave me a questioning look.

"This," I said quietly, giving his hand a squeeze.

He nodded with understanding. I reached my hand out to Tina. Positioning her crutches under her arms, she took it. Troy clasped the other hand Tina offered him. Standing in a line, we gazed out at the water.

"Close your eyes," prompted Tina. "And then, Troy, be still

and listen to the soothing movement of the waves. It's sort of like the music you play for your clients when you do a massage."

His smile was the last thing I saw before I closed my eyes. After a few moments, my heartbeat slowed, and my thoughts wandered. Holding onto Tina's fingers, I felt a difference in her grip. Gone was the fierceness of someone who wanted control. I opened my eyes just enough to observe her facial features soften. I was struck by both her beauty and vulnerability. My gaze met Troy's. We stared at each other for a moment and then I closed my eyes.

After more time passed, Tina sighed. "Thanks, Ann. I needed that."

I turned to her. "Your mother?"

"She called."

At the concern I couldn't conceal, she patted my arm. "Don't worry. I'm going to stay right here where I can work with Barbara. It's sad, in a way, that my mother will never be a real mother to me. She has never been, you know."

"Yeah," said Troy, placing a protective arm around Tina. "No mom should be like that."

They headed back to the hotel, and Vaughn and I walked down the beach away from them. I worked to keep my stride with his. It felt good to breathe in the tangy salt air and move in tandem with him. Seagulls and Caspian Terns performed white-winged dances above us, circling around and around like soft-feathered water spouts. Sandpipers skittered along the water's edge pursuing insects and small snails.

"I have just enough time to freshen up before the next shift of diners arrive," I said, checking my watch.

We headed back to my house.

"I'm going to call Ty and then relax by the pool. I've got to go over my script for the end of this movie." He paused and sighed. "And I suppose I'd better look at the stuff for the TV show. They want me back, and I think I should do it."

As we walked back home hand in hand, I was all too aware of the separate obligations we had—obligations that would always keep us apart. People often wondered aloud how long our relationship would last. Sometimes I did too. Then I reminded myself that Vaughn was a much different man from Robert. He wouldn't desert me.

Later, as I was preparing to leave my house, my cell rang. I checked caller ID. Liz.

"Hi, honey! How are you?" I said, clicking onto the call.

There was a pause and then Liz said, "Okay, I guess."

"But?" I prompted.

"But now Dad is saying he won't pay for me to bunk in with Angela and her friends in their apartment. He thinks I should live at his house and commute to school."

"And how would you commute?" I asked, feeling my insides grow cold.

"He said he'd give me Kandie's old car, that she wants a new one, anyway."

At the tearful sound of her voice, the Mama Bear in me rose up. With effort, I held back a snarl. " What did you tell him?" My forced calmness didn't stop the angry pulsing of blood in my body.

"I said I'd talk it over with you. That really pissed him off." Liz paused. "But, Mom, I do need your advice."

This time, I couldn't hold back. "Staying with Angela would cost less money than buying a new car for Kandie, who, as I recall, insisted on a new car only two years ago. And I think it's important to enjoy college life with your friends. Furthermore, you told me you might have a job on campus, working as a TA for one of your professors. And ..."

Liz's laugh stopped me. "Thanks, Mom! That's all I need to

hear. Besides, Dad only set this up so I'd be their live-in nanny. Robbie is a cute little boy, but he's totally out of control. Kandie won't discipline him, and Dad is overbearing with him."

I knew it was important not to put down a divorced spouse, but I wasn't feeling that nice. "You make it clear to him and Kandie that any money he's spending for your education was yours to begin with. And there was certainly more than enough set aside for you to live on your own."

"Yeah, I will. Oh, here he is now."

I heard muffled voices in the background, and then Robert's sharp voice penetrated my ear. "Ann? What did you tell Liz? Any deal I make with her is between her and me. Got it?"

"If Liz asks for my opinion, I'm going to give it, Robert. Got it?"

"I don't know what I ever saw in you, Ann," he snarled. "You're not the woman I married."

"Thank God," I muttered, hurt fighting anger.

"By the way, remember that ski lodge where we went on our honeymoon?" said Robert. "Kandie loves it."

Hearing the disdain in his voice, I had the urge to choke him. I drew a deep breath, forced my fists to unclench, and told myself to calm down. Neither he nor Kandie was worth wasting my energy on.

"Here's Liz," Robert said. "She wants to talk to you."

"I'll call you later when we can really talk," said Liz. "It's a mess here. Kandie is yelling at Dad and Robbie is crying. But, Mom? Thanks for your support. Sometimes Dad makes me so crazy I forget to think logically."

"Love you, sweetie. Happy Thanksgiving."

We hung up and I sat a moment, thinking back to my marriage. Had I been a doormat to Robert's wishes? His ego?

If so, I might have set a horrible example for Liz. I'd have to remind her from time to time to hold onto her own desires. Isn't that what mothers did for their daughters?

"Everything all right?" Vaughn asked, coming up beside me.

"It's Robert. He's trying to force Liz to live with him. And both Liz and I know why. He wants her to babysit Robbie, who, I gather, needs a lot more than a babysitter."

Vaughn rubbed my back. "Hey, Liz will be fine. She's got a mother to help her figure things out."

I leaned into him, unsure at the moment what, if anything, I could do for Liz. Maybe this is what parenting was all about. Teaching young children what you could, and then watching them struggle, hoping they'd learned something valuable from you.

CHAPTER TWENTY-TWO

The days following Thanksgiving remained busy. It was at times like this when I wondered why I'd ever gotten into the hotel business. Vaughn was a pretty patient guy, but even he chafed at the lack of time we had together. And I couldn't blame him. Some of our guests were easy to please, others were not. Rhonda and I prided ourselves in providing a lovely setting and top-notch service to them. It stung when people complained about the smallest thing.

On the Saturday after Thanksgiving, Rhonda lost her patience.

"What a bunch of crap!" Rhonda snapped at me after one of the waitresses returned a mostly eaten luncheon plate to the kitchen, claiming the guest had announced she wasn't paying for leftovers.

"That chicken salad was made fresh this morning. And look, she's eaten most of it. I'm going to tell her exactly what I think of her."

I grabbed hold of Rhonda's arm. "Cool it. That woman has a lot of friends in Naples. We can't antagonize her."

"You're right, but I'm tellin' ya, Annie, these people sometimes drive me crazy!"

I turned to the waitress. "Tell Mrs. Winston the meal is on us."

"But don't show her the dessert menu," said Rhonda. "She can go without."

At my look of disapproval, Rhonda sighed. "If she asks for it, give it to her. But, between us, I don't care if she ever comes back to The Beach House Hotel."

With the lunch rush over, Rhonda and I sat in our office going over my forecast and checking reservations. It was a tricky time of year. People were staying at home to prepare for the holiday season. To help fill the hotel, we'd advertised a special, pre-holiday spa package. It had helped us, but the big push into the high season wouldn't happen for a couple of weeks.

"Rhonda, I know how tired you are. Do you want to go home for a rest?" As outspoken as Rhonda was, she wasn't usually snappish at guests.

"No, no, I'm all right. It's Angela's situation that's made me so irritable. It breaks my heart to see her so unhappy. I swear if I ever again lay eyes on Reggie or his dreadful parents, I won't hold back. How could he just leave like that? Poor Angela has cried herself silly. Will tried to talk to her, but she clams up with him the same as she does with me. I'm going crazy worrying about her."

"I'm worried about her too." I wished I could say more.

"For the first time, I'll be glad to see her go back to school," said Rhonda. "She can be with her friends and forget that someone like Reggie ever existed."

I remained silent.

Rhonda sat up with a sudden start. "I think I felt the baby move." A smile spread across her face. "Oh, Annie! It's so exciting! I never thought this would happen to me. Not now." Her smile disappeared. "Reggie's mother was appalled when she found out I was having a baby. Do you think others feel that way?"

"Reggie's mother is such an iceberg I'm amazed she even had Reggie," I retorted. The look of disapproval on Katherine's face when she'd learned Rhonda was pregnant still made me angry. "Don't worry about what she or anyone else thinks. We had our daughters very young. Lots of women your age have healthy pregnancies."

"You're right. I can't let Katherine or anyone else ruin happiness for Will and me. Babies are such a miracle."

A tap on the door interrupted us.

Vaughn stuck his head into the room. "Thought I'd see how your afternoon is going."

I smiled. "Come on in. The lunch rush is over."

"Can I steal you away?" The look Vaughn gave me sent a message loud and clear.

"Go on, Annie. I'm here for a while," said Rhonda. She grinned at Vaughn. "Guess you need a little time alone, huh?"

He returned her smile. "I have to take advantage of every spare minute Ann has. I got a call from the director's office. I have to leave a day earlier than I thought and there's something I want to do before I leave."

I left the hotel with Vaughn expecting to walk over to my house. Instead, he led me to the hotel's white limousine.

"Where are we going?" I asked, surprised.

"You'll see." His smile was mysterious as he got in the backseat with me. Paul was driving.

"So you've hired the limo?"

He grinned. "Yeah, with so little time left I didn't want to waste it driving." He slipped an arm around me and brought me close.

I sighed. He was such a romantic.

Paul delivered us to one of the biggest marinas along the coast.

Raising my eyebrows, I wondered what Vaughn was up to.

"I wanted some peace and quiet with you," he said. "So I've rented a sailboat for a couple of hours."

"A sailboat? Who's going to sail it?"

"You'll see."

We got out of the car. I waited while Vaughn gave Paul instructions, and then he took my arm. As we approached the dock, a man wearing white shorts and a blue T-shirt came toward us. "The Lady Jane" printed in white block letters crossed the chest of his shirt. He saluted Vaughn.

"We're set to sail, sir."

"Aye, aye, Captain," said Vaughn happily. "Meet my lady, Ann."

The captain gave me a little bow. "Bill Withers. Welcome aboard."

He led us to a sleek, blue-hulled, single-masted sailboat.

"She's a beauty," Vaughn said to the captain. He turned to me. "She's a forty-six-foot sloop, a Bristol, I believe."

A younger man offered a hand to help me step aboard.

Gripping his hand firmly, I stretched a leg and hopped onto the deck of the boat, grateful to be wearing slacks.

A pretty, young woman came up on deck from below. "Hi, I'm Jane." She bobbed her head in the young man's direction. "And that is my husband, Chad."

I glanced at the captain.

"My father," said Jane, answering my unasked question.

He and Vaughn came over to us.

"It's a beautiful afternoon for a nice sail. The wind is about perfect. We'll motor out through the channel and set sail. Get comfortable."

I sat in the cockpit beside Vaughn.

He put his arm around me. "Thought you'd like a little break. Sailing seemed like the perfect way to spend a few hours with you away from the hotel." He winked. "She can be a demanding bitch, huh?"

I grinned. Hotel work never ended. Depending on its daily demands, being part-owner of even a small one like ours was either a joy or a pain in the behind.

As the boat got underway, I leaned over the side, watching the wake the boat made as it glided through the water.

We soon reached open water.

Working together, Chad and Bill hoisted the sails and set a course.

I leaned back against the cushions in the cockpit with a sigh of satisfaction as the boat responded with a steady movement forward. The wind in my hair and the warmth of the sun shining down on us loosened the taut muscles brought on by the stress of the past few days.

"Nice, huh?"

I grinned at Vaughn. "Very nice. I haven't done much sailing, but I love it."

"I'm glad. It's one of my favorite things to do."

A gray shape rose out of the water and then dove.

"Oh! A dolphin!" I cried with delight.

Moments later, a familiar-looking snout rose out of the water. Dark eyes along the sleek gray head gleamed as the dolphin stared at us, smiling as only dolphins can do. It swam in circles near us and then dived again.

I waited, hoping to see it again. Then, unbelievably, it rose straight from the water, arching its back before diving into the water once more.

I clapped. "Wonderful!"

"He's quite the show-off," said Jane, handing us each a bottle of water.

As if it heard her, the dolphin's smiling face appeared once more, drawing close to the boat. I leaned over the side of the boat and reached out a hand to touch its nose. Coming closer to the boat, the dolphin rose out of the water, nosed my hand and then disappeared.

"Wow!" said Jane. "I've never seen him do that before."

"Everyone loves Ann," said Vaughn, giving me a squeeze as

I settled in my seat again.

The wind, the waves, and the sun took their toll. I rested my head sleepily on Vaughn's shoulder. I don't know how long I'd snoozed before Vaughn nudged me.

"C'mon! Let's go to the foredeck. I want to show you something."

I eagerly made my way behind him, past the mast to the bow of the boat, where we settled on the foredeck.

Feeling the wind on my face, I stared ahead at the open water. Impulsively, I raised my arms and shouted, "I'm flying!"

Vaughn pulled me close against his chest and laughed in my ear. "Love it! Love you!"

I turned around and placed my lips on his.

Aware of his response, I deepened my kiss.

He groaned and pulled away. "You're killing me, woman!"

Self-satisfied, I couldn't help the way my lips curved. Robert and I had never had this kind of sexual relationship.

Vaughn's expression turned serious. "There's something between us that we need to get settled."

Alarmed by the change in him, I swallowed hard. He wouldn't look at me but stared straight ahead of him.

He shifted so that he and I were facing each other straight on.

"Yes? What is it?"

"Ann, will you marry me?"

Relief mixed with joy. "Yes! Of course, I will."

He kissed me soundly, surely. Then he fumbled in his pocket and drew out a small, black-velvet box.

I held my breath.

Opening the lid, he lifted out a sapphire and diamond ring that looked an awful lot like the royal ring Princess Diana and Kate, Duchess of Cambridge, wore.

I gaped at it. It meant so much more to me than a beautiful ring. With it, Vaughn, who could choose any woman, had chosen to spend the rest of his days with me.

"Are you ready to put it on?" Vaughn prompted, lifting it out of the box.

Tears filled my eyes. I nodded, too touched to speak.

He slid it onto my finger. "Perfect."

Though my cheeks were wet, I smiled. "You are perfect."

We reached for one another as Captain Bill shouted, "Better get back here, we're going to come about."

Laughing, Vaughn and I hurried back and sat in the cockpit, just as the boat swung around for the return trip home.

CHAPTER TWENTY-THREE

Preparations began for our second annual Christmas Open House at the hotel. Over the past two years, the guest list had grown exponentially. Now, we included dignitaries from Miami and other localities important to us, as well as other influential guests. It was an occasion for us to strut our stuff and recruit more customers.

Rhonda waved me over to her computer. "Look at this, Annie! A maternity dress for the holidays! Isn't it cute?"

I looked at the red knit dress with a white fur collar and hesitated.

"Just kidding," said Rhonda, arrowing down to a dark green dress that flowed easily from the model's shoulders. "This is the one Will liked. He thought the other one was a little too fancy for me."

"The green is perfect for you."

"What are you going to wear, Annie? Why don't you choose something red?"

With my dark hair, red looked good on me. "I'll look for something."

"I'll help you." Rhonda grabbed hold of my left hand. "Every time I see that ring flashing like a rainbow, I can't help smiling. Vaughn and I had the sailing trip all planned, you know."

I smiled. Rhonda was proud of the friendship she and Vaughn had formed.

We were perusing a clothing catalog, looking for a dress for me, when a knock sounded on the office door.

Tim stood in the doorway. "Can I come in?"

"Sure," Rhonda and I said together, sounding like a chorus.

"I wanted to talk to you," Tim began, looking unusually tentative. "I'm going to leave ..."

My heart froze mid-beat. *Leave?* We could never replace him.

"... the apartment and move in with my girlfriend."

Weak from relief, I sank onto my chair.

"Oh," said Rhonda softly, and I knew she was thinking of Angela. After Reggie left, Rhonda had hoped that Angela might have another chance with Tim.

"We understand," I said. "No problem, Tim."

"Uh, I'm wondering if we can talk about adjusting my salary."

"Yes," I said before Rhonda could object. I'd do anything to keep Tim. I was counting on his steady presence to help me when Rhonda had her baby. Then, Rhonda's time wouldn't necessarily be her own. And as always, I wanted to be able to spend more time with Vaughn. Gentleman that he was, he was becoming impatient with my lack of attention.

Tim took a seat. "By the way, Troy is interested in having the apartment. He'd be glad to pay rent, but I told him that maybe he could do extra work at the hotel in return for rent. Like you do for me."

"You mean when he's not busy with clients?" I wondered how many free hours he'd have. Ours was a small spa that could handle only a couple of clients at a time.

"Good idea," said Rhonda. "We can train him for front desk work, so we have more than Dave or Julie to back you up."

"I think Tina is going to move in with him," said Tim, glancing uncertainly at me. He was aware of Tina's story.

The thought didn't alarm me. I'd seen how protective of her Troy was. As the business in the spa began to grow, Troy had asked for permission to enlist Tina's help by acting as hostess to his clients and coordinating the schedule for the nail salon. At first, we weren't sure about Tina handling fussy guests, but after keeping a careful eye on her, we were satisfied. It brought out a different, more caring side of her. And I was sure if Barbara felt it wasn't healthy, as Tina's therapist, she'd say something to her.

Later, when I had a free moment, I headed over to the spa to see Troy and Tina. Funny, I mused, how that difficult, obnoxious girl had wheedled her way into my heart. With Liz and Angela away, I liked the idea of her sticking around.

As I entered the spa, I was greeted with a pleasant hello.

I returned Tina's smile. Sitting behind a small reception desk, she looked like the perfect hostess, showing enough toned body to be pleasing.

"Where's Troy?" I asked.

She indicated one of the closed doors off to the side. "He's with a client. We're starting to get traffic from the locals." She gave me a look of satisfaction. "He's really good. All the ladies like him."

Seeing that we were alone, I took a seat in a chair beside the desk. "Tim says that Troy wants the apartment here. He says you might move in with him."

Tina looked off into space and then turned her gaze to me. "I talked it over with Barbara. She thinks it might be a good way for me to learn to trust men. She met Troy and liked him." Her cheeks flushed a pretty pink color. "He and I haven't ... you know ... I guess you say ... gone to bed ... yet. Weird, huh?"

"Nice," I said firmly. "He strikes me as a very good guy. This is the way things might have been for you..." I let my words hang in the air.

"If I hadn't been forced into the movie business." Above her curled lips, her nostrils flared. "I never want to go back there, do those things. With my money out of my mother's hands, I won't have to."

"Does your mother know that?"

Tina shook her head. "She thinks I'm recovering from the accident. She doesn't realize that I'm recovering from her treatment of me."

I reached over and clasped her hand. "For what it's worth, I think you're a very brave young woman. It isn't easy to dump baggage." My smile was weak. "I'm still learning to let go of a few things myself."

"It's hard, huh?"

I grinned and pushed my grandmother's image out of my mind. "Yeah, it's freaking hard."

We laughed together.

"Are you going to be content to do this kind of work for any length of time? Doesn't it seem boring to you?"

Tina shrugged. "For the time being, it's teaching me how nice people can be. A lot of Troy's clients are older ladies who have no idea who I am. I like it."

"We're going to have to hire you officially," I said. "Come to the office and fill out the proper paperwork."

"Yeah? What are you going to pay me?"

I laughed at the teasing look she gave me. "We'll discuss it in my office."

Troy came out of the private room he'd been in. He smiled when he saw me.

"Did Tim talk to you about the apartment?"

"It's yours, but we need to talk about the financial arrangements. We'd like to offer you the chance to learn our front desk procedures and become a part-time team member in lieu of paying rent."

"Okay," he said agreeably. "And, Ann, Tina is going to move in with me."

"Yes, I know."

Tina turned to him. "Don't worry about paying rent. I've got enough money to pay rent."

He held up a hand. "I take care of myself. Remember?"

The smile that crossed Tina's face reminded me of the Cheshire Cat. I realized Troy had passed a test of hers and was even more impressed with the changes in her.

Long after I left them, I thought of my own relationship with Vaughn. He made a lot of money, but we'd agreed early on that our finances would remain separate. That's the way I wanted it. Even now, being officially engaged to him, I wouldn't take advantage of him. Though I might struggle from time to time and worry about the hotel's success, it made my life my own. My independence was important to me. After being overshadowed by Robert, who took credit for all the work I'd done in setting up the business he then called his own, I'd vowed to never let a man diminish me. Fortunately, Vaughn was a secure man who understood.

When I went back to the office Rhonda was busy on the computer.

"What are you doing?" I asked, taking a seat at my desk.

"Brenda sent a list of requirements for the royal wedding. Wait until you see it. It's a mile long."

I frowned. "Why is she so late sending this to us? I've reminded her a couple of times."

"She apologized, but said the bride has been difficult and wouldn't agree to everything her mother wanted until now."

"Is there anything on the list we should worry about?"

Rhonda turned to me with a worried look. "Two things. First of all, the number of guests has been cut. So now we can release some of those rooms, but it makes it a little difficult to provide privacy if we have a lot of other guests."

"What else?" I braced myself for more bad news.

"The Hassels want German food for the wedding dinner." She frowned. "I don't think Jean-Luc will be happy about that."

I let out the breath I hadn't realized I was holding and squeezed my hands together. Jean-Luc prided himself on his French continental cooking.

"You'd better tell him. Not me," said Rhonda. "I'll save any fight with him for later."

I sighed. "First, let's go over the rest of the items on the list."

Rhonda and I studied the Hassels' requests. Nothing else seemed too difficult. We could rent the two additional limousines they required, handle the reservations, and deal with the wedding planner they'd lined up, though I'd never heard of Lorraine Grace at Wedding Perfection.

Going over the details, I realized what a difficult situation lay ahead of us. Charlotte Hassel, the bride's mother, was apparently as much a bridezilla as her daughter Katrina. There was an imperious tone to the requests that spelled trouble.

I sat back in my chair. "We're going to have to be very careful how we handle this wedding group. Maybe we should hire a few extra people for the event."

"We can use more part-time service help for the holidays anyway. If we start training them now, they should be ready for New Year's and the wedding."

"Okay, you speak to Sabine and Consuela about hiring and I'll call the wedding planner. We can't waste any time coordinating with her. There are only four weeks before the wedding and a little more than three weeks before they all arrive." My stomach churned at the thought of what lay ahead. For once, I was glad Vaughn wasn't there to distract me.

When I spoke to Lorraine Grace at Wedding Perfection she

apologized profusely for not being in touch. "The contract was just signed," she explained. "Ordinarily, I wouldn't take on a client this late in the game, but as you can imagine, the draw of a royal wedding was too irresistible to turn down. I'm new in town and trying to build up the business I had in St. Louis."

"I understand the clients are difficult," I said, "which is why we want to work closely with you. When can we meet here at the hotel?"

"Let's do it tomorrow morning. I love The Beach House Hotel but I need to see the hotel from their perspective and take measurements of the dining room in particular. I'll bring my notes and we can go over everything then."

"That will be fine. Rhonda and I will both sit in on the meeting." Disconnecting the call, I felt much better about things. Though it was the first time Lorraine had overseen a wedding at our hotel, she seemed very capable. Her contribution would make a huge difference to us.

That afternoon, I went to see Jean-Luc in the kitchen. Observing him and noting the deference his staff gave him, I sometimes thought of him as an aging lion in his lair.

I approached him carefully.

He looked up from the paperwork he was studying. "*Oui*?"

I cleared my throat. "Jean-Luc, remember the wedding that's scheduled for January 5th?"

"The royal wedding."

"I know you were planning a special meal for them, some of your favorite French recipes but, well...because they're German, they want a traditional German meal."

I stepped back.

Jean-Luc slapped the counter with the palm of his hand. "*Mais non!* German food? *Merde!*"

I drew a calming breath and continued. "I've printed out what they want. You and Rhonda can work out the recipes.

Fortunately, the wedding party has been reduced considerably so you'll be able to do your usual, delicious meals for our other guests."

I handed him the menu and turned to go.

"It's not your fault, Ann, but this is a...what do you call it? A slap in the face to me."

"I'm sorry, Jean-Luc, but we do everything we can to please our guests, and this is one of those times."

He shrugged, and I left as quickly as I could.

CHAPTER TWENTY-FOUR

Lorraine Grace was the epitome of elegance when she arrived at the hotel for our meeting. Her hair, dyed a light gold, shone in a sleek bob. Her dark eyes were bright and all-seeing as she shook my hand and then gazed around the front entry with interest. She was dressed conservatively in a black linen dress with simple lines that covered a rather bony structure.

I introduced myself to her and explained that Rhonda would be with us shortly.

"Let me show you around the first floor so you can get a good idea of the setting for the reception and dinner," I said.

"Yes, I will need to do that," Lorraine said. "I need everything to be perfect."

"How did the Hassels learn about you?"

"Friends of friends, that sort of thing. Apparently, Joseph Hassel sometimes does business in St. Louis and mentioned this wedding." She smiled at me. "Small world, isn't it?"

"Oh, yes. We see that sort of thing with our guests all the time."

I showed Lorraine the library, the private dining room, the living area and then led her into the guest dining room.

"This space is very adaptable, easily changing from a casual setting for breakfast to a more elegant offering. Rhonda had her own wedding reception here."

"Good. I like the nice clean lines of the room. It allows me more freedom to do what I need to do to make the room the way they want it."

"And what would that be?" said Rhonda, joining us. She winked at me, telling me in her own private way that her visit to the OB had gone well.

A frown appeared on Lorraine's brow and was quickly smoothed out by an unenthusiastic smile. "In talking to the bride's mother I've learned the reluctant bride is very difficult. Concessions have been made. Bribery involved."

"And?" I choked on the word, dreading what was coming.

"And she wants a German *biergarten* effect, complete with centerpieces placed in antique beer bottles."

"What a bunch of crap!" sputtered Rhonda. "Our place isn't a tavern!"

Lorraine's hands fluttered frantically in front of her face like the wings of a distressed butterfly. "I know, I know. But this is where compromise comes in. I'm renting a number of potted palms that I will cover with miniature lights and place around the room in various spots as if the guests were sitting outside. And the glass bottles are in place of the beer steins the daughter wanted to be used in the centerpieces. Little by little, I'm being allowed to make changes. Next, I'll make sure we can use tropical flowers and white tablecloths."

Shaking her head, Rhonda sank down on a chair. "Why do I have the horrible feeling we're being gamed? None of this makes any sense."

I wanted to disagree with Rhonda but I couldn't. Something was off.

"You say she's a reluctant bride?" said Rhonda. "I think, to get back at her parents, she's making it as difficult as possible. Maybe we shouldn't take this on."

A look of panic filled Lorraine's aging face. "You can't back out. I've committed a lot of my own money to this project."

"You haven't been paid anything?" I asked, unable to hold back my dismay.

Lorraine shook her head. "Not until they get here."

Goosebumps sprinted up and down my back.

"Good thing we got something from them," said Rhonda.

I'd made a pest of myself by insisting a healthy deposit be made on the rooms they'd originally requested, but even then we'd lose out if the event wasn't held here.

"I need this job," said Lorraine. "I moved here with my husband, who's ill."

Rhonda and I exchanged looks of concern.

"We'll go ahead with it, but it won't be the same," I warned Lorraine. "The Hassels originally wanted to book the entire hotel, then only eight rooms. Now we've released half of those rooms, hoping we can sell them at the last minute."

"And they'll have to use the small dining room for the reception and dinner so as not to disturb any other guests," said Rhonda, getting to her feet. "C'mon, Lorraine, you'd better meet our chef, Jean-Luc."

I left them and went into the office to call Brenda.

A while later, Rhonda walked into the office. "What a mess. These people are royal all right. Royal pains in the ass."

"I called Brenda. She said the daughter is putting up a fuss about the wedding out of jealousy. It seems her little sister is the apple of her parents' eyes. And she is now engaged to the man Katrina once loved. They sound like a family that should be featured in Vaughn's soap opera."

"On a happier note, the baby and I are doing fine," Rhonda grinned. "Dr. Benson says he's growing well."

I perked up. "He? Did they do the test? Have you been told it's a boy?"

Rhonda shook her head. "Naw, in a couple of weeks we can have the test done, but I know it's a boy—a boy for Will. I feel it in my gut." She laughed and patted her stomach. "You know what I mean. Right here."

I chuckled. The excitement of Rhonda and Will's baby was a welcome relief from the worries of preparing for what I was sure would be the worst wedding ever.

The plans for the Christmas Open House moved forward. Dorothy Stern was handling the reservations for it. Each afternoon when she arrived at the office, she eagerly went through the mail and emails as if she were giving the party herself. Watching her, I couldn't help smiling. This sense of participation was something we encouraged in our help. Whether they were full-time or part-time, we asked that they consider the hotel their own. Amazingly, over the past two years, we'd had to fire only two people. Two others had left for personal reasons, but the remaining staff was loyal to us and to the hotel.

Now, with the wedding on the horizon, we'd taken on three new people. A housekeeper, a prep cook, and a bartender. With high season arriving soon, the months of January through April, they would be well used.

I did the last of a background check on the prep cook and satisfied that all was well, went into the kitchen tell Jean-Luc that he would start as planned.

Jean-Luc was growling to himself as he mixed a batter of some kind. I knew enough not to ask him what it was. Ever since he'd been given the menu for the wedding, he'd been spending time fiddling with recipes for *Wiener Schnitzel*, trying to make it more acceptable in his eyes. Now, a pile of very thinly sliced apples lay on the workspace next to him. The batter, I suspected, was the apple cake the bride wanted as her wedding cake.

"Miguel is all set," I informed him. "He's officially on our payroll."

He nodded and then stopped mixing the batter and looked up at me with pure disgust. "Ann, this wedding, I can't believe it's for real."

"I understand, but they've paid a lot of money so far to have it exactly the way they want it."

He shook his head. "*C'est terrible!* But for you and Rhonda I do it. Not for them!"

"Thank you, I appreciate it." I didn't blame Jean-Luc for feeling the way he did, but we had to go forward with the wedding plans as specified. If we didn't, and it was all too real, our reputation would be tarnished.

I left him and went back to the office. Year-end results would be needed within the month, and I wanted to get a head start on them.

The ringing of my phone pulled me away from my work. I picked up my cell. Smiling at the picture on my phone, I said, "Hey, Vaughn! How's California?" The last of the filming on the movie was being done there.

"It's going well, but there's something I need to tell you."

The ends of my nerves tingled with a warning. He normally didn't call in the middle of his afternoon. "Yes?"

"I met Lily Dorio for lunch, and we were photographed together. You know how rumors start out here. I wanted to give you a heads-up."

My mouth went dry. "Lily Dorio? After what she did to you? To us?" A sick feeling washed over me. Lily had let the whole world think she was carrying Vaughn's child. It had taken me a while to understand the downside of stardom and to try to deal with it. I still didn't like it.

"Lily said she needed to see me, that it was important."

"So, of course, you met her." I knew I sounded churlish, but I couldn't help it. This woman had almost destroyed our relationship.

"Yeah. It turns out she's suing Roger Sloan for child support and might need me to be a witness."

"But?"

"But now some reporter is claiming it was my child all along. Same old story."

I looked down at the engagement ring Vaughn had so proudly given me and closed my eyes. Doubt rolled through me like a tidal wave, destroying my sense of happiness. Life with Vaughn was never going to be entirely comfortable. Other women wanted him, or thought they did, and had no problem throwing themselves at him. I might not like Lily Dorio, but even I understood her buxom body was what some men dreamed of. Why should Vaughn be any different? We lived apart, and he was a virile man.

"Ann? You there?"

"Yes. I'm simply trying to understand."

"Understand? What's to understand? You know how I feel about you. You know about the business I'm in."

I cringed at the defensiveness in his voice. "Yes, of course, but all the fun and fantasy of it is sometimes difficult for me." To my ears, I sounded like a dull, boring woman.

"Ann, I love you. You know that."

His words tugged at my heart. He'd always made that clear. "Yes, I do."

"Thank you. You should also know I bumped into Tina's mother at the restaurant. She was sitting with a reporter I know. It can't be good."

"Thanks for the warning. I wondered how long it would be before she tried something else. Guess it's too hard for her to give up the good life her daughter used to provide for her."

"She's a very determined woman," Vaughn said. "Look, I have to go. I've got a conference call with the producers of the soap. I'm trying to get everything wrapped up so I can be there for the Christmas Open House."

"Good luck with it. I'll talk to you later."

We hung up without saying our normal, loving goodbyes.

I slumped in my chair wondering as I sometimes did whether I could ever be sure about a relationship again. Vaughn was as good a man as I'd ever met, but he didn't seem to mind all the attention he got from other women.

Rhonda came into the office carrying a small, cardboard box.

"What's that?" I asked.

"Our new brochures. The ones that show off the spa. They look great. Take a look."

She handed one to me. It opened to the section on our spa, offering special packages for new mothers. One of the photographs showed Troy massaging a woman's back. It took me a moment to realize it was Tina beneath the protective white sheet, almost unrecognizable with her hair completely blond and cut even shorter.

"Whaddya think?" said Rhonda, looking over my shoulder. "Troy looks great, and the spa does too."

I finished reading the ad. "Any prospective or new mother is going to love it! Good job, Rhonda."

She grinned. "Course I had to try everything for myself. I gotta tell ya, that Troy sure is good. He says he got special training to handle pregnant women, and it shows. I'm going to get him to teach Will how to do it."

We smiled at each other. Rhonda was enjoying every benefit of being newly pregnant, and Will, bless his heart, was her willing slave.

Before I went home for a pre-dinner-hour break, I headed to the spa to talk to Tina. Dressed in a short, tan skirt and a pink T-shirt with the hotel logo on it, she looked perfectly content behind the small reception desk. Seeing her this happy, I hated to break the news of her mother's interview to her.

I signaled to her to join me outside.

She left her station, and we walked out to the tennis court together. Taking seats on a bench in the shade, we faced one another.

I cleared my throat. "Vaughn saw your mother today. She was in a restaurant talking to a reporter. He wanted to give me, us, a warning because this reporter isn't someone he likes."

Tina replied solemnly, "She's mad at me. I told her I was out of the movie business. At least for the foreseeable future."

"I bet she didn't like that," I said.

"No, she screamed at me, told me I was a worthless piece of shit ..." Tina stopped talking and took several deep breaths.

I drew her to me.

Resting her head on my shoulder, she murmured, "Why is she that way? I keep asking Barbara the same question. I never did anything to her except be born."

I shifted so I was facing Tina. "She's a very sick woman. You understand that, don't you?"

Tina wiped her eyes. "Yeah, but it doesn't make it any easier."

"No, of course not. But you have a circle of friends who care about you, the real you. Not the movie star, certainly, but the person you've become." I gave her an encouraging smile. "It was a rough beginning, but we're all so proud of you."

"Guess I was pretty much an asshole, huh?"

"Pretty much," I said, brushing a lock of hair away from her face. "I don't know what the outcome of your mother's meeting will be, but we'll all stick together. Okay?'

Tina drew in a deep breath and let it out slowly. "Okay."

I left her and went on to my house. I'd been thinking about

Vaughn all afternoon and wanted another chance to talk to him. I'd let hotel business issues interfere with our growing relationship. I wished I could let go of my need to work so hard to prove an independence that might hurt me … us.

Stepping inside my house, I let the peace and quiet wrap around me like a protective blanket. It had become my haven from a sometimes too-busy life at the hotel.

I grabbed a bottle of water from the refrigerator and went out to the patio to enjoy a few moments of dying sunshine. Sunset in December happened early.

My thoughts naturally turned to Vaughn. I chided myself for my insecurity. Either we were together, or we were not. And aside from this aspect of our lives, I was happier with him than I'd ever been with Robert.

I was about to call him when my cell rang. Liz.

Delighted with the unexpected call, I chirped, "Hello?"

"Mom? You'd better sit down."

My pulse sprinted with worry. "What's the matter?"

"It's that … that woman that Vaughn was with last year. That Lily person. While you've been working at the hotel, he met up with her in California. It's all over the news."

My heart thudded to a stop. "What do you mean all over the news? What are you watching?"

"I'm at Dad and Kandie's house. She watches all those television shows about movie stars, and pictures of Vaughn and Lily came up." Liz's voice broke. "They're saying the two of them are back together."

"Hold on," I said, forcing a calmness I didn't feel. "Vaughn called me earlier to tell me about their luncheon meeting. Everything's okay. He might have to be called as a witness to a lawsuit Lily is making against the father of her baby. That's all that's going on between them."

"Oh." I heard the breath Liz released and then she said,

"Kandie was sure it was something else."

I reined in the anger that flared inside me. "Tell Kandie to mind her own business. She doesn't need to worry about me." I paused. "Not that she was ever concerned about me, especially when she was seducing your father."

"I know, I know."

"What are you doing at their house? I thought you were going to move in with Angela and her friends."

"Not until after the holidays. Besides, if I stay here for a couple of weeks, Dad says he's going to make it worth my while. I need money to make the move."

I pressed my lips together to keep from telling my daughter that Robert's promises were as empty as throwaway boxes. Maybe for her, he'd follow through. I hoped so.

"Don't worry, I'll make him pay," Liz said. "Watching Robbie is worth a lot. They can't keep a babysitter for long because he's such a brat."

"I'm sure you'll do fine with him," I said falsely. I'd only seen Robert's little boy once. He was cute as can be, but even as a tiny baby, he'd been difficult.

We hung up, and I sat a moment fighting frustration.

As I headed back to the hotel to help handle the dinner rush, I was surprised to see a group of reporters standing in the front circle of the hotel. One of our security guards was standing on the front steps, keeping them from entering. I ducked back into my house and called the front desk.

"What's going on?" I couldn't imagine the news about Vaughn and Lily was this big.

"They're after news about Tina," said Tim. "Apparently, her mother has made up a big story about Tina getting hurt here at the hotel. She's saying she's going to sue the hotel unless Tina signs up for the next movie she's scheduled to be in."

I felt the blood leave my face. Sinking into one of the

kitchen chairs, I gripped the edge of the table. The room spun around me. It was the worst position Tina's mother could place Tina in—choosing between helping us or taking the blame for hurting us. Her mother might be a bitch, but she was as shrewd as they come.

Bile rose in my throat.

CHAPTER TWENTY-FIVE

I was still fighting nausea when Rhonda called. "Ann, you'd better get over here. We need you to make a statement. First the Lily thing and now this. I've called our lawyer. He's on his way over here."

"I'll be right there." I stood on shaky knees, determined to save the reputation of the hotel and the people I loved. In these times of instant messaging, it was so easy for people to type in falsehoods. A lot of people used that to their advantage. Tina's mother, I was sure, was one of them.

I brushed my hair, put on fresh lip gloss, and closed and locked the door to my house. The thought of reporters invading my personal property sent chills racing down my sweating back. I was a private person sucked into situations like this due, in large part, to loving a very public man.

Behind my house a tiny space had been cut through the hedge, making it possible for me to get to the street unnoticed. I walked through the front gates of the hotel, past a couple of television trucks dominated by their large antennas and headed for the hotel. Immediately I was surrounded by bodies pressing microphones into my face. My small frame seemed to shrink in their midst. I fought claustrophobia and took several deep breaths to steady myself.

"Are you and Vaughn over? Is Tina here now? Is it true she's badly hurt and in the hospital? Did you know her mother is suing you? She says she's taking the hotel away from you."

I held up my hands to stop the shouting. "Give me a little time, and then we'll make an announcement. Please give me room to get to the hotel and inside. Then, and only then, will I attempt to answer your questions."

Tim broke through the crowd, grabbed my elbow and led me away from the howling and shrieking of the reporters. God! I hated them!

Feeling as if I'd been mauled, I entered the hotel. Rhonda ran over to greet me. Tim stood aside, looking worried. A few curious guests looked on.

"Oh, Annie. I'm so sorry. I know you hate all this publicity, but this is worse than I'd ever thought it could be. She's saying she's going to put the hotel under." Tears shone in her eyes. "We can't let her ruin us."

"Where's Tina?"

"Hiding out in Troy's apartment. I told her to stay there, that we'll handle everything."

"Is Troy with her?"

"He promised he wouldn't leave her side. She's a mess."

"You said Mike's on his way?"

"He told me not to talk to anyone until he got here. You too."

Michael Torson was a small man whose mild manners made him seem vulnerable. But to those he served, he was a quiet hero—shrewd, smart and quick-witted. People often called him Mike Tyson, a mix-up of names he enjoyed. A tenacious fighter, the name suited him. He'd been Rhonda's lawyer for years and now served both of us and the hotel very well.

"He's here," said Tim. "I'll go down to meet him."

Tim returned with Mike, towering over the man whose help we needed.

Mike brushed back a long, brown thread of hair and positioned it over the bare skin on the top of his head for effect. Studying us with toffee-colored eyes that sparkled with intelligence, he said calmly, "We'd better handle this quickly before things get out of control. Give me all the facts, and I'll see where we stand on this."

Rhonda clapped a hand to her heart. "I got a call from Dorothy telling me to turn on the television. She was watching *Hollywood Special*, that program about the stars, and Tina's mother was going to appear after the commercial. I raced into the lobby and turned on the television. Tim recorded it. Tina's mother came on, weeping and wailing and making up a whole bunch of lies about Tina and us. I'm tellin' ya, Mike, she's a lying bitch!"

True to his calm nature, Mike simply nodded. "I need to know to what specific lies you are referring. Let's go into your office, and we'll make a list of things we need to address broadly at this early time." He turned to Tim. "You'd better come too."

From behind the front desk, Julie watched us leave.

Inside our office, Rhonda turned to Mike with an angry flare in her eyes. "No one is going to ruin what Annie and I have built here with this hotel."

"Have you had contact with this woman before?"

"Yes," I said. "She came here a few weeks ago to try to get Tina to leave and go back to California with her. This was after Tina told her she wasn't going to be in her next scheduled movie, no matter what."

"Were threats made then?"

"She'd already threatened to sue us during a conversation Tina had with her mother," I said. "And then, when Tina wouldn't leave, she told us we'd be sorry."

"She's only interested in the money Tina can earn," said Rhonda. "She wants it for herself." Her lips curled with disdain. "She's done awful things to her daughter."

"Tina now has control of her money. Rhonda's husband,

Will, handles it for her." I suddenly realized how easily that fact could be twisted around to make it seem as if we were controlling Tina as her mother had once controlled her.

Mike and I exchanged worried looks.

"Okay, for the time being, I'm making a statement that will explain that a hotel as luxurious as this sometimes faces unwarranted and unjustified libelous claims and we have no further comment at this time. Ann, what do you want to state, if anything, about the relationship Vaughn Sanders and Lily Dorio have?"

I swallowed hard, trying to settle things in my mind. "Simply say that Vaughn and Lily are professionals who've known each other for a number of years." I held up my left hand. "I could show them this."

"That might still a few tongues." He took my arm. "Come, we'd better face the mob."

Standing in front of the crowd of reporters, I thought of Tina. Would she choose to come back to this constant interest in her, or would she decide to face her mother's challenge? I couldn't see a way out for her. Either way, she'd lose. That realization left me feeling sorry for her.

Grateful for his appearance, I listened to Mike expertly refuse to answer the reporters' questions. Standing on the opposite side of him, Rhonda looked as grim as I felt.

The questioning turned to me. I let Mike speak for me, repeating the message we'd worked on early. Now, he said, "As a matter of fact, my client and Vaughn Sanders are happily and recently engaged."

"Show us the ring, Ann!" a reporter cried out.

Then others began to shout. "When did it happen? What did he say to you? Did he get down on one knee?"

Reluctantly, I held up my left hand, and then quickly hid it behind my back. Showing it off made me feel shallow as if the ring he gave me was about its glitter, not its meaning.

Mike turned to leave the bank of microphones.

"Wait!" cried one of the reporters. "Where is Valentina? Why didn't she come forward? Is she already back in California?"

"As I told you earlier, we have nothing more to report on her situation. Her mother's attempt to sue us will follow the natural pattern of such things and will, no doubt, be thrown out of court."

Rhonda and I followed Mike inside and exchanged worried looks.

Mike turned to the small group of guests who had gathered in the lobby. "Nothing to be concerned about. This is our judicial system in operation. Even worthless claims have to be addressed."

"We love this hotel," said one of the guests. "If you need any witnesses to talk about the care we're always given, let me know."

I gave her a grateful smile. Stephanie and Randolph Willis, from Connecticut, were loyal, repeat guests.

"Thank you," Mike said to them, "but I don't think this case will come to that."

"Let's go to the office," Rhonda said. "I have a few more questions."

I led them to the back of the house. Opening the door to our office, I let out a cry of surprise.

"Tina! Troy! What are you doing here?" They were standing side by side against the back wall, looking like the hunted people they were.

"While the mob was gathered out front talking to you, Tina and I made our way along the side lawn to the back of the house and in through the delivery area." Anxiety drew lines of stress across his brow. His height and his obvious strength were reassuring.

He wrapped an arm around Tina's shoulders. "As soon as things calm down, I'm taking her to my parents' house. No one will think to look for her there."

Tina's eyes filled. "Troy's been a wonderful big brother to me." Tears slid down her face. "I don't know why my mother has to do these things. I'm going to fight her all the way."

"So you definitely don't want to do more films?" I knew how committed Vaughn was to his career and found it difficult to believe she'd simply walk away from all the money and fame.

"I ... I think so." Her hesitancy spoke volumes.

"She doesn't have to make up her mind on that now," said Troy. "Right, Tina?"

"If I ever go back to them, it will be without my mother around. I don't want her in my life. That I know for sure."

Tina jabbed a finger in my direction. "She's doing this now to get back at you as much as trying to make me work again."

"Me?" My stomach felt as if I'd swallowed a rock. "Why?"

"Because she knows I like you. You and Rhonda. She thinks you're the ones telling me to quit acting."

"But ..." I began.

"Bullshit," said Rhonda. "I say it's a guilty conscience buddying up to her greed."

Mike held up a hand. "We can speculate all we want here, but it's important to deal with the facts." He turned to Tina. "At some point, you're going to have to make a statement. But the three of us agreed that you needed more time to think things through."

"I need to talk things over with Barbara. She helps clarify my thinking."

"For now," said Troy, "she'll stay with my parents, away from the hotel, so guests here won't be bothered."

"Thanks." I wanted to hug Troy for his common sense. "In the meantime, make yourselves comfortable here in the hotel, away from the other guests."

"I have an idea," said Rhonda. "The truck from Reilly's Fish Market usually arrives at this time. We can arrange to have them drive you out of here and over to Troy's parents."

A grin spread across Troy's face. "Wow! This is like the movies. Right, Tina?"

She gave Troy a weak smile. "Not exactly."

"I'll give the kitchen staff notice that they're to let me know when the truck arrives," said Rhonda, hurrying out of the office.

"I'd better get back to my office," said Mike. "Let me know if anything else comes up."

Troy checked his watch. "I've got to get back to the spa." He turned to Tina. "See you later."

Tina and I sat, facing one another.

I was wondering what to say to her when Rhonda stuck her head into the office. "Okay, Tina. Your ride is here."

I walked her to the loading area behind the kitchen and watched as she climbed into the passenger seat and ducked her head. As the truck pulled away, I thought of the battle ahead of her and whispered, "Good luck."

"We need to make this fiasco work to our favor," said Rhonda, coming to stand beside me.

"The name of the hotel will come up in the news, along with pictures," I said.

"How about this?" Rhonda gave me a devilish grin. "A new ad campaign. The perfect place to escape from the bitch in your life."

I laughed. "Or this. The perfect place to hide out from the

pigs in the press!"

The relief that came from joking around calmed my jitters. Bad publicity before the holidays and the wedding could hurt us.

"You know, Annie," said Rhonda. "Maybe we should play up the fact that people can come here with a sense of privacy like we advertise. After all, Tina has been here for weeks without anyone finding out until today."

"Good idea," I said enthusiastically. "Let's work on a little promo piece for the local newspaper. Maybe others will pick up on it. I'll call our contact there."

With a renewed sense of hope, I phoned the *Sabal Daily News*.

Terri Thomas was everyone's idea of a gossip columnist. And she looked the part. Oversized, the elderly woman was known to make her way through rooms and around corners at any affair, seemingly led by her sharp, narrow nose. Her eyes, though appearing to be slightly red, seemed to see inside people, revealing their deepest, dark secrets. I, like most people who knew her, was uneasy in her presence.

"Ah, Ann," she murmured when she picked up her line. "Such a shame that Valentina and her mother chose The Beach House Hotel for their battleground. It could ruin a good reputation, you know."

My pulse stopped pounding and then went into overdrive. Stating a person's fears was one way Terri used to get people to talk.

I drew a deep breath, trying to think of how best to approach the situation. "Terri, as you know, our Christmas Open House is coming up. We want to be sure you'll attend."

"Of course," she said. "I wouldn't miss it for the world. Such a good source of information. But, Ann, we need to talk about your present ... uh ... situation. This is a chance for me to be right at the peak of national news."

I knew it was coming, but it still felt like a blow to my cheek. I hated this idea of *quid pro quo*. Scratching someone else's back to achieve what I wanted sometimes felt so cheesy.

"Well, I had thought that working together on a piece might be good for both of us," I said gamely. The truth was I'd do most anything to save the hotel.

"How about I come for an interview, and I'll bring a photographer to showcase the place?"

"Fair enough."

"Good. I'll see you in about an hour," she said crisply.

I hung up the phone and faced Rhonda. "It's a deal."

Following my interview with her, I ushered Terri to the front entrance. A pounding headache centered itself behind my right eye. Terri had quizzed me on my relationship with Vaughn, had her photographer take a picture of my engagement ring, and had pried as much information as she could out of both Rhonda and me about Valentina. Throughout it all, Mike had sat at our sides, acting as a mediator whenever Terri threatened to, lead us down a dangerous path of conversation.

"Let's hope Terri comes through for us," said Rhonda when I met her in the lobby. "She sure is nosy."

"At least we were able to shape the story somewhat." I hoped that after helping Terri, she'd do the same for us. A trade-off that might work.

My cell phone jangled in my pocket. I lifted it out and checked caller ID. Robert.

I slid the phone back into my pocket. No way was I taking a call from him. I could well imagine what nasty thing he had to say about us being sued. The jerk could gloat on his own.

"I'm beat, and you look exhausted," said Rhonda. "Let's go home. The staff can take care of the hotel this evening. It's a slow day."

"There you are!" Holding up a piece of paper, Dorothy hurried over to us. "Calls are coming in like crazy. We're booked solid for dinner, and people hoping to see Valentina are calling in for room reservations."

Rhonda and I looked at each other and groaned.

Dorothy's face fell. "I thought you'd be pleased."

"We are, we are," I said, thinking of the extra revenue while battling the headache of the century.

CHAPTER TWENTY-SIX

Like most moments of fame, ours soon faded, much to my relief, but Tina remained in the news. Lots of people wondered what her next move would be. Sadly, no one seemed to focus on the injustice done to her by her mother.

While all this was going on, Tina and I remained close, but I stayed in the background. I didn't want to give Tina's mother any more cause to attack us. And heaven knew we didn't want bad publicity. The wedding might be a strange one, but we wanted it.

Tina walked into our office one afternoon. Her shoulders slumped, her eyes full of sadness, she resembled a rag doll who'd lost her stuffing.

"I'm leaving," she said, sagging in defeat.

"Where are you going?" I asked, rising to my feet with alarm.

"You'd better not be going back to California," warned Rhonda.

Tina sank down into a chair. "I've got to get this mess with my mother settled. I want my brother to be safe and with me."

"What does she say to all this?" My mouth grew dry at the thought of Tina facing her mother alone.

A derisive laugh escaped Tina's lips. "My mother thinks it's all settled, that I'm giving in to her demands. But I'm not. My brother Victor is old enough to be able to choose to live with me instead of her. Once I know he's safe and with me, I can decide what I want to do with my life."

I gathered her into my arms. "You'll always have a safe

place here."

Tina rested her head on my shoulder. "Thanks. I know."

She turned into Rhonda's bosomy hug and then, with a sob, she raced out of the room.

As I lowered myself into my chair, my thoughts turned to my daughter. As much as I didn't like Liz staying with Robert, I knew he'd never intentionally be cruel to her. But Tina's mother was way too eager to hurt her daughter.

Rhonda clucked her tongue. "I feel so sorry for her."

"Me too. Hopefully, she'll keep in touch."

"By the way, Angela called last night," Rhonda said. "She's coming home right after our Christmas Open House. I was hoping she'd be here for the party, but she said she had a few things to take care of first."

My stomach lurched. Was it about the baby?

"Has she heard from Reggie?" I asked.

"Apparently, he phones her several times a day, but Angela refuses to take his calls. She says there's no point in trying to fit into his family after they were so rude to me. I don't blame her. I only want her happy, ya know?"

I nodded my agreement. We all did.

Maternal feelings swelled inside me as I stood in baggage claim, waiting for Liz to meet me. At the sight of her blond head and tall, thin body moving confidently across the floor, I ran to meet her. "I'm so, so glad to see you!"

Laughing, Liz hugged me back. "I'm so, so glad to be here!" she said, mimicking me with a teasing glint in her eyes.

It still sometimes amazed me that this beautiful young woman was my child.

"You look ..." we said together and laughed.

"Great!" I uttered.

"Wonderful," she said. Grabbing my left hand, she lifted it. "Let me see your ring. Wow! It's even bigger up close. When is it happening?"

I grinned. "Sometime in June. We haven't set a date yet. Not with all that's going on."

Liz threw an arm across my shoulders. "Nice, Mom. I'm so happy for you. Vaughn is one of the good guys."

Warmth filled me as I hugged her back. "Thanks, I think so too."

Arm in arm, we walked over to the baggage claim belt.

As we waited for her bag, Liz turned to me with a troubled look. "I tried to talk Angela into flying home with me, but she never picked up my calls or got in touch with me like I asked. There's something going on with her. I'm pretty sure it has something to do with Reggie."

"She's been upset since her visit at Thanksgiving. Reggie's parents were awful to Rhonda and her ."

"I heard his parents were real snobs, but Reggie didn't seem that way. Not after I got to know him." She shook her head. "How could anyone be mean to Angela? She's one of the sweetest people I've ever met."

"Hopefully, things will resolve themselves nicely," I said, not believing it for one minute. Liz's suitcase appeared on the conveyor belt, and to my relief, our conversation ended.

Liz rolled her bag to my Honda and loaded it in the trunk.

"Still using this car?" Liz said, buckling herself in.

I grimaced. "I can't afford anything new. Not yet. And if I need something bigger, I can always use the hotel's van or the limo."

"Kandie's van is real nice. I don't know why she needs something different." Liz shook her head. "She nags Dad all the time about everything. I don't know why he even stays with her."

I arched my right eyebrow at her.

"I mean it, Mom," Liz protested. "He's not happy with her. It's plain to see."

My shoulders rose and fell in an exaggerated shrug. I was not going to be drawn into that conversation.

As we pulled into my driveway, Liz sighed with pleasure. "Can't wait to take off this heavy sweater. Is the pool heated? I woke with a stiff neck this morning and want to soak a bit."

"I've got something you might like better. The spa is great, and Troy, who runs it, does a very good massage. Want to try it?"

The smile that crossed Liz's face answered for her. "After I get settled and changed, I'll walk over there."

"Okay, I'll call Troy and see if he has an opening. He's still trying to build our business."

While Liz unpacked and changed, I made the call and then put sandwiches together. BLTs were Liz's favorite.

Liz emerged from her bedroom, saw the sandwiches, and gave me a grateful smile. "Thanks, Mom." She glanced around with a mischievous grin. "OK, where are they?"

I laughed. "In a container. I'll get them out."

Chocolate chip cookies were another favorite of hers. I always tried to have them on hand for her visits.

We sat at the table chatting easily about events at the hotel.

"So Valentina is no longer here?" Liz said.

"To us, she's Tina Marks, which is her real name. And, yes, she's gone. Hopefully, she'll be back soon, with her brother. We don't know yet."

"When is Nell coming?" Liz asked, after taking the last bite of her sandwich. "I've missed being with her in DC these past few weeks."

"She'll be here in time for Christmas. I'll be anxious to see her. She didn't come for Thanksgiving because she went home with her boyfriend. As you might suspect, Vaughn is very curious about him. You've met him. Is he nice?"

Liz grinned. "Clint is a good guy and a real hottie—the kind of guy you wish had a lot of brothers."

It felt good to laugh together.

"Are you dating?" I asked, starting to clear the table. "You talked about a guy named Greg. Are you still seeing him?"

Liz shook her head. "There weren't any real sparks between us. Know what I mean?"

I smiled at her. Oh, yes. Whenever I was in Vaughn's arms, I knew all about sparks and the consuming flames that followed. We chatted for a while longer, then Liz left for the spa and, I returned to the hotel to help with the finishing touches for our Open House.

As I walked into the hotel lobby, I stopped and stared at the tall Christmas tree we'd put up right after Thanksgiving. A dramatic sight for hotel arrivals, it rose from the floor of the entry hall to the ceiling. Round glass balls of every color hung from the branches and were tucked into spaces in between. Clear-glass icicles hung nearby on the tips of the branches, reflecting the colors of the balls like slivers of rainbows.

"Always so pretty, huh?" said Rhonda, walking across the living room to greet me.

"I love it. It should be a lovely decoration for the wedding."

"Uh, about that." Rhonda gave me an apologetic look. "I'm afraid I let that little secret out."

"Rhonda ..."

She held up a hand to stop me. "I know we weren't supposed to say anything about it, but when Terri Thomas called to get an update on the party, I ended up telling her about the royal wedding. I didn't mean to do it, but you know how she gets you to say things you don't want to?"

Terri was a clever reporter, and Rhonda was proud of the

hotel. I just hoped Lorraine Grace at Wedding Perfection didn't find out, or worse yet, the Hassels.

Rhonda twisted her hands together. "The Hassels didn't want any publicity about it."

I wondered how best to handle the situation and decided to let it go.

Tim joined us, holding a box in his hand. "The candles have arrived."

"Great!" Rhonda clapped her hands. "Put them around. I want them everywhere!"

We left Tim and went into the kitchen to check on preparations for the party. With over two hundred people attending, it was essential to make and freeze what appetizers we could ahead of time. Consuela and Rhonda did a lot of the early preparation. On the day of the party, the entire kitchen crew would work together to prepare the fresh food.

Memories of last year's party filled my mind as I stood in the kitchen, surrounded by the tantalizing smell of cheese puffs baking. It had been such an exciting time for us, working together to make our first Christmas holiday celebration wonderful. Consuela looked over at me and smiled. Impulsively, I gave her a hug. Without her, I didn't know what we'd do. Steady and centered, Consuela was the person we could always rely on. Sometimes, I felt as if she and Manny were the parents I never knew and still missed.

After things were settled at the hotel, I hurried home, eager to share a meal with Liz. It was so nice finally to have her home with me.

Liz was in the kitchen when I entered my house. "Thought I'd make something special for dinner. It's a chicken recipe that Nell and I made a lot when I was with her in DC."

My surprise must have shown because Liz placed her hands on her hips. "What? You don't believe I can cook?"

"No, no, it's simply that you seem so grown up and so independent. It sometimes catches me off guard."

She laid down the knife she'd been using. "I am twenty-one. A real adult."

I hugged her. "Of course, you are." At her age, I was a married woman chasing a toddler around the house. Not a plan for her, I hoped. I wanted her to be able to fly on her own, free and easy, before becoming a wife and mother.

Liz's eyes sparkled. "I had the best massage ever. Troy is really good." Her lips curved. "And talk about hotties, why didn't you tell me he was so hot? I hope you don't mind, but I'm going out with him later tonight. He's going to show me around town."

I didn't know how much to say and then couldn't hold back. "Isn't he sort of going with Tina?"

Liz shook her head. "I asked him if he was seeing anyone, and he said no, that he and Tina were simply friends, more like brother and sister."

Dinner with Liz was a treat in so many ways. Good food, good conversation, and a good time filling my eyes with the sight of the daughter I loved so much.

I hid my disappointment when she rose from the table, ending our meal.

"I guess I'd better get ready," she said. "As I said, Troy is a really nice guy. Can't wait to see what he's like on a date."

While she dressed, I did the dishes and went into the office to check in with the hotel.

Liz stuck her head into my office and blew me a kiss. "See you later, Mom!"

I waved her off and sat thinking of Vaughn. Our wedding in June seemed a long way off. My thoughts turned to Angela. On a whim, I punched in her number, fully expecting to leave a message. The sound of her "hello" startled me.

"Hi, Angela, it's me. I've been thinking about you."

The sound of sobbing filled my ears. My heart fell to my feet. "What's wrong, honey? Tell me."

"It's the baby ..."

"Oh no! What happened?"

"Nothing," said Angela, between sobs. "I don't care what anybody says, I want this baby."

"Who is saying you shouldn't have it? Does Reggie know about it?"

"I don't want to disappoint my mother by having a baby like this. And, no, Reggie doesn't know about it. He wants to get together, but I've put him off. Once he sees me, he'll know. And, Ann, I love him, I really do, but I don't want him to marry me and then regret it."

I wondered how best to say it, then blurted out, "Don't you think you owe him the chance to make that decision himself?"

"That will have to wait until I deal with Mom. I've put off coming home until after the party because I don't want to upset her."

"You might be underestimating her," I said.

"Ann, you haven't mentioned it, have you?" The panic in her voice was unmistakable.

"No, but it hasn't been easy. Rhonda is not only my business partner; she's my best friend. In so many ways, I owe her the truth. But I realize it's not my truth, it's yours."

"I'll be home in a few more days, and then it'll all be out in the open." Her voice shook. "You're like a second mom to me, Ann."

"I feel the same way about you, honey. Don't worry. No matter what you do, you'll have a comfortable place here at the hotel."

"Thanks," said Angela softly and then I heard the click of the phone.

I hung up, thinking of mothers and daughters and how much we all needed one another. And I couldn't help wondering what Rhonda's reaction would be to Angela's news.

CHAPTER TWENTY-SEVEN

Vaughn walked toward me, a smile on his face. My heart lifted. The people standing around me in the airport waiting for newly arrived passengers melted away as we continued to stare at one another. My man, my love, was home. I ran to greet him.

He dropped his suitcase and swept me up into his arms.

"It's so good to have you home," I said, lifting my face for a kiss.

His lips met mine in a tantalizing combination of taste and feel. In the midst of enjoying his kiss, I suddenly realized people had stopped around us and were staring. I dropped my arms.

"Ignore them," growled Vaughn, but he too stepped away before clasping my hand in his and leading me away from the small crowd of people who'd recognized him.

"How are things in New York? Did the meeting go well?" In preparation for his return to the television show, he'd met with other members of the cast and the writers of the show.

He grinned. "The mayor of that crummy little town sure is a wily character. Believe it or not, I'm going to enjoy seeing what happens next."

"Ah, but while you're here, we're going to forget you're a mayor and treat you like any regular guy."

He grinned. "A regular guy in love with the cutest hotel owner I know?"

I laughed. "A regular guy who is the apple of someone's eye."

This friendly banter, the easy way it was between Vaughn and me, was something that was precious to both of us. As hard as it was to think of waiting until June before we married, I knew it was best to hold off until our schedules would allow us to savor the whole celebration.

During the drive to my house, I studied Vaughn out of the corner of my eye. He leaned back against the passenger seat and lifted his face to the sun. I longed to reach out and touch his cheek.

He cracked open an eye and turned to me. "What?"

"Just glad you're home, that's all."

A smile lit his face. "Me too."

At home, Vaughn easily lifted his suitcase out of the trunk and, hand in hand, we walked to the front of my house. With him beside me, the blue of the sky met my eyes with a brightness that filled me with joy. The fronds of the palm trees rustled in the breeze, whispering their welcome, and a sense of peace filled me. The tension in my shoulders eased as the problems that usually tore at me lost their grip.

We entered my house, and I called out to Liz.

No answer.

Curious, I went into the kitchen to see if she'd left a note in our usual spot. A white piece of paper was tucked under the catch-all bowl holding keys and clips and other junk. I lifted it and read aloud:

"Have gone on a friend's boat for the day. Say hi to Vaughn. See you later."

"So we're alone?" Vaughn's sexy smile sent a flurry of pin pricks racing up and down my body. Now I could welcome him home my way.

With my head resting on Vaughn's chest, I could hear the

slowing of his heart. I smiled to myself with satisfaction and felt my own body resume a more normal tempo. Making love with Vaughn was such a mixture of sensations, sweet and soft, pounding passion, gentle strokes, and almost rough kisses. I never tired of the various combinations.

"Sorry Nell couldn't make the party," said Vaughn, running his fingers through my hair. "I want her to get more comfortable being here at the hotel."

"I understand why she couldn't be here. The girls are at an age where their own lives and activities take precedence."

"Mmmm. Gotta admit I was a little disappointed that Ty and June couldn't join us. After the holidays, I want you to go to San Francisco with me. Think you can do it?"

"As long as it's before Rhonda's baby arrives, I can. She's hoping for an Easter baby."

He lifted my chin and looked into my eyes. "Are you sorry we can't have a baby of our own?"

I hesitated and shook my head. "No, I can't imagine having a baby at my age. But I'm happy for Rhonda and Will. Are you disappointed I can't have more children?"

"No, I'm grateful for the ones I have, but I don't want more. Besides, it gives me more time with you."

I checked the clock. "Speaking of time ..." I kissed him and reluctantly started to climb out of bed.

He grabbed hold of me and tugged me back against him. Grinning, he said, "I can make this real fast."

I laughed. "Not going to happen, big boy."

His eyes filled with mirth. "Later."

At the hotel, the atmosphere was abuzz with preparation for our Christmas Open House. The aroma of fresh pine lured me into the living room. Fresh greens adorned the mantel. A bar had been set up at one end of the room, and Tim was overseeing the storage of liquor bottles and racks of glasses behind the bar. During the party, he would assist the bartenders by supervising servers who would pass out glasses of champagne and sparkling water.

He noticed me and waved. I returned his greeting and went to check the dining room.

The waitstaff was dressing the tables with white linens and placing centerpieces I'd made of holly branches and white roses on each table. Small, white lights were strung among the beams of the ceiling, their wires spreading like glittering spider webs that seemed magical to me. Napkins and silverware, along with small china plates, were placed at one end of an extra-long buffet table, which sat at the end of the room ready to receive a bounty of food.

In the kitchen, Rhonda, Consuela, Carl Lamond, and Jean-Luc were preparing a variety of appetizers. Their fingers flew as they assembled little sandwiches, added items to toast rounds, and arranged little tastes on platters. Christmas music filtered into the room, adding to the whirring noise of mixers and other kitchen equipment. The aroma of butter, citrus, and chocolate filled my nostrils, a harbinger of the delicious food our guests would enjoy. The smell of turkeys cooking and the unmistakable aroma of a huge, steamship round of beef wafted from the ovens in a delicious mixture. Two whole hams rested on a table.

My stomach growled in anticipation.

Rhonda looked up at me. "Give Vaughn a proper welcome home?"

My cheeks warmed at her suggestive expression, but Rhonda was Rhonda, and I didn't care if she knew how happy I was to have Vaughn back with me. I waved at Jean-Luc, Carl, and Consuela, then went into the office.

Dorothy was taping a small candy cane to each of the new spa brochures we intended to hand out. A few reservations had come in already for our "New Mother Spa Packages".

After helping Dorothy complete the taping on the brochures, I sent her home to get ready for the party. Then I went to check on Ana and the housekeepers. They'd agreed to come back to the hotel in the evening to pass appetizers at the party. I needed to make sure they'd be here in plenty of time. If the party was anything like last year, the crush of people would be nonstop.

Later, when I returned to the kitchen, order was more or less restored. Sheet pans of appetizers filled a rolling pan rack, ready to be placed on serving trays. Jean-Luc and Carl were sitting in Jean-Luc's cubicle off the kitchen deep in discussion. Rhonda and Consuela were seated at the kitchen table, sipping glasses of water.

I joined them. "Everything looks wonderful. Can I do anything to help?"

Rhonda shook her head. "Everything set up? Housekeepers? Tim? Dorothy?"

"I've got everything at that end ready to go. The policemen directing traffic will be here before six. You two better go home and rest a bit before coming back."

"Yeah," said Rhonda. "I've got to put my feet up for a while. But don't worry, I'll be back here way ahead of the party."

Consuela got to her feet. "I'll go home and change."

I checked in with Tim. Satisfied he would be back at the hotel in plenty of time, I left the hotel to get ready.

Liz was at the house talking to Vaughn on the patio.

"Almost time to get ready for the party," I announced.

Liz gave me a teasing smile. "Rhonda said your dress is really hot."

"Oh?" said Vaughn, leering at me with exaggeration.

I laughed and went into my bedroom to get ready. Showing off the hotel was of more interest to me than showing off a new dress, especially one Rhonda had picked out for me.

Pulling the red dress out of the closet, I chastised myself for giving in to her. The dress was decidedly more daring than I usually wore.

After freshening up, I slid the silky garment over my head, tugging it this way and that to center the V in the front. The cut in fabric gave more of a peek at my breasts than I normally allowed, and I wished now that I'd bought something a little more conservative. Then my thoughts turned to Robert. He'd have refused to allow me to leave the house in this or in anything he thought inappropriate for the wife of someone in his position. What a crock!

Happier with my choice now, I clasped the pendant Vaughn had given me around my neck and slipped emerald earrings through my earlobes. The effect of the green jewelry with the red dress was a nice touch for the holidays.

Vaughn came into the room and let out a long, low whistle. "If it were only the two of us simply going out to dinner, I'd tell you to take off that dress right now. Guess there's no chance of that tonight."

"Not a chance," I said, pleased by the way his gaze lingered on me with interest. "Better hurry up and get dressed."

I went to check on Liz. When I knocked on her door, she emerged wearing a sleeveless black sheath that hugged her curves. The deep, dark color of her dress was in contrast to her long, blond hair, which met her shoulders in a simple wave.

"You look lovely, Liz," I said, hugging her.

Pleased, she said, "I bet Vaughn liked your dress. It's way cool, Mom. You know, when I was staying at Dad's, he kept talking about you. I think he really regrets leaving you."

I held up my hand. "Don't go there, honey."

Dressed in slacks and a sport coat, Vaughn walked over to us and offered an arm to each of us. "Ready to go, lovely ladies?"

Liz and I played along, each taking hold of an arm, and we left together.

As I stood with Rhonda at the front entrance of the hotel, I couldn't help thinking of all the changes of the past year. Our lives had been filled with the whirlwind of getting the hotel off the ground and keeping it going. I glanced at Rhonda. She wore a look of contentment that had been missing when we'd first met. But with Will's love, and now, the expected baby, her face glowed with health and happiness. The green dress she wore fell in folds across the belly she could no longer hide. Its color, rich and deep, brought out the sparkle in her dark eyes and highlighted the blond curls that escaped the knot of hair at the back of her head. Her smile came from her heart, which was as big and generous as any I'd known. She was so much more than a business partner to me.

Rhonda elbowed me, tearing me away from my private thoughts. "Guess who's here?"

I bit back a groan, smiled at a guest entering the hotel and focused on Brock Goodwin who was approaching the hotel with purpose. As he was president of the Gold Coast Neighborhood Association, there was no way we could avoid inviting him to the party. As much as Rhonda and I disliked him, we had to deal with his presence on occasions like this.

He climbed the front stairs of the hotel to us. Grasping Rhonda's hand, he bent and gave her a kiss on the cheek. "Happy Holidays. So glad I could come."

I stepped away as he turned to face me. He pretended not to notice and moved to my side. Bending down, he kissed me on the cheek. "So your little friend was Valentina Marquis? How naughty of you, Ann, not to let me know. We both wanted to be neighborly."

A sour taste filled my mouth. He was exactly the kind of man Tina needed to stay away from.

"Everything all right?" Rhonda asked, giving me a worried look as Brock walked away.

"It's just Brock being Brock," I grumped and turned to welcome the mayor of Sabal and his wife with a pleasant hello.

Later, after the bulk of the guests had arrived, I circulated in the downstairs rooms, making sure everyone had what they wanted. The happy buzz of conversation, the clinking of glasses, and the sound of silverware on plates was pleasing. People stood in conversational groups in the living room or sat in the dining room at tables with platefuls of food, chatting and eating. Once more I was struck by how well the seaside estate accommodated the workings of a small hotel.

"Penny for your thoughts," said Vaughn, coming up to me. I accepted his kiss and ignored the fact that female eyes followed his every move.

"It's nice to see so many people enjoying themselves here. It's what we work so hard for—happy guests."

"Liz looks delighted," he commented.

I searched for Liz in the crowd. Troy and a number of other young men surrounded her, and her laughter rang in the air like a bird's musical trill.

"She's lovely. I'll be proud to be her step-dad."

My heart filled with gratitude. I turned to him. "I feel the same way about Nell. Ty too, though I don't really know him." Thinking of our families as one, our June wedding couldn't come fast enough.

Rhonda came over to us and grabbed my hand with excitement. "The party's going well, Annie. A lot of people have spoken to me about our spa. The local women like the idea of getting a discount. Several others told me they're giving a spa package to their daughters or daughters-in-law as a surprise Christmas gift." A smile lit her face. "And they're so happy for Will and me. Can you believe it? Will and I celebrating like this at our age?"

I hugged her. "We're all are so pleased for you."

Tears came to her eyes. "I wish Angela was here. Thank God, she's coming home tomorrow."

I turned as someone called my name.

I was pleased to see Lorraine Grace. She walked over to me.

"Ann, I think we might have a problem. The Hassels are concerned about the lack of privacy here at the hotel. They'd been promised their wedding would be discreet, but they've learned about the incident with Valentina Marquis, and they don't like it."

"Don't worry," I said, choking back the taste of acid in my mouth, "I'll write a letter to them addressing the situation." We couldn't lose the wedding now.

"Thanks. That would be wonderful." Lorraine beamed at me. "Now I'm going to taste some of that delicious food of yours."

I watched her enter the crowd, wishing that just once things would go smoothly. Then I saw Terri.

She waved and rushed over to me. "So glad I could make it. This party always works so well for me. I've set up a special interview with the mayor."

"You won't say anything about the wedding, will you? If you do, it might ruin your chances of exclusive, privileged information when it happens."

Her eyes rounded. "Oh no! I won't say a word. At least, not directly." She hurried away before I could stop her with another word of warning.

After the last guest had left and the hotel was almost back to normal, Rhonda and I plopped down on one of the couches in the living room and faced one another.

Rhonda gave me a high-five. "We did it again, Annie! Another great party."

I sighed with pleasure as I flipped off my strappy heels. "I'm glad it's over, but it went well. We've got a lot of interest in the spa now. Having Troy give tours of it was his idea, and it worked."

Rhonda laughed. "Every woman under eighty can't wait for him to get his hands on her."

I joined in her laughter. Troy was charming. Even Liz seemed taken with him.

"What's going on?" Will asked, approaching us.

"Nothing," Rhonda and I said together, continuing to laugh.

Good-natured as always, Will let it go and gave Rhonda a loving look. "Ready to go home, hon?"

"Remember, Annie; I'll be in late tomorrow. Angela is coming in at noon, and I want to spend some time with her."

"Take as much time as you need."

Rhonda got to her feet with a groan. "Oh, boy! I'm gonna sleep tonight."

I rose and gave her a hug. "Nice job, partner."

Rhonda and Will left, and I went to find Vaughn. He was sitting out on the pool deck. The lights in the pool were lit, giving the water an iridescence that was both beautiful and eerie.

"Come have a seat," said Vaughn, patting a space next to him on the large lounge chair.

I stretched out beside him, fitting easily into the shape of his body. The glow from the pool washed our faces in blue light. At the sigh of contentment from his lips, I warmed inside.

Enjoying the peace and quiet after the noisy party, we cuddled, satisfied simply to be together.

When our eyelids began to droop, Vaughn tugged me up and out of the chair.

"C'mon, Sleeping Beauty. Time to go home."

We said goodbye to Dave, who was working on the night audit and headed to my house.

Staring up at the starry sky, I had the deep-seated feeling I was exactly where and with whom I was meant to be.

I whispered my thanks to the skies and gave Vaughn's hand a squeeze.

CHAPTER TWENTY-EIGHT

All morning, while I worked at the hotel making sure things were in order for our next wave of guests, my mind was filled with worry over Angela's arrival. I wished as I had so many times, that I could've talked to Rhonda about the situation, but I also knew the importance of keeping trust between Angela and me. With her emotions in such disarray, Angela needed to know she could count on me until she'd figured out what to tell everyone else.

I was in the kitchen discussing Christmas Day menus with Jean-Luc when my cell phone rang. Seeing the caller's name, I swallowed hard and answered.

"Annie, can you meet me at your house? I need to talk to you."

"Sure, is everything all right?"

"You know very well that it isn't." Rhonda's voice was as cold as the winter days I'd disliked so much in Boston.

"Rhonda, I ..."

She hung up before I could continue. My heart pounded with dismay. Woodenly, I told Jean-Luc we'd continue the conversation later, to give me a list of what items we needed.

I hurried over to my house, glad that Vaughn and Liz had planned on doing lunch and some Christmas shopping together.

As I drew closer to my house, Rhonda roared up in her red Caddy. I stepped aside and waited for her to get out of the car. Her red eyes and blotchy skin were telling, but it was the angry look she gave me that made my mouth go dry.

Standing in the driveway, she settled her hands on her hips and glared at me. "You knew! You knew! Angela told me you've known about her situation for some time, and yet you didn't tell me! How could you do that to me?"

"I'm sorry, but how could I not do that for Angela?" I said quietly. "I love her like my own daughter. She insisted I not tell you or anyone else until she'd worked things out for herself. I begged her to tell you, and she refused. She loves you so much, Rhonda."

Rhonda lowered her face in her hands.

I put my arm around her shoulders. "I'm sorry, Rhonda. I really am. You're my best friend, and I wouldn't hurt you for the world."

"Oh, I know that," she said, lifting her tear-streaked face. "It's that I'm so disappointed for her. She loves Reggie so much. And me? I could kill him with my bare hands. He and that family of his made it plain she's not good enough for him." She sniffed. "All because of me."

"Whoa!" I said, leading her into my house. "Let's not even think along those lines. Let's sit and talk it over."

I fixed two glasses of blueberry iced tea, and we took them out to my patio.

Rhonda looked around. "Where's Liz? And Vaughn?"

"Christmas shopping. I don't know who was more pleased with the plan, Vaughn or Liz."

"What's Liz going to think about Angela's pregnancy?" Rhonda shook her head. "Can you believe it? My daughter and I having babies at about the same time?" Tears filled her eyes once more. "I want Angela to be as happy as I am about having a baby. Ya know?"

I took hold of Rhonda's hand. "No matter what happens, that baby will be loved. You know that."

Rhonda's weak smile was filled with sadness. "It tears me

up to see Angela so unhappy, so unsure of herself."

"What about school? Has she decided what she's going to do about that?"

"Angela says she's going to take a semester off and then go back. That's what she was working on before she came home." Rhonda wrung her hands. "I never did go to college, so it's real important to me that she gets her degree."

"She's very bright. Perhaps she can take some computer courses for credit during her stay at home."

"But how can she go to school and raise a baby?" Rhonda gave me a long sigh. "It's all so complicated."

"What about Reggie in all this?"

"Angela has refused to see him or talk to him on the phone. But, Annie, he's gotta know about this. I suggested she call and invite him down here for New Year's Eve. Once he sees her, he might do the right thing."

"What is the right thing?" I asked her.

She shrugged her shoulders. "I have no friggin' idea."

Her sigh lifted in the air and fell. She got to her feet. "I'd better get back to the house, and then I'll return to the hotel."

I stood up and hugged her. "Why don't you stay home this evening? The staff and I will take care of everything."

She pulled me to her for a long hug. "What would I do without you, Annie? You're always there for me."

"So you're not mad at me anymore?"

She gave me a sheepish smile. "Naw, it's only the hormones talking and the shock of it all. I'd do the same thing for Liz if she asked me."

I walked her out to her car and waited for her to get behind the wheel.

"Guess we'd better get used to having babies around," I said.

"Oh, my Gawd! I've been so worried about Angela it

suddenly hit me. Her baby makes me a grandmother. I don't think I'm ready for that. One kid will call me Mom and the other Grandma? It seems like a bad joke, huh?"

I patted her arm. "We'll all get used to it. Just give it time."

"Maybe so. When Liz gets back, will you ask her to give Angela a call? Or send her over. I think Angela needs her more than she needs me right now. I was pretty upset."

She pulled out of the driveway.

As I watched her go, I wondered what Reggie would do when he got the call from Angela.

I was in the kitchen rinsing the glasses when Vaughn and Liz walked in. They were both smiling.

"Hello there! How'd the shopping go?"

Vaughn grinned. "I'd say that Santa and his helper were very busy. It should be a fun time."

"Yeah, we got the best stocking stuffers ever." Liz's eyes glowed with happiness. Earlier, we'd decided to concentrate on several small gifts rather than one or two expensive ones. Both girls would get much-needed checks but no other gifts except for their Christmas stockings.

"Angela is home," I said. "Rhonda is wondering if you'd go visit her, Liz."

Liz's eyebrows shot up. "What's going on?"

"The news is out, so you might as well know. She's pregnant."

"Wow," Liz said. "Reggie's?"

"I'll let her tell you all about it. Rhonda is pretty upset because Angela has refused to talk to Reggie or to see him. She's hoping he'll come down to the hotel this holiday season and help get things sorted out."

Liz's expression grew thoughtful. "I wondered what was

going on with her. Now I know. Is she going back to school? I was going to room with her."

"When is the baby due?" Vaughn asked.

"About the same time as Rhonda's baby. I'm not sure of the exact date."

Liz gave a low whistle. "I bet Ange is really depressed. That's why she wouldn't take my calls. Where are the car keys? I'd better get right over there."

I handed Liz the keys and turned to Vaughn.

"I've got a little while before I have to go back to the hotel to handle a private dinner. Want to take a swim? The pool is heated up to a nice temperature."

"Sure. Guess it's me and Liz for dinner, huh?" The disappointment in his voice made me cringe. It wasn't fair to him, but I didn't know what else I could do. The dinner was scheduled, and Rhonda was taking the evening off.

"Afraid so. Tomorrow will be a little easier. With two private parties in the house tonight, I have to be there." The 24/7 commitment to the business was something I sometimes chafed under. But it was reality and my life.

Vaughn and I changed into bathing suits and stared at one another in the middle of my bedroom. He was a few years older than I, and his body was trim and muscular and lean. He worked hard at keeping fit because cameras were cruel to actors. Gazing at him now, I thought he was handsome.

He moved toward me.

I lifted my arms for his embrace.

Snuggled up against me, I was fully aware of his arousal. I wrapped my arms around his neck and sighed with pleasure. Moments like this almost made our time away from one another worth it.

He slipped a hand down the front of my bathing suit. The tip of my breast tingled with his familiar touch.

Smiling, I pulled off my suit. Heart pounding, I watched as he tossed his bathing trunks aside. Confident, he lifted me up onto the bed. I lay there, gazing into those dark eyes of his, drawn in by the passion I saw in them. And then his lips met mine, and we began to move together.

We were up and dressed when Liz came through the front door, calling my name.

My heart pounded with dismay when I noticed her red, swollen eyes.

"Liz! Are you all right? Is Angela okay?"

Tears swam in her eyes. "It's all so sad. Angela loves Reggie, but she insists she doesn't want him to know about the baby. Rhonda made her call Reggie to invite him down to the hotel for the New Year celebrations. He told her he couldn't come, that he had a lot of deb parties to go to, and it was time for them to move on." Liz swallowed hard. "Angela's heart is broken, and Rhonda is mad as hell."

"She's going to have to tell him the truth. For one thing, it's the law." With my divorce from Robert, I'd learned painful lessons about truth, but in the end, having all the facts made things fair—not necessarily easy or fun, but fair.

"Rhonda thinks so too, but Angela said if Rhonda or anyone else tells him, she'll disappear and we'll never see the baby." Liz wiped her eyes. "She'll do it too. You know how stubborn she can be."

"Yes, but why does she feel this way?"

"Ange says she knows what she and Reggie had was special, and he's going to realize it without her trapping him with news of the baby." Liz shook her head. "I don't know what to think. They seemed really good together when they visited me in DC."

I let out a worried sigh. "As much as we might not like it, nobody else can make those decisions for Angela. Give her time. She'll come around. For the baby, if not for us."

"I hope you're right, Mom, because I've never seen Rhonda and Angela so angry with each other."

I didn't say anything more, but my worry grew.

CHAPTER TWENTY-NINE

Rhonda and I took turns supervising the rash of holiday parties at the hotel. Now that we'd become known for our lunches, we found ourselves busy most days hosting both lunches and dinners for outside guests as well as those staying in the hotel.

Jean-Luc and Sabine hung in there—Jean-Luc in the kitchen and Sabine overseeing the service of the delicious food he created. Julie and Tim were working well together, and Dave, bless his heart, stayed around the hotel even after he was relieved of duty as the night desk clerk. As grateful as I was to him for his loyalty, I realized it was time to bring in someone else to handle those duties when he was off.

Staffing the hotel was a little like the accordion effect of dense highway traffic—too many staffers at one moment, too few the next. But with an upscale property like The Beach House Hotel, it was important to have enough help at all times.

As I worked on payroll, I wondered how we'd manage without Rhonda for the early months of motherhood, but then brushed aside my worries, telling myself I'd address those issues after the holidays.

I hurried and finished up my work so I could enjoy a free evening with Vaughn and the girls. Nell had arrived that afternoon, and I'd planned a nice family dinner, just the four of us.

Outside, clouds floated above me in the graying sky like dollops of whipped cream. The first tinges of pink color from the setting sun highlighted their irregular shapes, tempting me to take some time to create cloud pictures in the sky.

Drawing near the house, I heard the giggles of the girls and realized that in spite of the cool air, they were in the pool.

Vaughn looked up at me as I entered the kitchen and grinned. "Ah, the princess returns to her castle."

Laughing, I went to him. "So how is the prince?"

"Glad to see you." He drew me into his arms. "Would you like a glass of wine? I bought a nice pinot noir to go with the salmon I'm going to grill."

"Great. I've already got the asparagus all set. Did you get the French bread I wanted?"

He nodded and gave me a pensive look. "Ellen and I used to love cooking together like this. And now I have you. How lucky can a guy get?"

"A lot luckier than this after the girls have left for the evening," I said, enjoying a flirtation with him.

He laughed. "I love you, Ann. Guess you know that, huh?"

I grinned. "Yeah, I love you too," I said as our lips drew closer.

"Oh no! Are you guys getting all romantic on us?"

Chuckling, we broke apart.

Nell, wrapped in a beach towel, came over to me and gave me a hug. Her eyes sparkled with pleasure. "Hi, Ann!"

I kissed her, struck as always by her uncanny resemblance to Liz. Two peas in a pod, they called themselves.

"Welcome! I'm so glad you could make it!"

She returned my smile. "Thanks. I'm pleased to be here. Holidays are for family, and I've missed being together like this."

Her words warmed me. She'd been supportive of Vaughn and me from the beginning.

Liz came inside, and after the girls changed into their

clothes, the four of us sat on the lanai, sipping drinks, and talking. Studying Liz, I admired her for how she'd survived all we'd been through. That same inner strength would, I hoped, be a help to Angela as she went through becoming a mother alone.

"So, Dad, I'm thinking I'd like Clint to meet you and Ann," said Nell, drawing me back into the conversation.

Vaughn leaned back and studied his daughter. "So who is this Clint Dawson?"

A dreamy expression filled Nell's face, adding a glow to her lovely features. "He's the man I'm going to marry." At her father's look of dismay, she held up a hand. "Don't worry. It's not going to happen soon. He doesn't even know it yet."

I laughed softly, along with the others. But I could tell how serious Nell was about him. She had the look of love about her.

I couldn't help thinking of Angela. Why, I wondered, couldn't Reggie have agreed to visit her? Was he already committed to the girl who lived in Palm Beach, the daughter of Katherine Smythe's friend, the girl Katherine wanted him to accompany to all those fancy deb parties?

Vaughn got up to start the grill. I went inside to set the table. I put aside my concerns for Angela, intent on enjoying the evening with my family.

Christmas, Hanukkah, and half of the Kwanzaa celebration passed in a blur of unprecedented activity, due to the hotel's growing reputation for fine dining. Our spring season was already filling up, which was both a joy and a worry to me. That's when both Rhonda's and Angela's babies would be born, leaving me to handle things on my own.

As I sat in the office with Rhonda, we commiserated about the lack of time we had for family. Vaughn had been great about my being unable to spend much time with him, but, genial as he was, he was getting tired of it. And Will was fretting about Rhonda working so hard.

"Who knew it would be so hectic?" said Rhonda, sighing and absently rubbing her growing stomach. "I've hardly even seen you. We've been like ships passing in the night."

"I love the success we're having, but we're going to have to bring someone in to help manage this place. Tim is wonderful at what he does, but he doesn't have the experience to handle the entire operation, and we can only do so much. After the wedding, we'll talk about hiring a general manager. Okay?"

"Yeah, someone who can manage the staff while we do the work behind the scenes." Her eyebrows drew together with worry. "I want to be there for Angela."

"Any more word from Reggie?"

Rhonda shook her head. "No, the little prick. I could murder him for what he's doing to her. Angela needs closure."

Nell left Florida the next day to celebrate New Year's Eve with Clint. Liz had already informed me she was going out with Troy, leaving Vaughn and me alone with guests at the hotel.

During a lull between lunch at The Beach House Hotel and the start of our New Year's Eve party, Vaughn and I were able to spend time alone at my house. I was stretched out on the couch, my head in his lap, talking about what the next year would bring when the jangling of my phone brought me reluctantly to my feet.

Leery, I checked caller ID. Angela.

"Hi, sweetie! What can I do for you?" I asked her.

"Ann, I need a big favor. I can't ask my mother, and Liz isn't answering her phone."

"Yes?" I was struck by the seriousness in her voice. "What is it?"

"Will you drive me to the airport? I don't want to go alone."

"What's going on?" I fought visions of her leaving home.

"It's Reggie. He's flying in. I promised to meet him."

A mixture of emotions gripped my body. "Does he know about the baby?"

"No, that's why I want someone to drive me to the airport. Once he sees me, he'll know. There's no way I can hide it. I'm showing now."

"So you want me there because ..."

"Because I won't be able to drive myself home if he decides not to stay," said Angela. In her soft voice, I heard the threat of tears.

"Of course, I'll drive you there," I said. "When is he coming in?"

"He should be there by the time we get to the airport. I didn't get his message until a few minutes ago. I'll head over to your house right now."

"Okay, I'll get ready."

Vaughn gave me a questioning look as I hung up the phone. "Everything okay?"

I shrugged. "I'm not sure. Reggie is flying in to meet Angela. She wants me to drive her to the airport in case he decides not to stay."

Vaughn frowned. "Not stay? I thought she was so sure about him."

"Me too. Now we'll see what kind of young man he really is—like his parents or like the kinder, better person Angela fell in love with."

"All right. You go. I've got a couple of things I need to do before the party tonight."

"Okay. See you later." I grabbed my phone and my purse and went outside as Angela pulled her little Beemer into the driveway.

She got out of the car and came over to me. Dressed in jeans and a loose knit white top, she looked charmingly pregnant. It wouldn't take Reggie long to notice the baby bump. I hoped he'd notice the love in Angela's sparkling brown eyes and the glow on her face that only pregnant women seem to get.

I hugged her, and then we climbed into one of the hotel vans. I had commandeered it while Liz had use of my Honda.

The drive to the airport was a quiet one. I tried to strike up a conversation but Angela's monosyllabic responses made me realize she wanted to deal with her anxiety privately.

At the airport, I parked in the short-term lot, and then Angela and I walked together into the terminal.

"Where are you to meet him?" I asked.

"In a corner of the baggage claim area, away from everyone else."

"Okay, then, I'll wait for you near the door."

Angela clutched her hands together and turned to me with a worried grimace. "Oh God! I'm so nervous."

I placed a hand on her shoulder and looked her in the eye. "Relax. Remember how sure you were of him. And, remember too, that no matter what happens, you have your family and friends behind you."

Tears filled Angela's eyes. She ran her fingers over the baby bump she couldn't hide. "Thanks," she said and walked away, her body rigid with tension.

I watched her go, rubbing my cold hands together to warm the nervous chill that had come over me.

Taking a seat at the end of a row of seats where I could unobtrusively observe her, I prayed things would go well. In the past, Angela had been so strong, so sure. Now we'd see if that confidence in Reggie would be borne out.

CHAPTER THIRTY

I saw Reggie before Angela did. He descended the escalator carrying a small backpack and looked around eagerly. With his fresh-faced look, he seemed so young. When he caught sight of Angela, a smile spread across his face and then quickly disappeared. His eyebrows formed a frown.

She waved and went to greet him.

The blood left Reggie's face as he drew closer to Angela. I held my breath as he gaped at her, his eyes wide behind the lenses of his glasses.

For a moment, I thought he might turn around and run away. Then, he dropped his backpack onto the floor and swept her up in his arms.

Sobbing, Angela lay her head against his chest, clinging to him. He lowered his lips to her head and kissed her dark hair. As she continued to sob, he stroked her back in comforting circles.

As I watched them, tears came to my eyes. Every bad thought I'd had of him disappeared. He was, I now knew, a better young man than I'd given him credit for.

They pulled apart. Angela swept her gaze around the room, finally finding me.

I waved.

She tugged Reggie over to me. "If you drop us off at your house, I'll get my car. Reggie and I need to go somewhere to talk."

"Sure." I held out my hand. "I'm so glad you're here."

He shook my hand. "This whole thing is quite a surprise."

He turned to Angela. "But we'll work it out. Right?"

Angela bobbed her head and gave him a bright smile.

"Aren't you supposed to be at some deb party tonight?" I asked him.

"Yeah, with Laurel Larkin. My mother and her parents are going to be pissed that I'm not there, but I'll call Laurel as soon as I can to let her know. She'll understand. She didn't want to go with me anyway. She's hot on some other guy."

His words wiped the happy expression off Angela's face. "Your mother is going to be unbelievably unhappy with me now."

Reggie put an arm around her. "After attending a number of these parties this season, I think it's all crap. My parents can't decide my life for me. I've tried to please them, but now I don't care. What they want for me isn't what I want at all."

I liked what he said, but I knew life wasn't that simple. "Your parents aren't the only ones you both have to consider. Rhonda is less than pleased with your and your family's conduct at Thanksgiving."

A flush washed his face. He kicked at the marble floor with a sneaker. "I'm sorry I left with them. I should've stood my ground." He faced Angela. "When you wouldn't take my calls, I had a lot of time to think things over. I thought I could move on, but I love you, Angela. I always have, and I always will."

Angela leaned against Reggie, her face wet with tears. Reggie closed his eyes and held onto her. Pulling a tissue out of my purse, I dabbed at my eyes, blotting tears of my own. It didn't matter that there were other people around us talking and moving about. It felt as if the three of us were on an island in the midst of them.

After a few moments, Reggie said, "Where's your car, Ann? We'd better go."

On the ride back to the hotel, Angela and Reggie cuddled

together in the back. Ignoring their quiet murmuring, I wondered how Rhonda would react to Reggie's appearance. I knew her well enough to know that she'd do anything to protect someone she loved. Would she give Reggie a chance to prove himself to her?

I pulled into my driveway and waited while Reggie gathered his backpack from the back seat.

He stood and faced me. "I understand that for a long time you were the only one who knew about the baby. Thanks for being such a good friend to Angela. I hope I can be your friend too. I'm going to need all the support I can get to face what lies ahead. But, Ann, I promise you I'll do what's right."

"That's wonderful, Reggie, but I'm not the one you have to convince. You'd better make sure that Rhonda is behind you."

"Yeah, I guess she thinks I'm an ass, huh?"

"Let's say you have a gigantic task ahead of you. But Rhonda is big-hearted, and once you can convince her, she'll be behind you all the way. Wait and see."

Impulsively, I kissed him on the cheek. "Now go get 'em!"

Angela, who'd heard the whole exchange, smiled at me. "Thanks so much! I'll see you tomorrow for dinner."

"Good luck," I whispered, hugging her close.

The New Year's Eve celebration at the hotel had been advertised as an old-fashioned, elegant evening. In keeping with the theme, I was wearing a long, silk sleeveless dress in a shade of blue that Vaughn swore perfectly matched my eyes. In his tuxedo, Vaughn looked like the star he was as he hosted a table of local politicians whom Rhonda and I had invited to join us.

I flitted back and forth between our table and those of our other guests, making sure everyone was happy.

Understandably, Rhonda had bowed out of hosting the evening.

As I moved about, I listened to the light background music of a pianist and a harpist. Their music accompanied the conversational hum of guests dining with satisfaction. Jean-Luc had outdone himself with a choice of Steak Diane, Sole *Meuniere* or Cornish Hens *a l'Orange*. The aroma of good food wafted throughout the dining room, which sparkled with tiny lights and other decorative touches that would be part of the décor for the upcoming wedding. Gaily colored paper hats and horns lay on a table, awaiting midnight.

As I looked around, I thought it was a lovely start to the evening. After dinner, a singer and jazz quartet would perform music for dancing. I couldn't wait for that to happen. Aside from the impromptu fooling around, Vaughn and I had danced only one other time—at Rhonda's wedding.

Later, with Vaughn holding me in his arms, moving to the music of old favorites, I let myself relax. Midnight would soon be upon us. Then we could salute the new year together with our guests. Afterward, we could celebrate in a much different way in the privacy of my home. The past year, full of ups and downs, was one I'd never forget. But this evening I felt stronger, smarter, and happier than I'd ever been.

The musicians stopped playing and announced it was time to go outdoors.

Vaughn grabbed my hand. Along with the other guests, we hurried out onto the edge of the beach where the neighborhood association was about to set off fireworks.

One of the men began a countdown: Ten ... Nine ... Eight ... Seven ... Six ... Five ... Four ... Three ... Two ... One!

Suddenly, sound and lights exploded. The dark winter sky filled with colors and shapes and popping noises. Vaughn bent down and kissed me. The flickering colors behind my eyelids were as magical as the fireworks in the sky.

"Happy New Year, Ann," Vaughn whispered in my ear. "Next year we'll celebrate as husband and wife."

"Yes," I said, smiling at him. "I can't wait until it's official. I hope sometime in June."

"If that's what you want, then you shall have it," he said, cradling me against his chest.

I shivered from the cool air.

Vaughn took off his jacket and wrapped it around me.

I looked up at him, drinking in the way he was looking at me. He might have liked the dress I was wearing, but I knew how he liked me best.

"Should we go home?" I said.

He grinned and winked at me. "What a good idea."

I checked with the hotel staff to make sure all was under control. Dave was supervising the clean-up operation. After I assured myself everything was as it should be, I joined Vaughn at the front of the hotel.

Vaughn took hold of my hand. "Tomorrow I want to talk to you about something."

"Not now?"

He shook his head. "It's so late, and it's something I want you to think about."

I hated being left in suspense, but I was too tired to do anything but agree to it.

Later, lying in bed waiting for Liz to come home, I couldn't help wondering what Vaughn had in mind. He'd sounded so serious. But even after I asked him to talk about, he'd refused.

I heard Liz go to her room, closed my eyes, and started to count silently from one hundred down, going slower and slower.

The next morning, I climbed out of bed, careful not to disturb Vaughn. Though Rhonda was handling the breakfast shift, I was anxious to talk to her about Angela and Reggie. I slipped on a light sweater and slacks, pulled a brush through my hair, and tiptoed out of the house.

Outside, the gray dawn sky gleamed with promise. A coat of dew lay on the grass, exposing the crystal-like webs that little nocturnal creatures had formed here and there. As I walked along, the palm trees rustled a greeting.

I entered the hotel quietly, hardly disturbing Dave who was busy behind the front desk. He looked up at me.

"Happy New Year!" I said softly and went on my way, careful not to make too much noise. With guests still asleep in their rooms, this was the time of day when I felt the hotel was mine.

The smell of cinnamon led me into the kitchen where Consuela was preparing the breakfast rolls that had helped to launch The Beach House Hotel.

I smiled at her. "*¡Prospero año nuevo!*"

"*¡Si!* Happy New Year!" she responded, returning my smile with a humorous glint in her eye.

I poured myself a cup of coffee and hurried into the office.

Rhonda was working at her desk. She stopped typing and grinned at me. "Happy New Year, partner! Last year was a wild ride! Let's hope this one will be a good year too!"

I hugged her and took a seat. "It's bound to be. For all of us. How are Angela and Reggie?"

"Okay, I guess. Sorry, I couldn't talk to you yesterday." She shook her head and sighed. "Will and I grilled the two of them about how things would be going forward. I have to admit Reggie was very apologetic for what happened at Thanksgiving. He told Will and me that he'd do anything to prove how much he loves Angela. When we asked him how his parents were going to take the news that he intends to marry her, he grew kinda quiet."

"So he intends to marry her?" I asked, taking another sip of the hot, steamy liquid in my cup.

"That's what he says. The proof will be in how he handles his parents. I'm more convinced than ever that he's a good guy, but having parents against the marriage is tough for anyone to handle."

"How's Angela in all this?" I couldn't stop thinking of the scene at the airport.

Rhonda shook her head. "My baby girl is so in love it's almost sickening. She's very proud that Reggie came through for her, that he loves her exactly like she believed. But I want her to be prepared to face Katherine's disapproval. That woman is a witch with a capital B, and no matter what, she'll always be the baby's grandmother and Reggie's mother."

I set down my cup of coffee and sighed. The situation was difficult. "Having observed them meet at the airport, I assure you Reggie's love for her is genuine. I even cried, for heaven's sake. But no doubt his mother is already furious. He ditched the girl he was to take to a deb party, a girl his mother wanted him to marry."

"Yeah, he called her from our house. She was real unhappy that it was such late notice." Rhonda clutched her hands together. "Oh, Annie! What am I going to do if Reggie decides not to go forward with Angela? It would kill her if he decided not to marry her after all. And what if they do get married and he leaves her? We both know what that's like."

"These are two young adults who, I suspect, will do what they want. Maybe the thing to do is to make sure they know we're on their side. Has Reggie given any indication of how he'd support a family?"

"Will talked to him." Rhonda's eyes shone with tears. "I was so damn proud of Will. He acted as if he were Angela's real father, demanding to know how they were going to be able to be together financially."

"Reggie told me he has quite a bit of money of his own, so they can manage until he graduates. Then he's going to look for a job in either banking or financial management."

Rhonda and I locked eyes. The smile I felt crossing my face was reflected in hers.

"Omigod, Annie, are you thinking what I'm thinking?"

"Oh, yeah."

The tension that had filled the room evaporated in musical, giggling notes.

I held up my hand. "But, Rhonda, you have to let them come to that decision on their own."

Rhonda's grin was infectious. "Yeah, but it's one of those times when we can plant the seed of that idea. Will and Reggie working together? That would be perfect."

"Don't forget that Reggie's father wanted him working in New York. And Arthur's an international expert."

"Expert? Did you listen to their conversation? My Will knows more than Arthur Smythe does about some things." Rhonda's lips thinned. "He's just as fake as his frickin' name."

"Remember, your daughter might have that same frickin' name," I commented, hiding my laughter as I watched the realization strike Rhonda.

"Oh, yeah, right. Maybe she could be Angela DelMonte-Smythe with a hyphen. That sounds better, don't ya think?"

"I think we'd both better stop planning the future for them."

"Yeah, you're right. But you want things to be the best they can for your kids. Ya know what I mean?"

"Yes, I do. By the way, did you know Liz and Troy are dating?"

A smile filled Rhonda's face. "Well, whaddya know. Very interesting. I like him, and you know how I feel about Liz."

"I'm so glad things are better, but I've gotta go." I rose. "I'll be back later. I'm going to fix breakfast at home for Vaughn." My eyebrows drew together. "He said he had something to talk over with me. But he wouldn't tell me what it is."

"Everything all right?" Rhonda gave me a worried look. "I know we've been so busy at the hotel you haven't been able to spend much time with him."

"That usually isn't a problem, but it's to the point of being ridiculous." On this visit, he'd been placed on the sidelines too many times.

I left the office and headed home, my mind whirring with different thoughts about the people I loved.

CHAPTER THIRTY-ONE

Vaughn was home alone when I returned to the house. "Liz left to have breakfast with Troy and his parents," he explained.

Dressed in jeans and a black T-shirt that showed off his trim body, he wrapped his arms around me. "Happy New Year, Ann."

I nestled against his hard chest. "And to you, Vaughn." Smiling, I gazed up at him. "It's going to be a good one. I know it. We'll be married."

He grinned. "Yeah, I'll finally get to make you a virtuous woman."

I played along. "You mean I'm not a decent lover?"

He laughed. "You're the best, properly naughty."

Satisfaction filled me. He'd freed a sensuous part of me that had been hidden for years and I ... well ... I liked it.

Serious now, I pulled away from him and gazed up into his face. "What did you want to talk to me about?"

"Sit down. I'll be right back. I've got to get something."

I poured myself a second cup of coffee and sat down at the kitchen table, feeling my nerves tighten.

Vaughn returned to the kitchen with a sheaf of papers. He took a seat opposite me. After clearing his throat, he said, "Things haven't gone as well as I thought they'd be on this visit."

My heart stopped beating and sprinted ahead. "What do you mean?"

"With you here at the hotel, we never seem to have quality

time together. Your mind is always on your work."

"Yes, of course. It's my job, my livelihood."

"But married to me, you wouldn't need a job. I can support us in whatever style you wish."

I felt the blood leave my face. "Are you asking me to give up the hotel? You know I could never do that!"

Vaughn reached across the table and gripped my hand. "Hold on, Ann. Listen to me."

I focused on him, aware of his worried expression. "What are you saying?"

"I can't keep going on like this."

I felt my heart drop to my shoes. I gripped my hands together, squeezing them as I tried to get a grip on the dismay that tore at my insides. "Are you saying you want to break up?"

"Not at all. What I'm saying is I don't want to live being in a constant battle for your attention. I'm willing to share top billing with another star, but I'll be damned if I'm hardly mentioned at all."

"What do you mean?"

"I go out of my way to be here as often as I can. Sometimes when it isn't even easy for me to do so. And when I'm here, I expect some of your attention. More than you've been giving me lately."

"But ..."

"I understand your fear of being left with nothing after Robert pulled his dirty tricks. And I understand your unwillingness to turn to Rhonda or me to bail you out financially. But I think it's time you had a little more faith in yourself and the future so you can relax and enjoy what success you have. Do you understand what I'm saying?"

I let out a long breath, seeing myself in a whole different way. I'd allowed the expectations of others to override my need to have a life of my own. A life I wanted to share with

Vaughn, the man I loved like no other.

"My god! I'm so sorry. Vaughn, I've been so selfish ..."

"No," he said. "You've been dedicated to your job. Now it's time to dedicate more time to us—to our life together. What do you say?"

I fought to hold back tears. "I say I love you more than anything in the world. I say I would do anything to make you happy. Understand?" The tears that had been stinging my eyes blurred my vision.

He put an arm around me. "Hey, honey, we'll work it out. I have an idea you might like. Here." He pushed papers at me.

I glanced down at a number of real estate listings. "What are these?"

"I want to buy a place that's just for you and me, away from the hotel."

My mind stuttered. "But I live and work here."

"Of course, you do. But we need to have private space, like Rhonda and Will do. That's all I'm saying. We each have our own careers. I get that. But I want you to understand that I need at least a piece of you that's just for me. I can't be expected to continue to live this way. I don't think that's unreasonable. Do you?"

My heartbeat slowed as I took in what he was asking. It wasn't unreasonable at all. In fact, it was a good idea. "Okay," I said. "Let's take a look at what you've found."

He got up out of his chair and moved behind me. Leaning over my shoulder, he pointed out the different features of five different properties in town. Each one was more spectacular than the other.

"What do you think?" he asked.

"I think I love you very much," I said, awed by the beautiful properties he'd selected. "You make me feel like a princess with a beautiful castle." The thought of what he was willing to do for us filled me with joy.

His lips spread into a wide smile. "You deserve everything I can give you. Which one do you like best? We can make an appointment to see it anytime you like."

Excitement coupled with awe. I held up a sheet showing the smallest of the estate-like homes. I knew the house. I'd once been in it for a party for charity. Situated alongside a tiny, private bay, it was the perfect choice for our family. When all the kids came home, there'd be plenty of room for them and yet, it would be quite comfortable for only the two of us.

"Vaughn, this is beautiful. I've been inside it. It would be perfect for us."

He sat down on a chair and faced me, his look of relief obvious. "I'm so glad you see my point of view. I know how important the hotel is to you, but I need a part of you too."

Tears came to my eyes. "You have no idea how big a part of me you are. Let's make this work. It's good timing. Rhonda and I have already talked about hiring a general manager. That will give both Rhonda and me more personal time."

"Great, that's settled then. I'll call and make an appointment for us to see the house."

The more I thought about living off-property, the more I liked it.

Between lunch and dinner hours, Rhonda's family and mine gathered in the small dining room at the hotel for our private New Year's Day dinner. We were in so many ways one family, I thought, as I took a seat at the table. Opposite me, Reggie and Angela held hands even as they sat down next to each other. With Vaughn on one side of me and Liz on the other, I felt whole. Rhonda and Will sat at either end of the long table, completing the sense of family.

Jean-Luc had prepared a roast of pork with a special ginger and brown sugar glaze, a recipe he'd picked up from one of the islands in the Caribbean. In deference to Southern tradition, black-eyed peas and a leafy green salad accompanied the roast, along with a mélange of other vegetables.

"So tell me again, what do the black-eyed peas signify?" Liz said to me.

"They're for good luck. And the green leaves of the salad are for prosperity in the New Year. It's a lovely tradition."

"Let's hope it works," Liz murmured, glancing at Angela and Reggie, who had eyes only for each other.

I squeezed her hand. "Yes, we've got to hope it all works out."

We were finishing dessert—apple tarts in pastry so light it simply flaked—when my cell phone rang. I checked caller ID. Tina. "Well, hello, stranger," I said. "How are you? We've been playing phone tag for a while now."

"I'm doing fine," said Tina, her voice lilting happily. "I have custody of my brother, and my new agent has found a film for me. Something very different, almost sweet."

"How wonderful! Though I guess that means you won't be coming back here." I couldn't hide my disappointment.

"Actually, I'm thinking of buying a house there after my next film." She chuckled. "If my financial manager approves."

I laughed. "I'm sure Will can find a way to make it work. He's a very clever financial manager. Trust me."

"Ann, I wanted to thank you and Rhonda for all you did for me. I wouldn't be in this good situation without your forcing me to see things as they were. And by the way, one of the agreements I made with my mother was for her to drop the lawsuit. So you won't have to worry about that. Thanks and Happy New Year to everyone there. Love you all."

She hung up, and I turned to the others and told them about the call.

"That's one happy ending," said Rhonda. "Let's hope there are more."

Reggie gave her a sheepish look. "My parents should be back from Europe tomorrow. I'm going to give them the news then."

There was a moment of silence, and then Angela said, "We can face anything together. Right, Reggie?"

A smile broke across his face. "Right, sweetheart. Together."

Rhonda and I exchanged worried glances.

The next morning, I awoke with a fresh sense of purpose. Vaughn and I were meeting the real estate agent that afternoon to tour the house we both loved. Now that the idea had been raised, I couldn't wait for the time when I wouldn't be so accessible to the hotel. I'd seen what a difference it had made for Rhonda, and I was ready to make the change.

With the holidays behind us, I wanted to work on final details for the wedding, so all would be prepared for the Hassels. They were due to arrive the next day.

Rhonda and I were at work in the office when the phone rang. I picked it up. "Hello?"

"Ann, is that you? It's Lorraine Grace at Wedding Perfection. I have terrible news. Charlotte Hassel just called me. She was practically hysterical. Her daughter has run away with another man. Needless to say, the wedding here in Florida is canceled." Her voice broke. "I don't know what I'm going to do with all the things I've ordered for the wedding— fresh flowers, hundreds of them, and all sorts of special requests they made of me."

"Can you cancel the orders?"

"Not all of them," she said. "I should've made them pay for everything up front. That's what I usually do. But I was carried away by the sound of royalty. Now I'm ruined."

"Surely they will pay you." My heart sank at the idea of getting stuck with any extraneous costs. And now we'd have to see about filling empty rooms at the last minute. My mind raced. "Lorraine, can we call you back?"

"Sure," she sighed. "I'll be here, trying to cancel as much as I can."

I hung up and turned to Rhonda. "The wedding is canceled. The Hassels' daughter has run off with another man."

"You're kidding!" She gave me an incredulous look. "What are we going to do about the rooms? And all that special veal we ordered for their *Wiener Schnitzel*?"

"I've got an idea," I said, unable to hide a smile.

Before I could tell Rhonda what I had in mind, a knock came at the office door. The door opened, and Angela and Reggie entered the room, holding hands. Angela was in a pretty green dress and Reggie was wearing a white shirt and gray slacks.

"Hi, honey! What's up?" Rhonda said to Angela.

A pretty pink spread across Angela's cheeks. She glanced at Reggie.

"We have something to tell you," he said, looking nervous.

"We're married," cried Angela. She held up her left hand. A gold band wound around her ring finger.

"Whaaaat? When? Where?" Tears filled Rhonda's eyes. "You went ahead and did this without me?"

"Hold on, Mom," said Angela. "We only wanted to make sure no one would come between us. I know you've always talked about a nice wedding for me, but this is what we needed to do."

"Without me?" Rhonda's wail was full of pain.

Angela went to her mother and hugged her. "Oh, Mom, I'm sorry, but if we hadn't done this, Reggie's parents would have tried and tried to force him to change his mind."

"I'm sorry too, Rhonda," said Reggie. "I love Angela and always will. I agreed to do this to protect her, not to hurt you."

Rhonda sat back in her chair. "Oh, my! What a surprise."

"I have an idea," I said again.

The three of them turned to me.

"We've just received news that the royal wedding has been canceled. With everything in place, let's make it a royal wedding for the two of you." I turned to Reggie. "I suspect a nice wedding here at the hotel would please your parents more than having you two sneak off to get married. In many countries, there is a civil ceremony and then a fancy wedding."

Reggie's expression brightened. "I think you're right. My parents can attend or not."

Angela beamed at her mother. "And then you can have the wedding for me you've always wanted. What do you say?"

Rhonda straightened in her chair. "I say we do it. We'll have the sweetest damn wedding Reggie's mother has ever seen. Let's get to it."

She stood. "Come here, you two."

Wrapping her arms around Angela and Reggie, she hugged them close. Tears leaked from her eyes. "Oh my! Now I have a daughter *and* a son."

Seeing the joyful expressions on their faces, I felt my own eyes sting with tenderness.

CHAPTER THIRTY-TWO

To give Rhonda time alone with her children, I quietly left the office. I had a sudden need to see my daughter.

I opened the front door to my house, anxious to tell Liz the good news. She was sitting in the kitchen with Troy, sipping coffee. I stared at the dress she was wearing, the white shirt on Troy.

"I guess you know about Angela and Reggie," I said, realizing what had happened.

Liz smiled. "Troy and I stood up for them." A dreamy expression filled her face. "It was the sweetest thing ever. They love one another so much." Her soft sigh was laced with romance.

Vaughn came into the room in his bathing suit, his hair wet from the pool. "What's going on?"

"A lot," I told him. "Angela and Reggie got married. But they're going to have a second wedding here at the hotel for family and friends. The Hassels have canceled the royal wedding because their daughter eloped with another man. So we'll exchange one wedding for the other."

Vaughn shook his head. "Whew! Love sure does complicate things sometimes, huh?" He pulled me to him. "Guess we'd better try to keep things simple."

"What does that mean?" I asked playfully.

He grinned. "It means when we have our wedding in June, it will be exactly the way you want it."

Liz turned to Troy and said in a stage whisper, "They're like this all the time."

Troy laughed. Standing, he said, "I guess I'd better get to work. I have an appointment in a little while."

Liz showed him out and returned to the kitchen.

"So, Mom? Will I be part of the hotel wedding too?"

"I suspect so. You'd better talk to Angela. Things are moving in a hurry. All the stuff Lorraine ordered for the royal wedding will probably be used for this one."

I turned to Vaughn. "I've got to get back to the hotel. See you after lunch for the house tour."

"What's this?" Liz said.

"Have Vaughn show you what we have in mind, and if you want to join us, that would be great," I said, giving them a wave goodbye.

When I got back to the office, Rhonda was on a call with Lorraine. I sat at my desk, reviewing the reservations chart, wondering how we could fill empty rooms.

Rhonda hung up. "Lorraine is thrilled to help us out. 'Course I knew she would be." She clutched her hands in a prayerful pose. "I want this to be perfect. For Angela and Reggie, and for me and Will."

"I'm sure it will be. The Beach House Hotel is known for putting on perfect weddings. Have you talked to Sabine?"

Rhonda shook her head. "I've sent her a text. Angela and I are meeting with her this evening. Angela is very happy she'll have a nice wedding after all, and Reggie is okay with everything." Her eyes filled. "He really does love her, ya know?"

"I know. It's very clear to see," I said. "Has he been in touch with his parents?"

Rhonda grimaced. "He called them right after you left. They were shocked, then angry. But they've promised to come to the wedding to make a *proper* appearance."

"Oh, dear. That doesn't sound easy. But we'll all help you

to get through it."

"Angela is going to ask Liz to be her maid of honor. And I think Reggie is going to ask Troy to be his best man. Angela doesn't want a big wedding, just a nice one."

"What about a dress?"

Rhonda grinned. "She's my daughter all right. She wants a white wedding dress and veil and everything. She's going to have Liz help her pick it out. Some of the newer styles make it pretty easy to accommodate her being pregnant. I told her to choose something with Liz, then you and I will take a look at it. The owner of Wedding Styles is a friend of mine. She'll help us make it happen."

"That sounds good," said Ann.

Rhonda let out a little yelp, and then a grin lit her face. "The baby just kicked. Busy little rascal." She shook her head. "Everything is happening so fast; I can't believe it. It wasn't too long ago the two of us were wondering what to do with our lives. Remember, Annie?"

I laughed. As Rhonda would say, it had been one helluva ride.

Liz joined Vaughn and me for a tour of the house Vaughn was thinking of purchasing. I was pleased to see her take an interest in it because I hoped she and Vaughn's kids would always feel free to spend time with us, and when they had children, they'd bring them to us.

The house was as I remembered it—elegant but not ostentatious. Five bedrooms, four and a half baths, a large kitchen, and a huge lanai were the features I liked best. Liz naturally went for the pool and spa. Vaughn, typical guy, loved the three-car garage. Outside, a lawn led to a private dock where a small day sailboat was tied up. The tiny bay, more like an inlet, had only eight other houses edging it, giving us a great sense of privacy—something that was important to Vaughn.

Liz and I wandered around outside while Vaughn talked to the realtor. When he emerged from the house, he grinned at us. "I've made an offer that the agent is pretty sure will go through. I couldn't take a chance on losing it."

"It's wonderful, Vaughn," I said.

He swept me up in his arms. "As soon as we're married, we'll add your name to the title."

A shiver traveled down my back and grabbed hold of my body. Robert had made such a promise and then not kept it.

Vaughn's eyebrows drew together. "Are you all right?"

I took a deep breath and reminded myself Vaughn was no Robert. He'd already proved it to me in so many ways.

"I'm fine," I said, smiling up at him. And I was. Vaughn was a generous man, and I trusted him.

I left Vaughn and Liz and headed back to the hotel. We were waiting to hear from Katherine how many rooms we should save for them for the wedding.

Rhonda was in the kitchen talking to Jean-Luc when I entered it. Rhonda gave me a grin. "Jean-Luc is very happy he can do something more French with the veal we ordered."

"*Mais oui*," he said, bringing his fingertips to his mouth and opening his hand with a flourish.

"Do we know how many people are coming?" I asked as Rhonda and I walked into our office.

"Katherine and Arthur have invited their friends, the Larkins from Palm Beach. That's it." Rhonda shrugged. "Angela wanted a small wedding, so I think it's going to be only the four of us plus Liz and Troy. And Consuela and

Manny are representing the staff from the hotel. Oh, yes. Dorothy, too. I knew we couldn't leave her out. She'd be heartbroken if she weren't invited."

"Nice. So, we'll give Katherine and Arthur the Presidential Suite?"

"And the Larkins can have the new Bridal Suite. Ange and Reggie are going to Naples for their first night and then on to Barbados. Angela and Liz can get dressed at the house."

"Sounds good. How are things going with Reggie?"

Her eyes sparkled. "He and Will have been doing a lot of talking. I'm hoping he'll consider doing something here in Florida after graduation. But I don't dare bring up the subject. The poor guy is worried about facing his parents, worried that they'll do something to hurt Angela."

"When are they coming here?"

Rhonda drew a deep breath. "Tomorrow night."

I was as nervous as she.

The phone rang. Rhonda picked it up, listened, and then got to her feet. "C'mon, Annie, we're about to see what Angela looks like as a bride." She grabbed my arm. "Can't wait to see what the girls picked."

Moments later, Rhonda pulled her car into the parking lot next to the bridal store. We got out and walked around to the entrance. The elegant storefront indicated the quality of dresses inside.

The inside was just as elegant. Light rose plush carpeting covered the floors. Creamy, fabric-covered couches and settees were scattered about, forming conversation areas. Coffee tables sat in front of some of them, displaying a collection of bridal magazines.

A woman in a gray skirt and écru silk top approached us with a smile.

"Congratulations, Rhonda! I hear you are about to

welcome a very lucky man into your family."

"Hi, Elise! You remember Ann from our parties at the hotel, don't you?"

She gave me a broad grin. "Indeed, I do. I understand you may be a client someday soon."

I returned her smile. Elise Talbott was one of those people who didn't miss an opportunity to do business. "Not right away. Vaughn and I are thinking of a June wedding."

"How nice," she said. "Come this way. The girls are having a little tea party, waiting for you to arrive."

The dressing area contained three large, individual dressing rooms outside of which sat a group of comfortable chairs. A silver bucket holding a bottle of champagne in ice sat on a small sideboard. A sherry decanter and a bottle of red wine were beside it. Next to the sideboard, a table held a coffee maker and a pot labeled "hot water." A leather box holding a variety of tea bags, cream, sugar, and lemon slices sat nearby. My critical eye was pleased by what I saw. This place had hospitality and class. Like the hotel.

Rhonda turned around and around. "Where are the girls?"

"Mom, is that you?" came Angela's voice.

"Annie and I are here, waiting to see what you've chosen."

The door to the middle room opened. Angela stepped out of it and stood in front of us. A wide band covered with crystals circled her body under her small breasts. The white dress she wore flowed from its high waist in gentle folds that met the floor. The simple scooped neckline showed off her beautiful skin, tanned by the sun. The crystal band above her waist was matched by a circlet she wore on her head. Silk flowers had been added to it, offset by Angela's shining dark curls. The beautiful, intricate handwork on the dress and the headpiece gave an elegance to the simple lines of each. Both were stunning.

Rhonda held a tissue to her eyes and gave in to her emotions. I wrapped my arm around her shaking shoulders and let her cry. When she could catch her breath, she lifted her face. "Oh, Angela, you are the most beautiful bride I ever saw."

As they embraced, Liz and I exchanged happy glances.

"What about you, Liz? Did you find something to wear?" Rhonda asked.

Liz turned to Angela. "Shall we show them?"

Angela grinned. "Go put it on."

I waited eagerly to see what the girls had selected for Liz. When she opened the door to the dressing room, I caught my breath. She too was dressed in white.

"It's gorgeous, but why white?" I asked.

"Ange and I decided if it was to be a true royal wedding, it should be like Kate and Will's wedding, minus a lot of pomp and circumstance."

The dress, though not as elaborate as Kate's sister's dress, held a lovely sheen as it hugged Liz's body. Though not nearly as elaborate as Angela's dress, it too had a scooped neckline and fell simply to the floor.

"It's stunning," said Rhonda, giving Liz a hug. "You're so beautiful, sweetie."

Yes, I thought, two beautiful daughters and two proud mothers.

CHAPTER THIRTY-THREE

All day, tension hung in the air like a piece of ripe fruit hanging from a tree, ready to drop at our feet.

Lorraine bustled about the hotel, thrilled that her royal wedding disaster had been saved by Rhonda. I checked on her progress from time to time. In the small, private dining room, she'd strung additional tiny lights across the ceiling. Against the dark green ceiling, and with the sconce wall lights dimmed, the lights resembled a canopy of stars. Using some of the fresh greenery and flowers from the original *biergarten* theme, she soon transformed the room into an outdoor garden. It was, quite simply, stunning, I thought, gazing around the room with delight.

In addition to decorating the small dining room, Rhonda had Lorraine decorate the rest of the hotel with floral arrangements. She'd also had her place the small palm trees she'd purchased for the royal wedding in the library, where Angela and Reggie would be married. Once more.

Studying the room later, I thought of how valuable that space had become. Politicians had held top-secret meetings there. Others used it as a gathering place. And now it would be used for the sweetest purpose of all.

"I don't want it said that we don't do things right," said Rhonda, coming up behind me. A note of defiance rang in her voice, and I knew how insecure she felt about facing Reggie's parents again.

"Everything's going to be fine," I assured her.

"Wonder what the Larkins are like. Probably as snooty as

Reggie's parents. Well, I say fuck 'em. I probably have more money than they do."

"Take a deep breath, Rhonda. You'll be fine."

She shook her head. "You're right, Annie. It's not like I even have to like them. We only have to get through tonight and tomorrow. Then they'll leave."

It was almost six o'clock when we got the message from Tim that our special guests had arrived. Rhonda and I stood and gazed at each other with apprehension.

"This is it," said Rhonda. "Stay right with me, Annie. I need you there."

"I'm here for you. Come on. Let's go."

We walked to the front of the hotel together, out the front door, and down the steps to greet Reggie's parents and their friends, Bettina and Chester Larkin. The men emerged from a white Bentley and hurried to open doors for the women sitting in the back seat. I recognized the air of disapproval from Katherine as she emerged from the car. I turned my attention to Bettina Larkin. A small, dark-haired woman with pretty features, she beamed as she gazed at the hotel's facade.

Rhonda and I moved forward to greet them.

"Welcome to The Beach House Hotel," I said, offering my hand to Bettina.

She shook my hand and then covered our grip with her other hand in a warm embrace. "I'm so happy I finally have the chance to come and see the hotel. I've heard nothing but good things about it. And," she turned to Rhonda, "I've heard the nicest things about the two of you."

"Thank you," said Rhonda in a subdued manner. "I'm Rhonda DelMonte Grayson, mother of the bride, and this is Ann Rutherford."

Bettina smiled at Rhonda. "I heard it was quite unexpected, this wedding. But what a beautiful place for one."

Katherine's face, I noticed, was a mask of uncertainty as she stood aside and listened to the conversation.

"So how did you hear of us?" I asked Bettina, curious as always about comments like this.

"Isobel Pennypacker is my next door neighbor. She raves about this hotel and what an elegant place it is. And she loves both of you girls."

Rhonda grinned. "Isobel and her sister Rosie come here all the time."

"Oh, yes," said Bettina. "I tried to tell Katherine ..." She turned to Katherine. "We're going to have a good time. Aren't we?"

I hid a smile as Katherine nodded obediently.

Arthur shook my hand, and then Chester Larkin introduced himself to me and asked about parking the car.

"I'll have Tim take care of it for you. To be safe, we'll put it in the garage."

"That'd be great," he said.

Bettina clucked her tongue. "Men and their toys."

"Won't you come inside?" Rhonda said. "Your rooms are ready for you."

We climbed the front stairs and paused in the front hall while Bettina walked into the living area.

Turning from one side to the other, she studied everything. "Did Laura Bakeley do the interior decorating?" she asked Rhonda.

"Yes. She's the best," said Rhonda. "I love her work."

"So do I," said Bettina. She turned to Katherine. "Why didn't you tell me it was so beautiful?"

"I ... I ..." stammered Katherine.

"It was a busy time," I said, rushing to help Katherine out

of the awkward situation. "You probably didn't get the chance to see everything."

Katherine shot me a grateful look. "Yes, that's it. I really didn't have the opportunity to take it all in."

Though I could feel her studying me, I refused to look at Rhonda, afraid I might give in to the giddiness I felt. "Katherine, let me take you and Arthur to your room. We've placed some refreshments there for you."

"And I'll show you and your husband to your room, Bettina," said Rhonda. "You can freshen up there. Cocktails will be served in the living room at five-thirty. Dinner is at seven."

"Where is my son?" Katherine asked.

"He and Angela are at my house," Rhonda said. "They'll meet us here for cocktails."

A frown furrowed Katherine's brow, but she said nothing more, simply gave her husband a tight-lipped look.

Vaughn, Liz, Troy, and I entered the living room a few minutes late to find a few hotel guests sitting together. Several others were coming in from outside after trying to find the green flash of the sunset. In a quiet corner, the Larkins were sitting and chatting with Angela and Reggie.

As we crossed the living room to them, Katherine and Arthur appeared behind us.

I turned around to acknowledge them. "Hi, again. You both know Vaughn, but you haven't met my daughter Liz and her friend Troy Taylor."

Katherine's features softened as her gaze settled on Vaughn. "Hello, Vaughn." She held out her hand. "It's so good to see you again."

He gave her a pleasant smile and took her hand. "And you."

As other greetings were exchanged, Arthur shook hands with Vaughn, studying him carefully.

We continued on to the corner of the living room.

Bettina looked up at us and gasped when she noticed Vaughn. "You're that man on television."

"Well, one of them," he said graciously, taking her hand. "Vaughn Sanders." He shook Chester's hand and then Reggie's. "I understand congratulations are in order, Reggie. You're a lucky young man."

"I know that, sir," said Reggie, putting his arm around Angela.

Vaughn leaned down and gave Angela a kiss on the cheek. "Best wishes, sweetie."

"Why don't we all sit down?" I suggested. "Rhonda and Will should be here soon."

"If you'll excuse us, Katherine and I need to talk to Reggie. Alone," said Arthur, giving his son a stern look.

"Of course, take your time," I said.

After they left, Liz and Troy signaled Angela to join them, and the three of them left to be on their own.

Vaughn and I took seats on a settee opposite the Larkins. A waiter promptly came over and took our orders for drinks and checked to make sure the Larkins were fine with theirs.

"Thank you so much for being part of this celebration," I said. "Your presence seems to be a great comfort to Katherine."

Bettina shook her head. "Katherine and I go back a long way, back to the time when we were in high school together. She came from a poor family, and I sort of took her into my group. She's very bright and can be a lot of fun, but I'm afraid she's never gotten over wanting to be in the right circles. It's too bad because as we all grow older, we realize it doesn't mean a hill of beans. Aside from that, Katherine is a sweet person, maybe a little ambitious for her son, but sweet nevertheless."

"At Thanksgiving, she and Arthur were very rude to Rhonda and her family," I said, unwilling to forget it. Even now the memory of their actions caused me to sharpen my voice.

"I can well imagine," said Bettina, "but be easy on her. She doesn't mean to be that way. Arthur isn't easy to live with, and she truly loves her son."

"Yes, I can see that," I said, warning myself to relax. "So tell me a little about you two. Chester, what is it that you do?"

"Besides playing with cars?" chided Bettina, giving him a loving look.

He started talking about his latest acquisition. Soon he and Vaughn were carrying on their own conversation, leaving Bettina and me to ours.

I discovered that Bettina was well known for her charity work with autistic children. "It started when our oldest child, our son Gregory, was diagnosed with these issues. My interest has grown, along with the burgeoning of this problem."

"What about your other children? You have a daughter, don't you?"

Bettina smiled. "Yes. Laurel. Aside from being a headstrong young girl, she's perfectly normal." She laughed. "Or I should say she's perfectly normal because she is such a determined young lady."

"Wasn't she supposed to marry Reggie?"

Bettina dismissed that idea with a wave of her hand. "That was Katherine's idea and mine. Silly of us, I know, because at Thanksgiving it became very evident they had no interest in each other."

I sat back in my chair, relieved beyond words that this sensible, kind woman was Katherine's friend—someone who would be a steadying force.

"Hello, sorry we're late," said Rhonda, interrupting our conversation. "I got a call from Lorraine and had to straighten out some things for tomorrow." She took hold of Will's arm and pulled him forward. "This is my husband, Will Grayson."

Introductions were made all around. As we were about to take our seats, the Smythes appeared with Reggie.

"All set?" I asked.

Reggie looked around and asked, "Where's Angela?"

"With Troy and Liz. I believe they went outside," I answered.

He left, and the eight of us adults sat in a circle. Arthur ordered his favorite scotch, and Katherine a white wine. After the drinks had been brought, Will lifted his glass.

"Let's toast the health and happiness of the young couple."

Arthur and Katherine hesitated for mere seconds and then joined us in raising our glasses.

"They're a darling couple," gushed Bettina. "And, Katherine, I'm so jealous that you'll be a grandmother before me."

The shock on Katherine's face was telling. I silently blessed Bettina for being so forthright and forcing Katherine to accept the facts as they were.

Bettina reached over and patted Katherine's leg. "You know, dear friend, it was never going to work—Laurel and Reggie."

Katherine's eyes misted but she gave her a smile. "Yes. I know that now. The important thing is for Reggie to be happy. Reggie and Angela, I mean," she added, giving Rhonda a polite smile.

"Yeah, you're right, we simply want them to be happy," said Rhonda. "I didn't think Reggie was good enough for Angela, but over the past few days, he's proved himself to me."

I wanted to laugh at the surprised expressions on the faces of the Smythes and the Larkins. *Good for you, Rhonda!*

"Here they come now," I said.

Watching the four young people walk toward us, I couldn't help wondering what the next months would bring. Two babies and a wedding and what more?

Vaughn caught my eye. I smiled at him, knowing whatever the future held, he'd be there for me.

CHAPTER THIRTY-FOUR

Sitting in a circle in the middle of the library with the other wedding guests, I felt like I was in a tropical garden. Lorraine had cleverly filled the room with plants and tiny lights and flowers of every shade of pink. A small fountain bubbled quietly in the back corner of the room, lending more tropical feel to the room.

Reggie stood at the head of the circle with the minister who'd agreed to officiate. Troy stood beside him.

Rhonda sat next to me, and Vaughn was on my other side. Manny, Consuela, and Dorothy sat beside us. The Smythes and the Larkins faced us, completing the circle.

The harpist Lorraine had hired began to finger the strings of her instrument. Soft, soaring notes filled the room. We all stood and turned to the doorway. Carrying a bouquet of pink orchids, Liz entered the room. In her white dress, she looked so beautiful tears stung my eyes. I glanced at Troy and realized from the tender look on his face that his feelings for her were real.

Liz moved opposite Troy and Reggie and waited with the rest of us for Will and Angela to appear.

As Angela stepped through the door, clasping Will's arm, a gasp filled the room. She looked positively angelic. The sound of harp music in the background made me believe it even more. The gown and the circlet on her head were perfect for her. Seeing only Reggie, she moved toward us, her smile lighting her face with joy. Unable as I was to tear my eyes away from her, I didn't realize that Will was crying until he turned to sit down next to Rhonda. Dabbing at her own eyes, she gave him a watery smile and said softly, "I love you."

He kissed her on the cheek and turned to listen to the minister.

I gazed at Vaughn, drinking him in with my eyes.

He grinned when he noticed me. "Next time it's us," he whispered.

"It'll always be us," I said, as sure as anything I'd never stop loving him.

Thank you for reading *Lunch at The Beach House Hotel*. The 3rd, 4th, 5th, and 6th books in The Beach House Hotel Series, *Dinner at The Beach House Hotel, Christmas at The Beach House Hotel, Margaritas at The Beach House Hotel,* and *Dessert at The Beach House Hotel* are available on all sites. If you enjoyed this book, please help other readers discover it by leaving a review on Amazon, Bookbub, Goodreads, or your favorite site. It's such a nice thing to do.

Enjoy an excerpt from my book, *Dinner at The Beach House Hotel*, Book 3 in the Beach House Hotel Series.

CHAPTER ONE

Rhonda DelMonte Grayson and I stood at the top of the front steps of The Beach House Hotel, the seaside mansion in Sabal, Florida we'd turned into an upscale, boutique hotel. As the limo rolled through the gates of the property, I crossed my fingers behind my back.

With Rhonda due to give birth in the next two months, I needed all the help I could get while Rhonda and her husband Will welcomed their child into their family and the world. Bernhard Bruner was our last hope of finding a suitable general manager for the hotel out of the group of candidates we'd screened.

"I hope we like him," said Rhonda. "The last two applicants we talked to were doozies. I'm tellin' ya, Annie, I'm not going to take any bullshit from a guy thinkin' he can boss us around."

I smiled, used to the way Rhonda thought and spoke. My

proper grandmother would shudder in her blue-blooded grave, but Rhonda wasn't even aware of the language that hid a big, loving heart.

The limo continued toward us.

"I hope *he* likes *us*!" I said, giving my crossed fingers a squeeze.

Below a lock of bleached blond hair that fell on her forehead, Rhonda's dark eyes sparkled. She elbowed me. "Here goes."

Before the limo even pulled to a stop, Rhonda and I eagerly made our way down the steps to greet Mr. Bruner. An older man in his fifties, he'd come highly recommended to us as the perfect choice to oversee a property like ours. But would he be willing to work with us?

We'd interviewed several other men who weren't exactly thrilled with the idea of having to work under the guidance of two women. But The Beach House Hotel was our baby, and we weren't about to simply hand it over to someone else—no matter how much we wanted and needed some time to ourselves.

Paul, our driver, stopped the limo, got out, and hurried around behind the car to open the passenger door.

A shiny black shoe appeared, followed by creased gray slacks. Dressed in a navy blazer, starched white shirt, and conservative tie, the man who stood so straight before us had a sharp, blue-eyed gaze. Beneath his nose, a trimmed mustache brushed the top of his lips. His stern appearance reminded me of my old, middle-school principal.

As we exchanged greetings, a black and tan dachshund jumped out of the car and sat at her master's feet, looking up at me with what I thought of as something of a smile. Charmed, I stooped to pat her head.

"And who is this?"

"Trudy," Bernhard said. "She goes everywhere with me."

Rhonda and I exchanged glances.

"Uh, we weren't told about her," said Rhonda.

Bernhard picked the dog up. She gave him a lick on the cheek and turned bright dark eyes to us, wagging her tail furiously.

"If it's a problem for me to have her here, we can end this visit right now." Bernhard's words weren't unkind, but there was no question as to his intentions.

I reached over to give Trudy another pat on the head and grinned when she licked my hand. I loved dogs, but Robert, my ex, had been allergic to them. And any kind of pet had been out of the question in my grandmother's formal home, where I lived after my parents were killed in an automobile accident.

Rhonda glanced at me and shrugged. "It's okay with me, Bernie."

Bernhard stiffened. "My name is Bernhard."

I placed a hand on his arm. "Among ourselves, our staff is quite informal. Rhonda likes to give people nicknames. It's a sign she likes you."

I held my breath as I waited for him to say something. If he and Rhonda couldn't get along, it would never work.

"All right. A few of my friends call me Bernie, but, in business, I like to use my full name." He set the dog down and stood staring at the façade of the hotel.

The two-story, pink-stucco building with its red-tile roof spread before us. I recalled the first time I'd seen it and how impressed I was with its design and features. By anyone's definition, the seaside estate was gorgeous.

"Can we give you a quick tour of the property?" I asked. "Normally we'd usher you in through the front door to give you an idea about the arrival that guests enjoy. But with the dog, and your long day of travel, you might want to stretch your legs and start the tour outside."

"Good idea," Bernie said. "I want to see everything."

Rhonda and I pointed out the putting green in the front circle of the hotel and led him over to what was once a large multi-car garage. Now, its second floor held an apartment for Manny and Consuela, the two people who'd been with us since before we opened our hotel, and an apartment for Troy, who was managing our day spa. On the ground floor, we'd set up a small laundry for towels and special linens, leaving some garage space still to park the hotel's limo and the occasional VIP's car. The day spa was attached to the building near the laundry. Behind it, there was a tennis court, a shuffleboard court, and horseshoe pits.

I watched Bernie's face for a sign of approval as he took in everything, but he gave nothing away. "Let's have a refreshing drink by the water," I said, "after which we can take you through the public areas and show you a number of rooms before we sit down and discuss the job."

Bernie nodded agreeably.

While Rhonda went inside to talk to Consuela, I walked Bernie around the side of the hotel, past the herb garden the chef had recently established, and out onto the beachfront. Beneath a palm tree, a ground-level, wooden deck held a few tables and chairs. Guests frequently had lunch there, or, in the evening, enjoyed a cocktail while watching for the elusive green flash of a Gulf Coast setting sun.

I was amused to see Trudy run off for a sniff here and there before dutifully returning to Bernie's side.

The late January day was cool for Florida, but Bernie seemed to enjoy the shade as he sat waiting for Rhonda to reappear.

"You're certainly welcome to take off your coat and loosen your tie," I said.

He shook his head. "No, that wouldn't do." He gave my sandals a disapproving look.

"We like our guests to relax and enjoy themselves. While a dress code for dinner is suggested, we all like a bit of informality during the day," I quickly explained.

He nodded, but didn't comment, making me wonder if the man ever relaxed.

Rhonda walked toward us, followed by Consuela carrying a tray of drinks and snacks.

Bernie stood as they approached.

"Bernie, I'd like you to meet Consuela," Rhonda said. "She and her husband Manny have been with me since my ex and I bought The Beach House before Ann and I converted it to a hotel. Consuela is a whiz in the kitchen, and her husband is well...my Manny around the house." Rhonda let out a raucous laugh.

Bernie's mustache twitched and a glint of humor lit his eyes.

At the sight, I filled with relief. Rhonda was Rhonda, and though it had taken me a while to get used to her ways, I loved her and her carefree manner.

Bernie sat down and watched as Consuela placed the drinks before us and set a plate of cookies and a bowl of nuts on the table. "Thank you, Consuela," he said, smiling at her.

She left us, and Rhonda described how the kitchen staff had grown after hiring Jean-Luc Rodin as chef to prepare evening and some luncheon meals, along with his sous-chef, Carl Lamond.

"It continues to be a growing operation," I said. "The locals like to come to the hotel to dine and hold special events, and we've encouraged them to do so."

"Yes, I've read all about dinner at The Beach House Hotel. You've got a fine operation," Bernie said. He slipped a cookie crumb to Trudy, who wagged her tail in appreciation.

"C'mon, let's show you around the place. I think you're gonna like it," said Rhonda, rising to her feet.

I smiled. Rhonda was as proud of the hotel as I was.

Inside, we explained how we'd configured rooms downstairs for the small, discreet, private meetings our VIP guests demanded. Bernie nodded with approval at the small dining room where senators and other government officials sometimes met and where guests could entertain and dine alone.

As we continued our tour, Bernie asked discerning questions about the property, guest services we offered, staffing issues, and other aspects of the hotel operation. I knew then he was truly interested.

By the time we'd shown him the entire hotel, including the Presidential Suite, the Bridal Suite, and a few typical guest rooms, Bernie seemed as excited as a reserved man like him could show.

"Well, whaddya think?" said Rhonda as we led Bernie to our office.

"You've got a very impressive operation here. I'm sure I can be of help to you."

The three of us sat at the small conference table in the office. After going over his résumé, probing his past experiences, and discussing his management approaches, Rhonda and I shared hidden smiles.

I checked my watch. "I realize you have another appointment. Thank you so much for coming here, Bernie." I rose and shook his hand. "It's been a very productive meeting. We'll get back to you as soon as we can. As we have told you and others, as part of the compensation package, any general manager we hire will be given the use of the small house on the property for his residence."

"That's very nice." He shook hands with Rhonda and smiled at both of us. "Thank you for your time. I'm sincerely interested in this position and would love to have the opportunity to work with you."

We accompanied Bernie and Trudy to the front entrance of the hotel, where we made arrangements for the limo to drive him downtown.

Standing on the steps of the hotel, watching his departure, I turned to Rhonda. "Well?"

Rhonda shrugged. "He's a little uptight, but I think we can get Bernie to loosen up. He's the best of the lot, Annie. His references are excellent, and his résumé is outta sight. Let's take a chance on him."

"Okay. Him and Trudy," I said, smiling. With Rhonda's baby due and our busy season upon us, we needed help. I just hoped by bringing Bernhard Bruner into the mix, we weren't about to make a horrible mistake. We'd made a few along the way.

About the Author

Judith Keim, a *USA Today* Best Selling author, is a hybrid author who both has a publisher and self-publishes, Ms. Keim writes heart-warming novels about women who face unexpected challenges, meet them with strength, and find love and happiness along the way. Her best-selling books are based, in part, on many of the places she's lived or visited and on the interesting people she's met, creating believable characters and realistic settings her many loyal readers love. Ms. Keim loves to hear from her readers and appreciates their enthusiasm for her stories.

Ms. Keim enjoyed her childhood and young-adult years in Elmira, New York, and now makes her home in Boise, Idaho, with her husband and their two dachshunds, Winston and Wally, and other members of her family.

While growing up, she was drawn to the idea of writing stories from a young age. Books were always present, being read, ready to go back to the library, or about to be discovered. All in her family shared information from the books in general conversation, giving them a wealth of knowledge and vivid imaginations.

"I hope you've enjoyed this book. If you have, please help other readers discover it by leaving a review on Amazon, Bookbub, Goodreads or the site of your choice. And please check out my other books:

The Hartwell Women Series
The Beach House Hotel Series
The Fat Fridays Group
The Salty Key Inn Series
Seashell Cottage Books
The Chandler Hill Inn Series
The Desert Sage Inn Series
Soul Sisters at Cedar Mountain Lodge Series
The Sanderling Cove Inn Series
The Lilac Lake Series

"ALL THE BOOKS ARE NOW AVAILABLE IN AUDIO on Audible, iTunes, Findaway, Kobo and Google Play! So fun to have these characters come alive!"

Ms. Keim can be reached at **www.judithkeim.com**

And to like her author page on Facebook and keep up with the news, go to: **https://bit.ly/3acs5Qc**

To receive notices about new books, follow her on Book Bub - **http://bit.ly/2pZBDXq**

And here's a link to where you can sign up for her periodic newsletter! **http://bit.ly/2OQsb7s**

She is also on Twitter @judithkeim, LinkedIn, and Goodreads. Come say hello!

Acknowledgements

I wish to thank my writer friends and family members for their encouragement, especially Lynn Mapp for her friendship and insight. It means so much to me. And as always, I wish to thank my husband, Peter, whose business career has always been in the hospitality industry. His insight and continuing support in so many ways have made it possible for me to keep writing the light, fun stories I love to tell. Love you, Man!

Made in the USA
Middletown, DE
02 June 2022

66496824R00187